HANSEL'S BEAR

EROTIC SHIFTER FAIRY TALES BOOK 4

USA Today Bestselling Author
YVETTE HINES

Hansel's Bear

Erotic Shifter Fairy Tales

Yvette Hines

Copyright © 2014 Yvette Hines

All rights reserved.

ISBN: 150564478X
ISBN-13: 978-1505644784

This is a work of fiction. Names, characters, places, and incidents are products of the author's imagination or are used fictitiously and are not to be construed as real. Any resemblance to actual events, locales, organizations, or persons, living or dead, is entirely coincidental.

All rights reserved. The unauthorized reproduction or distribution of this copyrighted work is illegal. No part of this book may be used or reproduced electronically or in print without written permission by the author.

Hansel's Bear
Copyright © 2014, Yvette Hines
Cover Artist: JS Design
Editor: Bernadette Schane

This book is licensed for your personal enjoyment only. This book may not be re-sold or given away to other people. If you would like to share this book with another person, please purchase an additional copy for each reader. If you're reading this book and did not purchase it, or it was not purchased for your use only, then please return to bookstore and purchase your own copy. It is illegal to upload books without the publisher's permission to share sites. Thank you for respecting the hard work of this author.

DEDICATION

To my readers who have screamed, hollered, harassed and supported the Erotic Shifter Fairy Tale series. Thank you for loving Den County Were-Bears as I do. One day, SASSE Readers, we are going to have to take a road trip to the Redwood Forest.

This year has been a year that has been crazy, stressful and exhausting on both an emotional and spiritual level, but I thank all of my friends (Pascha, Inayah, Darby, Bernadette, Eileen, and Charmagne) and family for their support. To my writer friends (Di, Aliyah, Stephanie, Serenity, Latrivia, Pepper, Tiana, Sienna, Erosa and Denise) that have supported me and shared in the multiple pains of loss I went through this year, thank you and I love you all.

Most importantly, to my daughter who is waaaay too young to read my work, but she has been my champion. Keep writing little bear, keep writing.

CHAPTER ONE

"Is everyone ready?"

Greta heard Cord, the new Mayor of Den County, call. She hovered on the edge of the lake in a long line of other Were-bears, young and old. Anxious and excited, her toes flexed and dug deeper into the moist sand around the river as cool mud of the early morning oozed up around her feet. The smell of fall permeated the air with the rich scent of pine and earth and the muskiness of the multiple redwoods. The weather was changing and becoming cooler. She loved it.

"Remember, the first one to catch a salmon is the winner." Cord's booming voice announced to the participants, which were most of the Weres in Den County—except for the pregnant females who stood around observing and judges. Rena, who had become one of Greta's good friends during the hibernation months, was one of those unable to join in on the riotous fun. Cord and Rena were expecting their first cub any day now.

Glancing over her shoulder, Greta spotted Rena rubbing her protruding belly.

Rena caught her gaze and smiled then nudged Riley, Theo's mate, who was just as round and plump with her second offspring—their fourth child. Rena and Riley both held up their hands and presented crossed fingers to her, showing her they were wishing her luck that she would win.

Unable to stop the smile stretching her mouth, Greta nodded her friends a thank you.

Turning her head, she glanced down the line of the other waiting contestants. Her cousin and business partner Dainton was next to her whispering words of encouragement to Ebony, who everyone hoped would eventually become her cousin's bond mate. Dainton seemed at peace with Ebony not being ready yet to receive his third bite, even though it had been several months since she'd come to Den County. Greta knew the woman and could sense she was holding back from the final decision for a reason.

Having her own issues and secrets, Greta respected the woman's privacy and let the couple work it out on their own.

To the right and left of her stood adults and children alike dressed in swimming apparel wanting to win the competition. However, Greta was more determined this year to gain the first salmon as they leaped and jumped through the rough water. This stream was closer to the edge of the county and eventually weaved its way through town toward the Den County Lake and was a part of the Upper Sacramento River that flowed down from Mount Shasta. At this time of year, the Chinook Salmon were making their way back to Shasta River to spawn. And the Weres of Den also collected a portion of them for winter stock and the First Moon Festival coming up.

"Remember, everyone, no shifting."

Greta knew Cord repeated that more for cubs would weren't in control of their bears yet and would shift during emotionally high moments—anger, extreme sadness and excitement. The smaller children, not having the strength to fight through the current yet, were only allowed to go but so far into the water.

He informed the more mature bears of the rule because the contest would be over way too soon if claws were allowed. Bare-handed was more of a challenge when catching salmon because the fish were not only quick, but slippery. Claws always made that challenge easier.

"Get those salmon!"

That was exactly what Greta was waiting to hear. Running and splashing through the rushing water she kept her focus. There was a large flat rock in the center she had to get to once she had her salmon. She'd been practicing the swim and dive through the violent waters all summer. Weres were excellent swimmers, so she knew she had to be the best and fastest. Especially since she had a slight hindrance compared to other Weres. Her ankle had started out stiff, but loosened up quickly, more evidence of her training for this moment.

Every year a male Were was declared the winner, but she refused to let that happen this time. She was winning it for all the females of Den. She never allowed herself to dig deep enough to discover why it was so important to her this year, but it was.

Once the water was rising up beyond her thighs, she dove in. The crisp cool water surrounded her and brushed along her body like icy fingers. Her scalp tingled from the cold. It didn't deter her but felt exhilarating.

Beneath the water salmon were everywhere. Instead of attempting to grab hold of them as she witnessed others doing, she kept swimming toward the victory rock. Breaking through the surface, she could hear the laughter and peels of screams as people splashed, chased and goaded each other. She kept to herself. A few strokes away from the rock she started her chase.

One salmon after another eluded her grasp. The change in temperature was causing the icy water to numb her fingertips. After more than fifteen minutes, she growled in frustration. She knew that someone may have already caught one and could be swimming toward the rock to rise up and declare their triumph.

Taking a few breaths, she forced herself to calm down and recall how she had caught the trout that were always in abundance in the lake during her early morning practice time. Out of the corner of her eye, she caught site of Dainton and Rorke pounding through the water several yards away. They each had a fish in their grip.

Until they reached the rock she still had time. Filling her lungs with air, she plunged beneath the water and floated on her back. Pushing against the water she sank deeper. The salmon on the surface were few, but the ones closer to the bottom, those avoiding easy capture, were more plentiful.

She was bumped and brushed by one determined fish after another but she waited with her hands relaxed over her chest until just the right one came along.

Then it happened. One swam directly up the center of her body and just as it started past her face, she seized it. Closing both hands around it tightly, she held onto the slimy, wiggling and bucking aquatic craniate.

Turning over, belly down, she began to kick hard with all her might. Unable to use her hands for fear of losing her catch, she swiveled her hips and worked her legs through the current. Finally she broke through the choppy foam caps beside the rock.

The two men were close and more people were moving in with their prizes as well. Greta knew she had mere seconds to act. Shoving the salmon to her mouth, she sank her teeth into the top directly about the short fin. She swung both her arms up and aimed for the hard edge. She could barely feel the rough surface through her numb fingers. But, she held on and located the dip in the back of the rock that she had discovered a few weeks ago. Rorke was already starting his climb when she planted her foot onto a short ledge beneath the surface and launched upwards.

It gave her the advantage and she found herself on the flat top first. She scrambled to stand as Rorke had one knee up on the rock and was about to rise.

Wheezing and trembling, she quickly snatched the fish from her mouth and held the plump, male salmon high in the air.

"We have a winner! Greta Armel!"

"Well, I'll be damned." Rorke was holding a large fish in his hand as he stood up beside her on the rock.

Greta began jumping up down. Before she knew it, she was swept off her feet in a tight hug by her cousin Dainton.

"Congrats, Greta!" Dainton cheered.

Hugging him back she laughed and took in all the smiling faces of the Weres still in the river praising her.

"I did it! I did it!" She was overwhelmed by the pride and joy that swelled up inside her. Even with all her training, a big part of her never believed it was possible for her to win.

Setting her back on her feet, he kissed her on the cheek.

A loud, fierce roar split the air. A sound so piercing Greta's heart stopped as she leaped, almost slipping off the rock.

No one had to be told it was a bear even though the animal could not be seen through the dense forest.

Tension mounted as every Den County Were present turned toward the opposite side of the river. The property didn't belong to Den. Adults went on full alert.

Some raced toward the children as others moved rapidly in the direction of the obviously angry bear. Were or full bear they didn't know.

By the time the band reached the river's edge, some had shifted into bear form while others raced on foot. All of them sniffed around the air searching for a foreign scent to track.

Fanning out, they all moved cautiously into the depth of the forest. Finally someone spotted something.

"Over here." Tim Bjorn, the Mayor's cousin called out.

The Den residents there hustled to him and witnessed the deep gouges through the bark of the tree. Claw marks.

People were murmuring and growling at the evidence.

Greta watched Cord break through the throng.

Stepping up to the tree, he investigated the four slashes. Leaning in, he sniffed the marks and around the tree. "A Were." He declared and frowned.

"From Den?" Someone questioned.

That would have been strange if a Den Were had been on this side of the lake and not participating in the competition. Not only that, but where was the bear?

"A drifter." A deep voice called out.

Everyone turned in the direction of the person who had spoken. Theo Kodiak stood with his arms folded over his wide chest and a frown creasing his face, mirroring everyone else's.

"True." Cord gave a hard nod. "Everyone catch the scent and fan out by twos. Let us know if you find anything." Fixing his gaze on her, the mayor said, "Greta, head back to the others on the shore and let them know what is going on."

"Okay." She gave him the appropriate response, however, she felt as if she couldn't move, her feet felt rooted to the ground like the tree before her. The icy water from her hair, bound in a high ponytail, dripped onto her bare shoulders and rolled along her back becoming warm as it collected the temperature of the elevated heat of her body.

She was hot, not because she a Were and her bear gave her an internal temperature of over one hundred degrees, but the heat in her blood had spiked. It raced like a flame on a kerosene line. Something was happening to her. Her body was responding as if she were about to go into mating lust. An ailment that had *never* happened to her.

Everyone dispersed and moved around the tree in various directions on the hunt. She was thankful they were distracted by the situation and that none of the males had picked up on it. The last thing she needed was to be explaining.

Greta stared at the claw marks. Four of them,

ripping deep into the tree to the point the reddish-blonde of the inside of it showed clearly through the dark red-brown bark. It wasn't the markings that had her stuck in place, but the smell. The identifying scent of the Were.

Even though she was standing about two feet away from the marred Redwood, the fragrance of woodsy cashmere crossed the distance and wrapped around her—like a vise. The memories that flooded her mind were memories she had buried so deeply over the years that they were twisted visions of fantasy and reality. Some good, most bad.

Her first step was a tentative one back, away from the tree. She shut her mind down on whatever images were attempting to resurface. One step became two and soon she turned and was high-tailing it back across the stream.

She told herself she was only rushing because her mayor had given her a job to do and she wanted to perform it quickly. However, the truth followed behind her like a ghost from life past.

"Greta, what's going on over there?" Rena moved to her first, followed by the remaining Den residents, mostly females, children and the older generation that had not participated in the competition.

Inhaling deeply, she filled her lungs with the crisp air that wasn't saturated by the Were's fragrance across the way. Feeling calmer, more clear-headed and stable of body, Greta filled them in on what had happened.

"What? Some wild shifter is stalking around?" A shiver shook Ebony's body as she wrapped her arms around her waist. There was a shadow of apprehension in the new shifter's gaze that only was reflected in the smaller Were's eyes.

Greta knew this was all new to Ebony. The only thing the new resident and shifter knew were the friendly inhabitants of Den. But Greta was all too aware that there were dark dangers that lurked too close at time to the county border. Barely more than five years ago, a violent werewolf pack had attacked Theo's first wife. The Were-bears of Den had rallied together and gone after them, killing off most of them and chasing away the few that were left with a warning. And that had only been a few years since the incident that had happened to her.

"Whoever it is will be found and taken care of if it is needed." Now Greta was the one trembling at her own words, but she balled her fists tight and kept her response to herself. *What in the hell is going on with me?*

~YH~

It was her. It was her.

Racing blindly through the woods, he finally reached the clearing where his motorcycle was parked. He wasn't running because someone was pursuing him, but because of the feeling of possessiveness and rage that had come over him. Squeezing his eyes shut and shoving his hands deep into his hair he battled with himself—bear and mind.

His response to what he had seen before him was uncalled for. He wouldn't be surprised if he'd brought that entire sleuth on his trail. As a lone Were, he wasn't ignorant of the rules and guidelines that others lived by, clung to for security. Experience had taught him over the years that it was best for him to go it alone. Not to depend on the aid of others. He had his own back and that was the only thing that mattered. That and his mission.

He needed to get out of there. This detour had not

been a part of his plan. For years he'd been set on a solitary goal. It was finally so close that he could feel it in his grasp. There wasn't time for side trips. Distractions.

That's what she would be to him, even after all these years.

His bear hadn't forgotten her. It was the reason his bear had led him off the main drag of the highway and into the forest as soon as he'd picked up a trace of the scent that seemed all too familiar. All because his bear was chasing the scent of wildflowers and raindrops. Not just any raindrop, but the natural robust smell they took on once they settled in the heart of a prairie. Her scent was sweet, refreshing and earthy. No one else compared.

But, it was time for him to go. Leave her be. After all this time it should not have grated his soul to see her in the arms of another. She deserved a good and peaceful life. During the time she had been absent from his life he'd wished for her happiness and thought about her swollen with cubs. He just never gave a face to the mate that would be with her, by her side. Now he knew and that ripped a hole in his heart. And that feeling had pissed him off more than seeing her excited, and radiant as she was held in another's arms.

Getting on his Stateline from the left and taking hold of the handlebars, he balanced the weight of the bike as he knocked the kickstand up with the heel of his boot. Moving with an automation that had been a part of his travel for years, he pulled the clutch then started up his classic ride with a flick of his right thumb over two buttons.

When it roared to life, pounding his body with heavy vibrations, he wasted no time to head off. The area needed to be dust in his side mirrors and sealed in past memories he only allowed himself to recall on nights he was too exhausted to fight them.

Less than a mile down the road his view was drawn to one of his mirrors as the sight of multiple bears and men broke through the forest and onto the road in full sprints after him. He might be on a reconditioned Honda but it was faster than even a bear could run.

He'd disturbed their celebration and it didn't take genius for him to determine they wanted answers and possibly his pelt. The honorable thing would be for him to stop, pull over and provide answers. If he did that, he might get to see her. One more time. See up close how she had changed over the years.

Was she one of the shifted bears in pursuit of him? The raging wind blowing past him hindered him from picking up her scent. He knew it was for the best.

His bear clawed at his gut to turn around, go back. But he didn't. Couldn't.

That kind of thing wasn't his style. If he wanted something like that, he would have located his old sleuth instead of continuing on his solo path. With a twist of his right wrist he accelerated until the group was just a speck in the distance.

Keep on task. You're too close to achieving your goal. Over and over again he reminded himself, not willing to risk allowing his bear a moment of space to change his mind.

~YH~

"Did you all find him?" Riley questioned as she walked up to her husband, Theo, with their three kids in tow behind her.

Theo shook his head and pulled his wife to his side as he stared toward Cord.

Greta watched the mayor strut from the water, his face showing deep lines of concern. "We got eyes on the rogue Were, but he got some distance on us because he was on a motorcycle."

When Rena moved closer to him, he took hold of her hand but kept his gaze scanning the faces of the Den residents.

"Do you think the Were is out to cause harm?" Someone called out in the large crowd.

"I'm not sure. However, he was headed away from town. That leads me to believe the possibility that he'd stumbled upon us and isn't interested in anything further." Cord's dark gaze was shadowed.

Greta's core began to ache at Cord's words. She knew it was for the best that the person stayed away. However, even as she thought it, the restless bear inside of her didn't seem to agree.

"What do you want us to do, Mayor?" Rorke asked, standing off from the group with his back supported by a large tree.

"I'll head back into town and meet with the sheriff. I want everyone to keep an eye out and increase your routine property checks. After I get with Sheriff Smokey, send out information on the CBs."

Multiple responses of agreement and understanding went out as people began to disperse and gather their families for home. The arrival of a stranger had placed a damper on the event and Greta could feel the concerned energy coming off the inhabitants in waves.

No one was more concerned than she.

"Greta, you alright?"

She recognized Dainton's voice, as he moved up alongside her. She turned to face her cousin on her father's side. "Sure. Why wouldn't I be?"

He must have picked up on something in her voice, because he lifted an eyebrow at her then lowered his gaze to her arms.

It was at that moment she realized she was briskly rubbing her hands up and down her arms. She had been feeling chilled to her core since the group had returned. Unaware of her own actions, she'd been attempting to warm herself.

Dropping her arms, she shrugged. "Everyone is a little thrown off by what happened."

"Of course." Thankfully, Dainton allowed his question to drop. Like everyone else in town, her cousin knew part of what had happened to her when she was younger. "Look, I'm going to head into town with Cord." Pulling his hopefully soon-to-be-bonded mate to his side with an arm around her shoulder, he continued, "Do you mind if Ebony heads to the house with you and your parents?"

"Not at all." Greta looked at her new friend and the newest employee at the consulting firm she and Dainton ran. "Don't worry, Ebony, everything will be okay." It made her feel more calm acting as protector for another. Every word she told Ebony, she told herself three times over.

"I believe that." Ebony fingered the damp lock behind her ear as she gazed over the raging stream toward the other bank and the forest beyond. "It's just that it has only been a few months since I even knew what a Were was and that I was one. Now, to discover that there are wild, vicious ones out there..." A quake rocked her voluptuous form.

"Daunting. But we don't know that he's vicious, just not one of our sleuth."

Ebony stepped in closer. "Did you hear that roar?"

she whispered.

Oh, yeah. Greta thought as her bear whined from within. "Come on. My mother makes the best honeyed bananas foster in Den County. I think it is just what we both need."

Smiling Ebony nodded.

"Thanks, Greta." Dainton kissed Ebony, whispered some private words in her ear and then was off.

By the golden flecks in Ebony's gaze, Greta could only assume it was something naughty. Shaking her head, she looped her arm through the other woman's and headed to a path through the woods. "Come on, Ebony. Let's go get you something warm, sticky and sweet."

"Sounds good to me."

To Greta as well. She was anxious to get home and be secured in her parent's house surrounded by things that brought her comfort. Now more than any other time she needed it.

CHAPTER TWO

What the fuck am I doing here? Hansel sat on his bike two hundred yards away from a sign that read Den County. TRESPASSERS UNWELCOME.

Almost fifteen hours ago he'd had this area in his side mirror as he continued on his quest. However, he'd made it to a small city about twenty miles away and stayed out under the stars in the park. He could have gotten a room at one of the hotels, but he needed the open air to think. There was a war going on inside of him. A struggle between him and his bear, an unrest. He could almost feel the animal prowling around his core.

He had never been as close to his goal as he was now, yet he couldn't drag himself further. Couldn't keep pressing on to victory, because of one thing—her.

She was the reason he'd awakened and left the park at five in the morning and journeyed back up the road where he'd come from. With the sun just barely starting to rise and lighting the sky to a soft orange and pale purple he'd started his ride up and cruised toward the turnoff for Den County.

He had no doubt he would be spotted. In Were communities, even greater than small town USA, they didn't take well to outsiders or what they would consider to be disruption to their lives. A single male Were-bear was a definite problem. It was still early and the area only had a few people driving around, unlocking businesses. However, if the number of people he'd seen out at the stream was any indication, this place had an ample number of residents.

It only took thirty minutes to drive down Main Street and park his bike in the middle of the long wide strip of Paw Tracks Street before the Fur Fill, which stated in small letters that it was some kind of general store. However, peering through the big windowpanes on the front of the store, he would have described it as a grocery store, plain and simple. However, maybe they sold more than groceries.

He shrugged and waited. After swinging his leg over his ride, he leaned his backside against it, digging his heels into the dirt for purchase just in case things got a little hairy before they got friendly. Pulling a strip of smoked salmon jerky out of his saddlebag, he gnawed on it patiently. Waiting.

A door across the street opened and someone stepped out and eyed him. The first person to stride toward him was a Were who was not only big but wide—built like a typical Were-bear. No one had to tell him who he was, the uniform and badge proclaimed it clearly.

"Morning. Can I assist you with something? You lost?"

The big burly guy stopped a few feet away from

him, so Hansel could read the name on the bronze badge. Hansel had pretty good eyesight, as did most bears, and could clearly see the stenciled letters on the glass door of the place the male had come from—Sheriff's Office.

Hansel didn't even have to take a wild guess, Sherriff Smokey was boldly engraved on the badge.

"No, sir." Hansel continued to tear off chunks of dried meat between his teeth as he kept his other hand resting at his side, the heel of his palm pressing into the leather of the seat. He swallowed. "I generally don't find myself lost. I go where I intend to end up."

One side of the uniformed were-male's lip curled slightly.

Hansel was impressed the man didn't let out a growl, a warning to his flippant answers.

"Well, let me ask a more direct question. What are your *intentions* in Den County?"

A few other people began to move in closer and gather around behind the law male. Hansel could see multiple trucks and cars moving with swiftness into town.

Yup. Word had gotten out quickly. *There was a stranger in town.* Would he be friend or foe was probably the question going through all of their minds.

That was still to be determined in *his* mind. However, he didn't come here for trouble. Trouble was already waiting for him sixty miles up the highway. He was here for one thing...one person.

Scanning the growing bodies of men and women observing him, Hansel did a slow check behind his back and sure enough there were two men standing practically shoulder-to-shoulder like a human wall. Most likely they had positioned themselves there to keep him from fleeing as he had yesterday. But, he had no plans of going until he got what he'd come for.

The men were the two on the rock in the middle of the stream with the woman. Hansel's bear clawed at him as he met the gaze of the dark-haired male standing beside a blonde male.

Hansel dragged in a long, deep breath through his nostrils as he put a leash on his bear. Answers were what he needed, but he wouldn't get them if he started a brawl on Main Street.

He returned his gaze to the were-male before him. "I'm here to check up on a friend."

"Well you sure have a strange way of dropping in. You frightened our children and some of our elderly with all that noise you made yesterday," the lawman said, his voice gruff.

That couldn't be helped, Hansel thought but kept his silence. A comment like that would spark more questions than the five hundred these folks already had.

"What friend is it you're looking for? Let's get them out here so you can conduct your business and be gone."

The sharp, hard glare from the male before Hansel spoke volumes. He wasn't welcome in town.

"Name." The lawman asked.

~YH~

Greta rolled over to her side in bed and pulled the covers over her head. She was awake. She had been up for hours since she'd awakened from a dream/nightmare. It had been years since her mind had returned to images she'd worked hard to keep buried. Since two in the morning she'd found herself on a mental sit-and-spin remembering things she was better off never having recalled.

However, her bear declared that wasn't completely true. Even though some of the things she remembered were frightening, there was something…someone that she felt altogether different about. Over the years, she'd told herself she wanted to forget and erase everything…however, that wasn't the case. It wasn't true.

Him, she could never forget.

Him, she occasionally sat alone on the bank of the stream and allowed herself to bring up his image. His face. What he would look like now.

His scent had saturated her soul and even though she hadn't smelled it since the last time she'd seen him, it was there. A part of her.

He had the smell of warm, woodsy cashmere. It had been that smell in the woods yesterday that had gotten her in a quagmire of emotions.

She was grateful today was her late day for work and she could attempt to reclaim the sleep she'd been denied all night. Taking in the darkness beneath the covers, she slowed her breathing and concentrated on clearing her mind so she could lose herself to the sandman's power.

Knock. Knock.

Nooo. She groaned.

"Greta, are you up?" her papa-bear, Manni Armel's muffled voice came through her closed room door.

She wondered if she didn't answer him if he'd go away. Her parents knew her schedule. She kept it posted on the refrigerator as she had done since going to work with her cousin years ago. Manni and Rita had kept a watchful eye on her, Greta didn't mind. Most of the time.

"Wake up, dear." It was her mother's voice coming from the other side of the comforter under which Greta had buried herself.

"Grrrr." She snatched the covering down and rolled to her back, staring at her mother.

"Don't you go growling at me." Her mother stood beside her bed dressed in her jam-making apron with her hands on her hips. "It's the Sheriff you can give your temper to when you get to town."

"Why am I going to town?" Greta didn't have plans to go anywhere but to la-la land located in the warm bed she was currently in. "Whatever you need me to pick up, I'll get it on the way home."

"Sheriff Smokey radioed in, Greta. He needs you in town immediately." It was her father, a big dark-skinned gray-haired were-male, who spoke.

Shoving herself to a seated position, she fingered her messy long ebony strands away from her face and scratched her head. Letting loose a loud yawn to show her parents just how exhausted she still was, she met their gazes. "I don't see any reason Den's sheriff would need me. Right now. What can't wait until later this afternoon?"

Her father rubbed the smooth skin of his head and his gaze shifted away from hers.

That loss of eye contact made the heavy worried feelings she'd been battling all night settle heavily in her stomach. Her father was always upfront with her.

"Papa-bear?"

"Look, dear, apparently there is some dispute happening in town right now. You're the only person that can settle it."

"Me?" She looked from left to right. She didn't have a significant role in town, like sheriff or mayor, nothing that was so important a town decision would rest on her shoulders.

"Yes, Greta. Now up and out." Her no-nonsense mother waved her out of bed.

Heeding her mother's urging, she crawled out of bed, feeling more like a contrite sixteen-moon girl than the grown female she was now. Her ankle was tight and a twinge shot through it as she put her weight on it, proof of her over use of it yesterday. "Is anyone planning to explain to me what is going on?"

"I'm sure you will discover all the answers you need soon enough. Dress quickly, you can ride into town with your father."

A parental escort. This was getting worse by the minute. Padding into her bathroom as her parents exited her room, Greta wracked her brain in an attempt to figure out what could be going on. If her dad didn't want her to drive into town alone, that meant it was not only serious…but possibly dangerous.

Twenty minutes later she was showered and dressed and sitting beside her father in his truck eating one of two honey biscuits her mother had prepared that morning. Greta would have preferred the full spread of breakfast her mouth had watered for, but apparently there was no time for a proper meal.

"Dad, is there something you can tell me about what is going on?" She tried her small innocent voice on her father. It always worked to soften him to her side, especially when she was in trouble for pulling some teenage prank with her were friends.

"I don't know much, Greta. Instead of me giving you the bits and pieces I know and you surmising the wrong situation, I believe it is best we just wait it out. We'll be in town soon." He reached across the seat and patted her knee.

Damn, it didn't work. Whatever information her dad had, he was holding close to his chest.

"Tell me. Do you think Chase Furfield or Simeon Grizmen will start pursuing you more seriously after that big catch and win of yours yesterday? Maybe even Lenny Gobi."

She let out a laugh followed by a groan. "Oh, gracious papa-bear, neither I hope." Both of the men annoyed her. They were best friends who competed over everything. Their arguments always ended in an arm wrestling or a grappling match. Dating either one of them would make a girl exhausted.

"I think you could handle them. Chase is doing well at the lumberyard, he just made shift leader. And that Simeon will be taking over his family's meat curing business." Her father couldn't keep the corners of his mouth from twitching in humor.

Greta knew he was trying to keep the mood light; she played along for the sake of time.

"You know, papa-bear, maybe I've judged their silly antics too harshly. I need to take more of a serious look at the two of them. They are very easy on the eyes. I'm sure you and mama are ready for me to get out of your house and start providing you with grands."

That got her father's fur all ruffled. "Hell if my daughter will settle for either one of those two nincompoops."

"Just think. My life would be full of laughs." Turning to him, she gave him a small innocent smile. "Don't you want me to be happy? Chase or Lenny would be an excellent choice for that."

"Only if you wanted to be in the next town that had the closest nut house. I swear those boys have knocked more than one screw from each of their brains." Her father shook his head in disgust.

"Well, then papa-bear, just for you. I'll just have to wait and see who the Great Spirit brings my way."

Her father frowned and eyed her sharply as he glanced away from the road briefly. She noted in his deep onyx gaze that he knew she'd played him.

Winking, she reached over and patted his knee as they turned onto the road that led into town. As they progressed toward the center of Main Street, her father started to slow his truck as they both spotted the large crowd gathered in the road.

"What in the hell?"

Her father took the words right out of her mouth. Whatever was going on it was major. By the time on the truck clock it was barely seven in the morning and the number of people and vehicles around made it appear closer to noon and a lunch rush.

A few people turned and pointed in their direction as her father drew the truck to a complete stop.

"Since everyone seems to be waiting for me, I guess I can't stay in the truck."

"Guess not." Her father reached across the seat and squeezed her hand. "I'll be right here."

Giving him a quick nod, she opened the door and slipped out of her father's high cab. As she sank to the ground that ominous feeling returned in her stomach. It didn't help that the crowd seemed to part wider with every step she made. She could hear the murmurs from the county folk around her, but she didn't really pick up on enough clues to understand what they were talking about.

"Greta?" It was Sheriff Smokey's deep baritone voice.

"Here she is sheriff." Someone called out and seemed to urge her forward with a hand to her back.

Greta had the urge to turn and snap at the person, but she restrained herself.

"Great. Now we can get all this settled." The Sheriff stepped through the crowd toward her. He was a handsome older male. He'd been single during all the years she had known him, but recently he had reconnected with her parent's neighbor's daughter—the love of his life. That woman was also the mother of Rena, one of Greta's good friends who'd moved into town after finding her own mate—Cord, the new mayor.

With the overflowing love in his life, the Sheriff displayed more smiles than he had with his previous gruff exterior. However, the deep-set frown in his face reminded her of the old lawman he had been. That increased her nervousness.

"What can I do for you, Sheriff Smokey?" She kept her cool, with all these Were's around her, they would be able to smell her anxiety.

Sheriff placed a gentle hand on her shoulder. "Do you know this Were?" He stepped to the side.

Instantly her knees went weak and her heart raced. It wasn't because of his handsome face. Boy was he good looking. He had a strong squared jawline, a thick bottom lip below a slightly thinner upper lip and long dark hair that hung in waves, way past the collar of his t-shirt. The male had shoulders as wide as any other were-male in town, but he gave her thoughts and images she should not be having with so many people standing around her. It was his eyes that drew her and locked her in. Basic Were-bear black…yet they seemed to share secrets with her. Know things that she had never told her family. That knowledge made her shiver with fear, not caring that everyone around her could probably sense it.

No, she didn't know his face because he had grown up. A lot. But she would never forget the sweet woodsy scent that was his alone.

"Well, Greta?" This came from Dainton her cousin who nudged her shoulder.

She must have been standing there dense and silent for too long.

The sexy Were before her smiled. Well if that's what one could call the left corner of his mouth twitching and lifting a few millimeters.

"Yes. Maybe...yes." She licked her lips, trying to control the stumbling over her words.

"Which is it?" Dainton's tone was low with a slight rumble, proof that her cousin could sense her discomfort.

The intruder from her past was quick to pick up on the situation as well because he ended the nonchalant pose he had maintained against his motorcycle and took his full height. However, he never took his gaze away from her.

Not wanting people to misunderstand her feelings, Greta rushed on. "I'm sure he's not here to harm anyone."

"How do you know him?" The Sheriff knew the story of her disappearance and just like her parents, he was overprotective of her.

"What's his name? He refused to give it to us." Rorke, one of the males in the crowd standing behind the visitor, called out.

Damn. She shoved her hands deep in her jeans pockets. To recall his name would mean she would be forced to go into deep memories she had worked hard to suppress. Ones that were beginning to ooze out from under the locked door of her mind. Sweat beaded up on her skin and began to roll along the center of her chest.

Shit. Oh, shit. She wasn't a nervous person by nature. She had always considered herself to have a strong disposition, but this situation was altering her very nature.

"Hansel. It's Hansel." Stepping up, he took hold of her arm and began to pull her through the crowd gathered around them.

Needing to escape, she allowed him to lead her away from her family and friends.

"Where the hell do you think you're taking her?" That growl came from her father.

Hansel didn't even pause in stride as he shouldered his way out, making a lane for them.

"I'm alright, papa-bear." Greta called out to him over her shoulder as she moved her feet in a swift pass to keep up with Hansel's long strides.

Leaving his bike he strutted down the center of Main Street daring cars and trucks to hit them.

"Where are we going?" Greta asked, keeping her focus away from the heat of his touch, which she could feel through her shirt.

"The hell if I know. Don't know this town."

Males. She shook her head. "Go left," she advised.

They weaved their way through oncoming traffic, which she was pretty sure by the stares they were getting as vehicles passed them that it was busy because by now everyone had heard that an outsider was in town and they came to see what was going on.

"If we keep straight down this road it will lead us to

the park entrance." Once they were along the sidewalk, she tugged against his hold. "I can walk on my own."

He stopped. Looking at her, those deep intense black eyes now had small chips of gold in them.

Seeing the tinge of color caused her core to tighten. Quickly she stepped back, thankful that he had let her arm go.

"Sorry, I'm not trying to frighten you, Greta." His voice was a husky timbre.

Cars still whipped by and she glanced toward the street, seeing they were still in full view of the townsfolk. "I'm not scared. Look let's get a little more privacy." Not waiting for him to follow, she started walking again. When she entered the park she didn't stop until she got to one of the picnic tables at the edge of the playground. Thankfully it was too early for parents to have their young playing along the jungle gym equipment.

"Why did you come here?" She stood beside the table pressing her hands flat on the smooth, crafted wood that she knew her friend Rorke's family company would have made.

"Look at me, Greta."

Damn, his voice, just like his eyes and body, were all too beguiling. Her mind attempted to convince her not to turn around, to protect her emotions from the rushing memories that she was sure were soon to come once the floodgates were open. However, her body had a will of its own.

Turning, she faced him. He was too close. Not close enough for her to feel his body heat, but if she took a step they would be sneakers to boots. "What now?"

"Say my name."

"Wh-at?" She stuttered.

"I never believed I would see you again. Your face and everything that I knew about you has haunted my mind both day and night over the years. I've thought about the sound of your voice saying my name." He spoke in a low, confident, commanding voice, "Say it."

Biting the inside of her bottom lip, she tried to step back but the edge of the table pressed against her ass leaving her unable to put more space between them. "Hansel." The name tumbled from her lips, the bomb that shattered the dam.

Her body began to tremble as images and nightmares poured out into her mind. Things she'd fought to forget, things she'd worked hard at containing…memories better left packed away.

"You happy now?" she growled.

"Ye—" He reached up, as if to touch her face.

She swatted his hand away. When she had first been returned to her family, she'd allowed her parents to hold and console her that first night. Then she'd put a wall around her mind and emotions dealing with the situation and would not discuss it.

Undeterred, he gripped her shoulders and pulled her body forward. His gaze searching hers. "I'm not happy if my presence has caused you pain, Blackberry."

That nickname had been what he'd called her the one time she had shifted after she'd been captured and tossed inside a cage, injured. That memory was sweet and horrific all at once.

"Well, it has." She placed her palms flat on his chest and pushed.

He didn't budge. Dragging her closer, he pressed his mouth close to her ear and spoke, "Talk to me."

"N-o-o." She didn't talk to anyone about what had

happened. The smell of him and the heat of his body brought comfort and a high level of desire she'd never known.

"You know you can trust me." The warmth of his breath caressed the shell of her ear.

She sank her teeth hard on the inside of her bottom lip holding back the whimper that tightened her throat. There was nothing she could do about the cream that drenched her labia and pooled in her panties. The park around her was starting to have a golden haze. Even though nothing like that had ever happened to her before, she wasn't ignorant of what it meant. But, why now...why Hansel?

Males in Den had tried to get her attention too many times for her to count, but none had caused this reaction. Now this male from her haunted past showed up and her hormones were going haywire.

Hansel's growl rumbled along the side of her neck as he lowered his head and buried his nose against her skin. "Blackber—"

"Stop, Hansel." Catching him unaware, she shoved him away and moved quickly. Once the table was between them she said, "Why did you come here?"

His features were drawn tight as he gripped the sides of the wooden top, his golden gaze locked on hers. "It wasn't my intention. I didn't even know this was where you were from. I was passing through."

Folding her arms under her breasts, she tilted her head and said, "You should have kept on through."

He stood there, silent for a moment. His gaze roamed from her face along her throat to her breasts now perched high on her forearms.

Her nipples tightened and pressed into her bra in response. Keeping herself and him on the topic at hand, she lifted her arms until they covered her bosom.

The gold in his eyes had faded somewhat when they met hers again. "Look, Blackberr—"

"Greta."

One thick, well-shaped brow arched high. "Blackberry," he declared.

Taking up the challenge, she set her hands on her hips. "Greta. That's my name. Use it or find your bike and get back on the highway outta here."

Those large, strong hands of his tightened on the edge of the table. She could almost hear the wood starting to crack. However, she wouldn't budge from her words. Hansel didn't scare her physically, but emotionally she wanted to run like hell was behind her.

With one sharp nod, he gave in, "Greta."

Damn, she should have allowed him to keep calling her the nickname. The rich, seductive slow timbre he used to whisper her name made her thighs ache. Made her mind play images of what it would be like to wrap her legs around him and feel him thrusting deep inside of her.

Not good, not good, not good. This were-male, made her body desire to play in an area she'd never ventured into before.

"Now that we have established my name, how soon can you get out of town?"

Assuming his full height, he shrugged. Maybe he just needed to see that I was okay. That I had *survived* the ordeal we had both gone through. I had survived, hadn't I?

"I was considering hanging around a few days."

What? "Why? I'm fine." She held her arms out allowing him to take in her unscathed form.

Quickly she realized it was the wrong action. Hansel's gaze moved along her form, taking in everything from her face to her thighs. He followed the path in the wake of his stare.

She lowered her arms. "Your curiosity should be satisfied." Turning, she began walking toward the entrance of the park, ready to leave this male and her past in the past. "You'll want to get out of town ASAP. Den residents don't like trespassers." She tossed over her shoulder.

"In your perfectly executed exit, did you consider I may be here for me?"

His words stopped her in her tracks. She faced him on a slow pivot but kept her silence.

He hadn't let her get far from him, because he was only a couple steps away from her. Evidence that he wasn't just allowing her to walk off.

"That I might need this, Blackberry."

There went that damn name again. She ignored it for the moment. "Why would you need it? It's apparent you got away as well."

One long step closed the gap between them. He wasn't touching her, but she could feel the heat of his body surrounding hers.

"Sometimes getting away doesn't free you."

He was correct. She couldn't bring herself to part her lips and admit that to him. To anyone. It was barely a confession to herself. It had been almost fifteen years since the incident, yet she still carried the scars in her mind. "Look, Hansel. I would love to be your therapist…truly I would," she droned on, "But, I have responsibilities, people who count on me…a life. Unlike you I can't just take leisure rides around the country seeing old friends."

Resting his fists on his hips, he shifted his weight to one side. "Well, I'm glad you've been able to let it all go and get a life." He leaned in and sniffed. "Unmated as it may be."

Her lower jaw dropped, leaving her mouth agape as she stumbled back from him. "Etiquette! In Den we don't just go around sniffing people when we feel like it." That actually wasn't the truth. Were-bears lived by their sense of smell. However, they normally were more subtle about it.

He released a low chuckle that rumbled through the air, however it sounded humorless. "You know where I'm from, the ways in which I was raised."

Hell, yes she knew. "Look, I can't do this." She shook her head. "Not now…" not ever she wanted to add but didn't.

"Then I'll just hang out until you're ready." He called after her retreating form.

"Good luck with that. No B & B or hotels in Den County." She yelled out without turning around. Getting far away from Hansel was her aim.

As she kept walking, she focused her attention on her delicate hearing and tried to pick up any trace that he was following her. The only sound was her own steps along the sidewalk. Satisfied, she almost sighed with relief until she spotted the group at the entrance of the park bold as day, showing that they may have allowed her to walk away with the stranger, but they still had her back.

"I'm fine!" She called out as she strolled right past Cord, Rorke, Sheriff Smokey, her father, and her cousin. "Dainton, don't we have work to do? I'll see you at the office."

Shouldering her way through the big men she

moved with force and purpose leaving the overbearing men of her life to do whatever the hell they wanted to as long as they stayed the hell out of her way. She was aching for a fight, she was hoping that someone in town would just push the right button or step in her way and she would lay them out flat. It wasn't that she was angry, but there was so much energy and tension pumping through her blood that she wanted something to do with it.

Sex. Her bear growled inside of her.

"Yeah, right." Even though she knew that part of the tension she felt was her intense and passionate attraction for the outsider Were. However, in the years she had entered adulthood, she had not taken any of the males in town up on their offer to roll around in the forest or sheets. She didn't know why, because there were a lot of good-looking males in town. Females were always panting or discussing whom they wanted to screw or had recently screwed. But, none of them interested her.

None of them turned her knees backward or curled her toes. Not like Hansel.

Her bear attempted to urge her to go back to him by flashing scenes of her laid out on top of the table naked with the long, dark-haired male thrusting deep inside of her as the hot sun beat down on both of them.

She groaned and her legs buckled slightly, but she kept a tight hold on her resolve.

Trying to distract herself she nodded at people as she passed by them headed to the office.

Fifteen minutes later she made a left onto Snout Lane and crossed the parking lot to the front door. She didn't have to use her key, since the office door was unlocked.

"Hey there. Didn't expect you until later, sunshi—" Ebony was coming out of the copier room and stopped midsentence. "Wow, girl, you look like you want to shift and maul a hiker."

Greta laughed at Ebony, her co-worker and cousin's mate...well, sort of mate. Dainton had gone down to San Francisco for a meeting and had come back with a female Were...who hadn't know she was a Were-bear. Ebony Scrooge didn't know much about their kind so had agreed to come with Dainton to learn more about who she was. However, with that agreement Ebony had refused to mate with Dainton until she'd shifted.

It was a bone of contention between the lovers, because Dainton wanted to give Ebony the last bite and make her his permanently, but Ebony refused outright.

"Ebony, I'm pissed." Greta made a beeline to her office and claimed her chair behind the desk.

"I can see that." The stylish were-female leaned against the doorjamb. "Dainton shot out of the office over and hour ago after a call from Cord about some outsider in town looking for you."

Shoving her hands through the twist of her hair, Greta groaned. "Well, he found me."

"Who is he?" Ebony moved deeper into the room.

Reclining back in her chair, she avoided her friend's eyes and stared out the window. "Do you mind if we don't talk about him? I'm a little talked out at the moment."

"Absolutely. But, how about we escape the males of this town and go to the lake tonight for some girl time and drinks. I hear Riley got a couple bottles of honey wine from Shardik Farms."

"Two to ten drinks sound good about now." Greta

leaned forward and turned on her computer.

Ebony laughed. "Well, hold off a few hours. I'll call the other ladies and see who's in."

She gave her a small smile. It was all she could muster up at the moment. "Thanks, Ebony."

"Hey, since I've been here, you ladies have shown me that these are the kind of things friends do for each other." Ebony winked at her and moved toward the door.

It had been true. Ebony had been a successful businesswoman, but a loner. She didn't have family or friends and kept to herself with the exception of one friend. The same friend that had set her up with a mystery date that had gone sideways and she'd ended up caught in a mating heat with Dainton.

Pulling up the reports she had to work on that day, Greta began counting down the hours until nightfall. Maybe getting drunk would help her bury the memory back in the vault of her mind. And hopefully by then Hansel would have made his way out of town.

Hopefully.

Hopefully not, her bear countered.

CHAPTER THREE

He had wanted to follow every step of Greta's full swaying hips. When she walked away in irritation, there was a subtle hitch to her purposeful steps. He knew where that notch in her gate had come from. It was not extremely noticeable, but he had been intent in his observation of her, taking in every change that life had gifted her with over the years.

As a young girl she'd been pretty, cute and scared. Her big black eyes had practically taken up most of her face. What had remained had been filled with the thickness of her lips.

However it was evident in so many ways how her body had developed into adulthood. A curvaceous beauty with ample breasts, rounded thighs and enough body that a Were-male could easily get lost in it for hours. As an adult female, her wide eyes had a saucy tilt to them at the outer corners and her lips were still wide and pronounced in her round face, beckoning a male—him—to kiss them. He desired to see them turn up in a smile or parted in passion.

The deep nutmeg complexion of her skin tempted him to run his tongue over it, tracing every path to her pleasure.

He yearned to see all her ebony hair spread out on sheets as he thrust deep inside of her.

A groan came out of his mouth.

His bear panted. *Mine.*

The intense, erotic and visceral response to Greta shook his core.

As a youth, he'd felt a bond to her, but he'd only seen himself as her protector.

Not this…this—

"I hope you have the answers you came for." The Sheriff stood blocking his path with his hands planted on his hips before a smaller crowd than had gathered around Hansel when he'd parked in the heart of town. However, none of the male faces had become any friendlier.

Hansel's focus had been so intent on Greta that he hadn't realized he had migrated out of the park.

"And you can get back on your bike and go." The additional comment came from the male, Hansel recalled, as the one he had seen sweeping Greta into his arms at the lake.

Why was he still hanging around? What was his relationship to Greta?

Mine. He bear growled scratching and clawing inside of him…wanting out.

Hansel kept a lid on his temper, he wasn't afraid of any of these six males, but he didn't come to fight but to talk with Greta. Ensure she was okay.

Taking his time as he continued strolling toward the group at the mouth of the park, Hansel said, "Not really. So, I'll be around until I do." Stopping a few feet before them, he shot his gaze to the Were that had dared to touch Greta.

"Listen up, Hansel…right?" The Sheriff began.

Shifting his attention to the lawman, he gave him a sharp nod.

"We don't want any trouble in Den—"

"Didn't come to bring any." Hansel folded his arms over his chest, keeping his heels planted wide, just in case trouble started.

The same male from the lake stepped up, aligning his shoulders with the sheriff's, and took on the same stance as Hansel—not challenging, but a definite show of force.

Hansel's bear dug deep in his core. And Hansel was tempted to shift, not to kill the male, but just to let some fur fly. He felt tense and agitated on so many levels he felt he couldn't even see straight.

"Good to know. However, since it doesn't seem that Greta wants anything more to do with you, I think it's best you continue on down the road." The lawman turned as if his words were the final decision.

This Were didn't know him. Hansel had stopped taking orders and allowing anyone to dictate to him where he could go and what he could do. "Don't think so."

Three words that might as well have been a gun going off.

Both the Sheriff and the hugger stepped forward growling.

Vision going red, Hansel lowered his arms and released a loud piercing sound of his own. Daring one of them to shift.

"Let's keep our heads about us now." Another male

standing at the fringe of the group stepped forward and placed a hand the male's chest. "Dainton, I know you want to protect Greta, but this isn't the way. You know if she got wind of you fighting all through the park on her behalf she'd have your ass."

"So, what...you just want me to stand back and let him press his way on her?" Dainton swung his gaze from the mediator back to Hansel.

"No. But, don't go defending her before she even calls out for help." The male with the apparent voice of reason, faced Hansel fully. "I'm Cord, the Mayor of Den County." He held his hand out toward him.

Hansel stared down at the palm offered as he took a few deep breaths to get his bear back under control. Not wanting to disrespect the first offer of kindness in the strange county, he gripped it and gave the mayor's hand a firm shake.

After they parted, Cord continued, "How long do you plan on staying in town?"

"Hadn't decided. A lot of that depends on Greta."

"Hm." That came from Dainton.

Cord shot Dainton a hard look before addressing Hansel again. "I understand. However, if it takes beyond sun down for her to give you the time of day again, there's no place for you to rest your head here. We're kind of a closed community and like to keep it that way...if you can understand."

"I do. It won't be the first time I slept beside my bike under the stars." Hansel wanted to make it clear that he was not leaving the town until he was good and ready. He was tired of making that clear to these men and Greta. *He* would say when it was time for him to continue on his journey.

Cord sighed and scratched his head. Hansel could

actual see him warring with his thoughts at the impasse. "Sheriff Smokey will have to be the one who gives permission for that."

Sheriff stepped up. "I don't want the Den folks uneasy about some strange Were-bear hanging out in the park day and night. I suggest you find another city to bed down tonight and just come back in the morning and try to approach Greta then."

Hansel cocked his head to the side. "That doesn't wo—"

"I swear you males don't have the manners the Great Spirit gave out."

"You guys will have the park turned upside down without a thought."

Two older women, with silver-streaked hair, one white and one black came shoving through the group of males. All the males appeared to take a step back and look a little bashful.

Interesting.

Cord took hold of the white woman's shoulders as if trying to halt her progress toward Hansel. "Grandma, this is no place—"

"Oh, pipe down, Mayor. We're just trying to show this male a little Den County hospitality. Right, Genma?"

"Right, Octavia." Genma, the older black woman smiled at him. "Have you eaten?"

"I'm sure you're hungry." The woman who was called Octavia shook off the hands of the mayor and moved up alongside her cohort.

He couldn't recall ever having grandparents and the last time anyone showed him such sweet, motherly kindness wasn't even a clear memory in his mind. "Um..." Hansel wasn't sure what to say, he felt befuddled. He wanted to give these two ladies the same kind of reticent treatment he'd easily displayed to the males, but he was finding it hard. He'd never struggled with such awkward emotions. "Sorta."

"I bet you haven't." Genma declared.

"Look, Ann over at Gobi's Diner makes the best smoked salmon fritta you've ever put in your mouth." Octavia stepped to him and wrapped her arm through his.

"And the honey butter on the rolls." Genma took hold of his other arm.

"Ladies, I don't think this is going to solve the issues." Sheriff Smokey stepped into their path.

"And what you all were growling and scratching about was?" Octavia moved and tugged Hansel forward.

"We don't want to keep Rita waiting any longer at Gobi's." Genma declared as she continued in step with the older woman, dragging him along with them.

"What's my wife doing over there? I don't want her involved in this until I know what the were-male's aim is with my daughter." A tall black male with short curly gray hair blocked their way.

Greta's father.

Hansel eyed the Were, seeing the resemblance not only in Greta's nutmeg complexion, but her eyes and nose as well.

The older females moved right around him as if he were but a small consideration. "Manni, Greta is her daughter as well. She has every right to get to know this fine male bear." Octavia patted Hansel's arm.

Looking from left to right at the two bulldozers as they led him from the park and to the main road, he felt more nervous about sitting with them in a diner than he had before a group of males ready to shift at any moment.

The were-males continued to grumble behind them about meddling were-females, but Hansel noticed that none of them stepped forward to stop the older females. No rescue for him.

He was good at fighting, defending himself with fist or claws, but what these seasoned females wanted from him, conversation, he had no recourse.

Keeping his silence, he allowed them to guide their progress, waiting to see if he would be presented with a way out.

The two females kept a lively discussion about events coming up in the county that he had no clue about. Ten minutes later they entered the restaurant.

It was packed with people enjoying breakfast and conversation.

Someone stood up and waved at them from a back table.

"There's Rita." Octavia released his arm and weaved through the tables, smiling and stopping occasionally to speak to people as she passed them.

Genma kept a firm hold on him, as if she were concerned he would bolt if she turned him loose.

He probably would have.

"Hi, this is Hansel…he's new in town." Genma would say when she paused to address someone who asked her a question.

It shocked him how they were presenting him to people as if he were a wanted guest. Like they'd invited him for a holiday stay.

It didn't escape him that the females of the town grinned and nodded, while the men eyed him suspiciously. No one had to tell him that the entire county had been informed about his presence and about him having a private conversation with Greta in the park.

"Rita, this is Hansel..." Octavia stared at him as if she were waiting for him to fill in the blank.

"It's just Hansel." He'd had a family name, even remembered it. When he used it, it just brought pain and memories he didn't want to deal with, so he left it off.

"Well, just Hansel, I'm Greta's mother, Rita Armel, and it is nice to meet you." She placed a hand on his shoulder as warmth filled her gaze.

"You too, Mrs. Armel." He felt unsure of himself and he didn't enjoy that feeling at all. He'd never met a female's mother before in his life. The women he associated with, mostly non-Weres, were women he just got with for a night or two of physical release.

She waved her hand before him. "None of that, Mrs. stuff...just Rita. Sit."

He waited until the females had claimed their seats then took the seat across the table from Rita as Octavia and Genma sat to the left and right of them.

"Well, well, well...I see you all got our county stranger in here finally." A woman with an apron approached the table all smiles and smelling of sweet honey and buttery fried eggs.

"If it were up to the males of the county they would let him starve to death, Ann." Genma shook her head.

"How they expect a person to have any kind of discussion on an empty stomach is beyond me." Octavia fluffed her short silver-blond hair.

His stomach chose that moment to sound off loudly. That piece of jerky he'd eaten well over two hours ago was long gone.

"I hear you, son…" Ann laughed. "I'll have Lindsey bring you out a plate of my frittata."

"Don't forget a bowl of those rolls." Rita winked at her.

"You got it. Anything for you ladies?"

Everyone ordered drinks only and Ann went back through the diner, hugging and smiling at people along the way.

"You're going to enjoy the First Moon Festival when it comes around."

He frowned. "There's a festival coming up?" Celebrations, of any kind, were something else he'd never been a part of. He always kept to himself for the holidays.

"In a few weeks, there sure is." Genma said, her eyes lighting up with excitement.

"Sorry to disappoint you ladies, but I probably won't be around here in a few weeks." He could only allow a day or two off his journey. He couldn't risk losing the headway he'd made.

"We'll let time take care of itself." Octavia added, not appearing at all discouraged by his response.

"Greta will be Den County's honoree at the festival." Rita's knowing black gaze met his.

The waitress chose that moment to arrive with a tray filled with their four drinks. Warm tea for Genma and Octavia, water for Rita and his coffee with extra honey. Most Weres had a sweet tooth, however, his was more prominent than most. He figured it was because he'd been denied small pleasures such as treats for so long in his adolescence that his body made up for it.

"Thanks." He nodded at the young were-female with Lindsey stitched in cursive on her uniform blouse.

"Anytime...Your food should be up soon. *Anything* else I can get for you in the meantime?" The heat in her gaze and the come-hither smile on her thin lips didn't leave any doubt what Lindsey was offering—fun in the woods.

She was attractive with her pale skin and red hair, but his body didn't even stir for her. Especially not with Greta so close. His bear had one focus and one only—Greta Armel.

"I believe Franklin is signaling you. We don't want to keep you from your *job*." Genma flapped her hand as if shooing away a bothersome fly.

Lindsey's seductive smile dropped as she scurried away to another table.

"You were saying about Greta, Rita?" Octavia guided the conversation back on the path it was before the waitress showed up.

"Ah, yes, yes, my daughter will be the honoree at the festival. Her getting that fish the other day was a big deal."

Octavia rested a hand on her bosom. "No female has ever won it before. Impressive."

"Won what?" Hansel asked.

"The salmon catch competition you witnessed the other day." Genma lifted her teacup to her lips and sipped, her gaze never wavering from his.

He almost felt like blushing hearing the woman bring up the fact that he'd been hiding in the woods observing the love and fellowship of their community. However, he schooled his features, kept them blank as he cleared his throat. "Oh, was that what was going on?"

Nothing about yesterday had even registered in his mind except Greta, seeing her after so long. Then that other male's arms around her. He rubbed the back of his neck calming the hairs that had risen there.

"Yes. We do it every year. It is great fun. Only unmated Were-bears can compete." Octavia smiled as Lindsey came back carrying a basket, saucers and his plate of food. "Thanks, dear."

"Welcome." After the quick mumble, Lindsey rushed away, not even giving Hansel a glance this time.

"She'd make Tim Bjorn a lovely wife." Rita flipped back the cloth folded in the basket and pulled out a roll.

"I was thinking the same thing." Genma set a roll on her saucer.

"I think I'll plan a family dinner next week and invite her over." Octavia was practically beaming.

"A perfect idea." Rita declared. "You must try the bread, the honey butter is Ann's special blend, she doesn't share it with anyone."

Pulling a roll from the basket she held out to him, he thanked her. Sinking his teeth into the warmth, his taste buds came alive as the syrupy sweet and salty blend met his palate. Never in all his life had he sampled something so good.

"It is just that good." Rita giggled.

Hansel realized he'd moaned. However, his embarrassment didn't stop him from finishing the bread in two bites.

Octavia set another roll on his saucer with a wide grin.

The scent of the eggs, kale, smoked salmon and diced tomatoes and onions beckoned him. He'd been on the road for the last couple months nonstop following one lead after another with only jerky and convenience store snacks to satisfy him. Now, with such fine fare he found it hard to contain his pleasure.

The first forkful had his lids sliding shut. Fluffy, smoky goodness. His bear was in heaven. It had been too long since he'd enjoyed salmon...and fresh, smoked salmon was a delight he'd missed immensely.

"Good?"

"Almost too good to be true." He opened his eyes and met Rita's.

"Fantastic. A male should have a delicious meal to greet him when he comes off the road." Genma smacked the table.

"I'm very grateful for this." He ate more. "Too soon I'll be back to my regular grub."

"Well, let's hope that won't be for some time from now." Genma placed a hand on his arm.

Pushing away the empty plate, he drank his coffee as he reached for his second roll. "Sorry to disappoint you. But, I think I've already overstayed my welcome." He'd attempt one more time to speak with Greta, but if she shut him down again, he could see no reason to stay. No matter what his bear wanted.

"Nonsense. Are you needed back home for something?" Octavia broke a bit of bread off and popped it into her mouth.

Home. That was a word he never associated with himself. "No home."

"Sleuthless?" Rita frowned.

He a part of a sleuth was just as foreign as a home. He shrugged.

"Then you must stay here. Get to know Den County and the Weres here." Octavia laid a hand on his wrist.

"Not sure if that's a good idea." The whole time he'd been there he could feel the male patrons' stares unwavering on him. Since his back was to the wall every time he glanced beyond the older females at the table with him, he'd meet another piercing stare. *Leave. We don't want you here.* Those were just a couple of the statements clearly evident in their gazes.

"Oh pooh, I disagree." Genma took hold of his hand. "I think a little rest and friendliness is just what you need."

Hansel looked past the elegant black woman and connected with eyes that held a twinge of red at the ring of the irises. A blond were-male sat with two others, perched on the end of their chairs as if they were just waiting for Hansel to do something wrong, untoward and so they could pounce.

Unfazed he slipped his hand from under Genma's. "Thanks for the offer. But I was already informed that Den didn't have places for outsiders to even spend the night. I don't mind laying in the woods at night, but I don't see myself being able to get much rest with having to keep one eye open." He let out a humorless chuckle.

Genma laughed.

Rita smiled.

Octavia tapped her lip, her brow lifted slightly, as she sat as if pondering a puzzle.

Placing his hands on the table, he began to rise.

"We know the perfect place," Octavia erupted as she set her gaze on Genma.

"We do?" Genma's eyebrows lifted.

"Tell me. I want in on it." Rita leaned toward Octavia who sat across the small square table from her.

"The first Den house." Octavia smacked the table and bellowed out a laugh of pure joy that had many heads turning in their direction.

"You're right, why didn't I think of that. It makes sense." Genma's smile was so wide it practically reached her ears then she fell into gleeful excitement with her friend.

"You mean where you two stayed a few months." Rita nodded her head, more to herself than to the other ladies. "You're so brilliant Octavia. We spent all that time getting it cleaned and straightened up for you two, now it just sits abandoned."

Hansel wasn't sure what these women were referring to. Their coded conversation went so rapidly he didn't even attempt to follow it. He sat there feeling as if he was waiting for them to say his name, even though they were discussing him. His mind pondered. Even if they did have somewhere for him to stay while he attempted to speak with Greta, 'Should I stay?' kept popping into his mind. It was clear Greta didn't want anything to do with him or to discuss their past together.

Maybe I should leave well enough alone.

No. His bear nudged him mentally and caused his core to tighten in resistance. This wasn't the first time he and his bear were at odds over what to do where Greta was concerned.

Finally, Rita's gaze settled on him. "It's time to go, Hansel."

"Yes, ma'am." seemed to be the only response. Fishing his wallet out of his pocket he slipped out funds to cover the bill.

"We invited you. We should pay." Octavia rose to her feet and began to reach inside her purse.

Placing a gentle restraining hand on her arm, he shook his head. "The day I sit at a table with three gorgeous females and allow them to foot the bill for my food, I will throw my bear fur down in front of a human fireplace." He tossed the money down.

The three older were-females shivered at the image of his words.

Octavia and Genma gave sharp nods.

"Let's go." Rita led the way out of the diner.

"Come back again, soon. You're welcome here anytime." Ann stood at the door greeting more guests as they left.

He gave the woman a wink, not committing himself to anything.

~YH~

"Oh, my, I needed this." Greta lay back in the soft grass and enjoyed the cool breeze along her skin as she balanced her wine glass on her belly with one hand.

"Me too. I love my kids at the school and my three at home, but there are times when I just want to shift and go for a long run or lose my mind." Riley rubbed her swollen belly. "With number four on the way I am sure a mental institution already has a room reserved for me."

Rena laughed, lying on the other side of Greta. "Hey, you have me a little scared over here."

"You're only on one…don't get scared until you catch up with Theo and I." Riley tossed out.

"Before this turns into a full offspring conversation I'm getting more wine…can I top you off, Greta?" Ebony rose from the ground and went a few feet back to the picnic basket filled with wine and nibbles.

"Absolutely." Greta downed the last swallow of her second glass of honeyed wine and held it up high awaiting her refill.

They had been out there about thirty minutes just lying around in the dark listening to the calming flow of the lake. They were downstream from Genma's house, but away from any other houses.

Tranquil peace. Greta was glad she'd agreed to this moment with her friends.

Ebony filled her glass from the jug of Shardik-made brew, slightly unsteady she splashed a drop on to Greta's cheek.

"If you're going to pour it on me...at least aim for my mouth." Greta smiled up at the pretty black woman with the birth-marked, gray streak in her hair.

Ebony's giggle slid out easily, proof she was a little tipsy. Usually her co-worker and friend was too serious for her own good. "True. No need to waste such good wine."

"So, tell us, Ebony. Since you don't want to talk about breeding...when are you going to allow that sexy Dainton to mate with you..." Riley leaned up on her elbows and glanced back at Ebony.

"Yeah. Make you his officially. You have that Were twisted." Rena added. "Bring me a bunch of grapes when you come back over here with your answer."

"And cheese." Riley added.

Greta kept quiet as she sat up to drink down a gulp of wine. She didn't enjoy the direction of the conversation. She wasn't pregnant or close to being anyone's mate. Not that she usually gave either issue much thought. However, having Hansel show up in town had her body completely on edge with need and made her mind display an occasional image of her life with a male to love her.

But she wouldn't fool herself into believing that Hansel was here for love. The male was a pseudo-brother. They were siblings of tragedy. For that reason alone she had to be glad he had heeded her words and left town.

"I don't know." Ebony plopped down hard in the grass beside Rena, drawing Greta's attention back to them.

Thankfully away from her own wayward thoughts.

"We know you care for him. It's evident on your face every time he walks into the same space you're in."

That was so true. At work, Greta had walked in on the couple at least twice with their faces locked together and hands caressing and cupping. They were combustible, ready to singe anyone that got near them.

"Yeah, I do. Probably even love the big lug of a bear." Ebony put her glass to her lips and downed half of her drink in one gulp.

"Then what's the problem?" Rena maneuvered her round body into a sitting position.

"What are you waiting for?" Riley remained stretched out, rubbing her swollen belly.

"It's…it's—" Ebony's words broke off as she stared out at the lake. Her mouth opened as if she was going to start again, but she closed it and shook her head and sighed.

Greta understood Ebony's emotional frustration. Even though their situation was extremely different, she comprehended the internal war of bear and mind.

"It's okay, Ebony." Rena placed a comforting hand on Ebony's shoulder.

"No, it's not." Ebony burst out crying.

That caused them all to freeze. Such open, raw emotions from the reserved, professional female had the three of them momentarily dumbfounded.

"I can't shift. I can't shift." The tears rolled unchecked down Ebony's face.

Rena scurried across the ground to her and pulled her into a hug. Greta watched as Riley joined in, her heart breaking for her cousin's mate. She, unlike the other three ladies, had been raised as a Were-bear, knew what was expected of her. Trained in her shifting skills and methods from birth, she could shift with barely a thought or breath.

However, she didn't belittle her three friends. Riley was a home girl bitten at a young age by Theo, but raised unaware of the Were gene in her blood until she'd met him again. Rena was a half-blood, with a mother who had felt rejected by Den's sleuth and set out on her own to live a 'human' life, leaving her daughter ignorant of her heritage until Rena's bear had come calling.

Yes, unlike them she knew whom she was, inside and out. There were just darker thoughts that haunted her heart and mind.

"It's okay, Ebony." Riley rubbed her back.

"That first shift is a bitch. It happened to me without me even realizing it was going on...I thought I was dreaming." Rena gave Ebony a kind smile.

Ebony wiped her eyes and blotted her cheeks with the back of her hands. "I don't know what's wrong with me, I keep getting emotional like this."

"You better not be breeding. Two pregnant friends that can't drink with me when I've had a rough day is enough." Greta pointed a finger at Ebony.

The ladies laughed, which seemed to break the tension some.

"Thanks, Greta." Ebony gave her a small smile.

A nod and a sip was her response. She had really tried to lighten the mood more for her own sake than for Ebony's. There was little doubt in her own mind that if she gave in to her emotions, even if in support of her friend, it may start the firestorm brewing inside of her since Hansel's appearance in town. Correction, since she'd picked up his unique scent in the woods by the river—woodsy cashmere notes.

A scent both masculine and delicate. Why couldn't he just have a simple musky spice like all the other were-males around Den. To her, none of the other males even drew her attention by their scent, let alone made her heart race and her belly tighten with the thought of it. She drank some more wine and dropped back to the ground with a groan.

"How do you do it?"

The three females went silent around her, cluing Greta into the fact that they may have been awaiting some sort of response from her. Rolling along the grass she stared at them. "Do what?"

What had I missed?

"You know… shift?" Ebony asked. "It happened while Rena was sleeping after a marathon of sex with Cord and that's no help for me. Dainton and I have torn sheets up numerous times and—"

"Hey!" Greta waved her hand vigorously before Ebony. "My cousin…don't need details about you guys's sexcapades." Her bottom lip was feeling a little numb and she could hear her words slurring a little. She almost smiled at the thought that drunkenness had begun to finally set in.

"Anyway. After all the gymnastics I still open my eyes in the same form I went to sleep in." Ebony's sigh was heavy.

"Hm." Greta nodded, the world tilted some. "I see how that could bother you."

"Theo took me through the paces. However, by then

I was already breeding so I think that may have helped give me strength to shift." Riley's shoulder lifted and fell.

"There you have it. Get Dainton to help you. Right paw, left paw, back paws, breathe." Greta giggled at her own childish instructions and choked some on her dink as she finished it off and pushed to her feet. The ground felt unsteady for a moment but after a few deep breaths it righted itself.

"Be serious, Greta. I was so sure of everything in the corporate world. Never doubted myself. If there was an issue I solved it. The envy of many." She glanced out toward the lake. "However, now, I feel out of sorts. Uncomfortable. This Were-bear thing is still all too new." Then she looked back and met the gaze of each of them slowly. "But, I want to find a way to do this shift thing myself. For myself and to make Dainton proud."

Moving across the lush grass, Greta squatted before Ebony feeling a little jealous of the love this person had for her cousin and the fact that she was getting an intense love in return. "I'll help you."

"Tonight?"

"Uh, no." Greta stood up again, too quickly, and ended up on her backside. "If I even considered it I think shifting while drunk would cause my bear to bring up my dinner."

"I'm not feeling well about now either." Ebony frowned into her still half-full glass.

"No more wine for the two of you." Rena took Ebony's glass then Greta's and went to the basket. She tossed the remainder of Ebony's drink into a bush before putting them away.

"Well, I guess we all need to head home." Ebony

stretched her arms over her head.

"Not yet." Riley spoke beside her.

"What's up?" Greta lowered her arms and glanced from Riley to Ebony who now stood beside her.

"We put this little lakeside party together for you." Ebony reminded her.

"Tell us about the hot, sexy rogue bear in town." Riley folded her arms under her breasts and waited.

"Not much to tell." She glanced back at Rena hoping to get some support from her ex-neighbor and friend, who now lived with her mate Cord instead of her grandmother Genma. However, she could see there was no reinforcement there, since Red, a nickname of Rena's, was strolling toward her with curiosity lighting her gaze.

"Where'd he come from?"

"How do you know him?"

"What does he want from you? Why is he here?"

The three females fired off questions so fast Greta wasn't sure who asked what. It didn't matter because if she had it her way, she wouldn't be answering any of them.

Rubbing her face, trying to buy time and sober her mind, she sighed in frustration. Why did everyone want to talk about him? Couldn't they just leave it all alone, he was gone now. Situation over.

"It's complicated." She lowered her hand and walked to the water's edge.

"Is he dangerous?" That soft, light voice was Riley's.

The answer to that easily tumbled out. "No."

"Okay. Did you know he was coming to Den?" Ebony came up alongside of her.

"Hell, no. If I did I wouldn't have been here." She faced the trio.

"Your history with him is that bad, huh?" Ebony touched her upper arm.

Sympathy was evident on all their faces. She recalled that since all of them were transplants from other places way outside of Den they weren't aware of the situation that had happened when she was younger. Most of the time she was grateful for that, because she never enjoyed the watchful gazes and sympathy of the townspeople when they looked at her. However, tonight with all the inquiry she could easily lump her three friends into the same pile with everyone else. Curiosity.

I just want to leave it all alone. Forget about Hansel and everything else. It's best that way.

"It's complicated." It seemed like she couldn't get past that one statement, nothing else clever would come to mind, especially with it sauced on honeyed wine. Human alcohol didn't have a lot of effect on Were's, so she had been told since even the idea of her taking her 'wandering years' after her earlier absence was not even a remote possibility. Be that as it may, fermented with a hint of apple juice was a completely different situation that could muddle a Were-bear's brain easily. Greta moved away, a little unsteady on her feet.

She started making sure all of the remnants of their snacks and wine were put back into the basket Rena had brought. Rising with it in hand, she stared at her friends. "Honestly, I don't know what to think right now. My mind is all over the place. Hansel is from a time in my past when I didn't know if I'd ever see Den County again. "My parents, my friends….everything I knew had been lost to me. Hansel was the only person—" She had to correct herself, recalling they had only shifted to human form once back then. "Bear that I could cling to. He was my saving grace in too many ways for me to list without allowing that part of my memories full reign in my mind. I refuse to do that." Taking a deep breath she walked back to the place by the lake where they still stood.

"I know it's not much, but I thank you all for tonight. I needed it. Now, I'm going to find my bed, I hope," she giggled. "And put the last couple days in the past."

She hoped they understood and would share with their mates that this discussion was now closed.

"We can respect that." Rena hugged her, then took the basket from her hands.

"Life doesn't always follow the straight line we draw." Ebony embraced her next. "Hell, I'm a perfect example of that."

They all laughed.

Riley stepped to her last. "If you need me, I'm always up for a couple hours away from the animal farm."

Greta shook her head and smiled. She knew Riley loved being with her kids and the ones she taught at the school. Her friend was a child magnet.

"I'll remember that." With an arm around Riley's wide waist she headed back to the opening at the end of the path that led to this remote side of the lake.

All the ladies got into their individual vehicles and started them up.

"Aren't you headed out, Greta?" Ebony leaned over the open door of her sports car. It was a vehicle that didn't fit in Den County any more than Ebony did when she had first arrived months ago.

"In a minute. I feel like a run."

"One day that will be me." Ebony's voice held hope, but her eyes tilted down a little with sadness.

"Yes it will. I'll see to that." Greta gave her a thumbs up.

After a wave, all her friends drove off, leaving her and her truck in the clearing.

Taking a breath, she filled her lungs with the cool night air. She hoped that shifting would shake off some of the uncertainty in her mind, maybe even give her some much-needed direction for her life.

If Hansel's appearance had done anything, it had made it evident to her...possibly all of Den as well, that Greta Armel's life had been in a stasis, on pause since the moment she'd returned to the secure embrace of her family.

Yes, she'd grown up and was a responsible adult Were with a job, but other than that she hadn't progressed in life. She still resided with her parents and was promptly at the table most nights for dinner. When she was off, she helped her mother around the house, gardened, and baked and canned items for hibernation time. A moment like this, when she was alone in the woods would *never* have taken place, before Hansel.

She'd always told herself she wasn't afraid to be out in the Redwood Forest by herself. Running free through the big trees. However, deep inside she knew it wasn't true. Even now her mind played tricks on her telling her that if she shifted someone would materialize out of the trees and get her.

Gulping down the anxiety she moved to her truck and began to undress. She needed to do this. *Had* to do this. Today was the day she would prove to herself that she could let the past go and that she was ready to move forward. Maybe luck would have it and she would participate in the Bear Run. Maybe it was time for her to allow an unmated male to catch her.

Hansel.

She ignored her bear—that door was closed. Once she'd left her office, she hadn't seen him or his motorcycle anywhere in town. That Were was long gone by now.

Sweater, shirt, bra, boots, jeans, panties and socks all went in a neat pile on the front seat of her truck. It was a clear sign to anyone who happened by her truck that she had shifted on her own and was out and about in bear form. It was unlikely that anyone would be around on this side of the lake, even those out doing night checks would have no reason to search out this area. Maybe Sheriff Smokey because it was still a part of Den County, but nothing much was on this side of the lake across from Genma's cabin.

"No more stalling." Just as she'd told Ebony, calling her bear was as easy as breathing.

By the time she exhaled she was on all fours. The tingling of her skin and the burn of her shifting bones were only a distant sensation.

Growling and pawing the dirt her bear rejoiced at being out. Digging her claws deep in the rich, heady soil she showered the front grill of her truck with broken earth.

Starting out at a steady pace, she allowed her bear senses to take over her liquored-up brain.

The smell of pine and the sweet spice of mulch greeted her as night birds called out to their mates. She could hear small animals scurrying about hoping not to get picked off by evening predators. At that moment an owl hooted and Greta knew it had located its prey.

The rich, woodsy must of the redwoods would always smell like home to her. Racing to one of the tall, thin, but thick trees, her bear aligned her back against the firm spongy bark and pushed up and down. Nothing like a good deep scratch along her spine.

She was thankful that her bear didn't get too into the base tree rubbing, because she could have been there until sun up.

Lowering her front paws to the ground she began a steady trot. Greta didn't even attempt to determine a path, just enjoyed the cool breeze caressing her dense bear fur.

Catching a whiff of a scent, her bear began to pick up speed. Paws pounding only the forest floor as if on some single-minded mission.

Greta rejoiced inside, loving moving through her county without fear or hesitation. She may have to make a night or early morning run her weekly thing.

When her bear came to a sudden halt at the end of a path, Greta's heart began to pound, hard.

Her bear sniffed the air.

Trembling started deep in her core for two very different reasons. She couldn't recall the last time she had been to this place, maybe months before her abduction. She'd played out there frequently with other young Weres.

It wasn't the small cabin, now appearing fresh and rebuilt, not like the dilapidated place it had been when she was smaller. Back then, they had worried that the roof and walls would cave in on them at any time. Then that frightful day happened, a day that was worse than wood slats falling on her head. She would have much preferred that over what did take place. A game of hide and seek had gone wrong. A glacier-like bead of sweat sliced along her spine. She shivered.

Even as the chills almost paralyzed her there was warmth that spread through her body and melted her from the inside out. It wasn't the cabin that sent her body into overdrive, but the woodsy cashmere scent that did.

Her bear inhaled a second time, slow and long as if pulling in the aroma in like needed oxygen.

The heat took over and caused every fiber of her being to respond with a throbbing ache.

A grunt and a snort. "Whooh…whooh…"

Immediately she responded, shifting back to human form to silence the call of her bear. Why would it do something that?

Naked, agitated and still a little tipsy she turned to escape.

"Greta?"

The deep male voice caused her movements to freeze. She prayed that her body was hidden enough by the shadows, maybe he would just believe she was a figment of his imagination.

"Your beautiful skin may be brown and dark, but it isn't the color of night."

Oh, damn.

Instead of turning to face him, she darted behind a nearby tree and peered around it at him. "Hansel, what are you doing here?"

He stood in the arc of the light from the porch. She could see him clearly. He had a full satchel slung over his shoulder and his arms folded over his massive chest. The male's presence was too overpowering for words.

The tall, sexy, trim bear of a male. He wasn't as huge or wide as some of the were-males in Den. But, he had no less imposing of a form. No one would look at him and see a weak Were or easy prey. Most likely the dark intensity of his gaze, the crease deep set between his dense eyebrows or the tight position of his strong square jawline would convince them he wasn't one to be messed with.

However, none of his 'back off or I will shift on your ass' looks were a distraction for her to keep her gaze from roaming. When he had been younger, his dark brown hair had just reached his shoulders in oily disarray. There had been smudges of dirt along his face and chest. Now his hair went way beyond his shoulders and shone healthy in the light, appearing soft...touchable.

"Please come out, Greta."

"Why are you here?"

"I was getting ready to settle down for the night, before the gift of your presence."

She could hear the light tones in his voice even though there wasn't any hint of a smile on his lips.

Why did I think about his lips? Her gaze settled on his mouth. They were not anywhere as thick and wide as her own, his own perfect shape. Slightly on the thin side, but well-shaped in a stretched bow. They had a pale pink tint that complimented his golden tanned skin very well. The coloring of his skin this late in the year was evidence that he spent long hours outside, most likely on his motorcycle.

"I'm no gift to you." Her hands gripped the rough trunk of the tree. "This is private property of Den County...you're still trespassing. I suggest you hop on your bike and ride out of here...all the way out of the city limits."

"I don't think I'll do that."

Frustration heated her blood as she stomped her foot onto the soft soil. "Hansel, don't be obstinate. Sooner or later the males will realize you are holed up out here and there will be trouble." She tapped her forehead against the tree and sighed. "I don't want to see you hurt."

"You care about my well-being?" The seductive texture of his voice drew her.

Peeking around at him, she shook her head. "I don't even really know you."

He took a step in her direction. "Yes you do."

"No. I don't. But, I owe you…my life. So, this is my repayment. Leave from here."

"You don't owe me anything." Another step.

He was still several feet away from her hiding place, but the closer he came the harder it was for her body not to ache and her bear not to push her to go to him. However, that was not going to happen.

"Innocent one, I would have given my life to see you free of that place. No one deserved that hell."

However, he had been in that place long before she had arrived. "Please….Hansel, if you care anything for me…leave."

"I can't." His long steps ate up more of the distance between them. He stopped and held his hand out to her. "Come out."

"Go," she countered.

"No." His hand stayed steady.

"No."

"Would you feel better if I told you I had permission to stay here as long as I needed to? So, no one is going to fly out here to send me away."

"By who?"

"If you come out I'll tell you all about it."

"Even if I wanted to, I'm not dressed."

"Of course you're not. I saw your bear. Amazing brown bear." He lowered his hand to his side.

Her belly flipped at his words, a clear indication that her bear was inside of her preening with pride and rolling around. "Don't try to flatter me."

"I can't make that promise. There's been so little joy in my life I have to appreciate it when it is before me."

She understood some of what he had been through.

"This—us, isn't a good idea."

"Maybe." He glanced away from her. The light from the porch was capturing his side profile, showcasing a hint of the shadows of uncertainty in his gaze.

That look caused her heart to sink a little.

Setting those dark eyes in her direction again, he said, "I'm not going until you come out. I've seen you naked before, I don't see what the big deal is."

"I was nine. We were both kids."

"True. Will you be more comfortable if I took my clothes off too? Make things even." He reached for the hem of his t-shirt and began to raise it.

Her bear panted, excited to see all he was hiding under the layers.

"No!" She stretched her arm out, palm up.

Chuckling, he dropped his shirt and it fell back in place, riding at the top of his jeans pockets. "Hold on. I think I have something in my bag you can use." He shoved the strap from his shoulder and opened it. He reached in and removed something and tossed it at her. "Put this on."

Catching the soft material she shook it out. It was a blue-striped button-down shirt, a bit wrinkled.

"It's clean."

"I can smell that." She started to put it on and her

acute sense of smell not only picked up on the lavender fragrance of the laundry soap, but under that the sweet, earthy notes that were Hansel. The shirt was big, but just long enough to fall below her backside—just below.

"Better?"

She fastened all the buttons up to her breast and stepped away from the tree. "A little."

"Good. Now, can we go inside for coffee?"

"Sure." She shrugged and headed toward the door. Evidently coffee was exactly what she needed, because she must still be feeling the effects of the honeyed wine if she didn't turn tail and run as soon as she realized Hansel was somewhere around. However, chances were that if she did try to escape he would have just shifted and took chase. Better to get the conversation over with so this imposing male from her past could be on his way. For good this time.

CHAPTER FOUR

She walks in beauty like the night.

He was haunted by those words of a poem by Lord Byron he'd heard so long ago, when he sat in a coffee shop and they happened to have a poetry night. At the time it hadn't meant anything to him. Just background noise as he perused local newspapers for the men he was hunting.

Now they made sense. Greta's steps were cautious but sure. The swing of her full hips seemed to catch the light just right and played with his desire for her. He met her at the porch and reached around her to open the door. Her scent, wildflowers and rain showers, greeted him. He paused, not turning the knob yet, and inhaled deeply.

His bear sighed as if just being near her gave him a sense of calm — home.

Home was a word he didn't even know, it didn't fit with him. However, he yearned for it as he stood by her.

Shaking that off he allowed her to enter the small cabin.

"Wow, they have really done wonderful work on this place." She moved into the living room and turned in a slow circle as she took everything in.

He was glad he'd started a fire before he went out to get his bag containing the few things he traveled with. There weren't many items he felt that he needed to sustain him.

"I was told they had recently made improvements to it." He dropped his stuff beside the single chair and took in the profile of the female before him. Her shoulders appeared drawn up and there was a tension filling the room. He wasn't sure if just being around him was the cause of it.

"Take a seat when you're ready. Can I get you that coffee I promised?"

The fire he had started in the small grate made the room toasty, romantic. However, he told himself not to allow his mind to roll in that direction. Even though seeing how his shirt barely covered the lower part of her ass made him hard as ice. Those thick brown thighs showcased for him made him want to cross the short distance between them and glide his hands then his tongue up them until he reached the hidden treasure covered by the shirt.

The room around him had a hint of a golden hue. He barely caught the groan that started to slip from his lips.

She glanced at him over her shoulder, catching him in her ebony gaze.

If she were just a little closer he'd be about to see if there were a few metallic flakes in her own eyes. His cock twitched. Maybe while he was in the kitchen he'd place a few ice cubes down his pants. He took a deep breath to clear up his vision.

Big mistake since it brought her scent to him again.

"So, you learned to cook?" He question was just the distraction he needed to get him back on track.

"No. Coffee is the beginning and end of my skills." Another male may have chuckled at her comment. However, it was a small reminder to him about their connection. Where he'd spent his youth and why she may have been shocked to discover he had culinary skills.

Her sigh was low. "I'd like a cup please." She rubbed her arms over the sleeves as she faced him. "One dollop of sugar please."

With a short nod he left the room. Evidently she didn't have a sweet tooth like him. In the kitchen it wasn't hard to spot the coffee pot on the small counter. The only other thing beside it was a tall crockpot and a toaster. All the appliances were new, another sign that the place had been given a new face inside and out. He wondered for whom the place had been made ready, especially in a town that didn't open easily for strangers.

Pushing the power button on the coffee maker, he opened one of the four cabinets to locate all the items he would need to brew the coffee. His mind journeyed to the three grandmotherly were-females he'd had the pleasure of meeting. Genma, Octavia and Rita had shown him sincere kindness he'd never experienced before—feeding him and ensuring he had a place to rest his head.

Don't get used to it, he warned himself, taking out two mugs and honey as the pot began to percolate. He wasn't staying in this town. Just passing through. A lot sooner than he'd thought since the Great Spirit had seen fit to present him with Greta at his doorstep.

Coffee done, he walked with two cups back down the short hall to the front room. There were only two other rooms in the place, the bathroom and the bedroom. He knew there was a large bed inside from the short tour he'd taken before going back to his motorcycle for his things.

Don't think of a bed while Greta is in the cabin. "As you requested with one honey drop."

She gave him a small smile as she claimed the mug he offered her. "Thank you." Cupping her hands around the ceramic she stood in the same place.

"Please have a seat. I'm sure your bear could use a rest after being out and about." He waited to see which seat she would take before he sat.

It didn't surprise him that she lowered herself into the single chair. She wanted to keep a distance between them.

Smart female.

Settling into the center of the couch across from her, he sipped his extra-sweet drink and allowed her some time. She must need it the way she stared into her mug…as if she were awaiting a small animal to pop up from its depth.

"What's going on inside that beautiful head of yours, Blackberry."

Tilting her head up, she cocked an eyebrow up at him, taking issue with the nickname.

He gave her a wink and a small smile and drank more coffee. He'd much prefer to see the spark of annoyance in her gaze than the anxiety that seemed to fill it.

"This is the place."

To ask 'what place' never crossed his mind as he leaned forward and set his mug on the table between them. With the history between him and Greta, what they had experienced together, some clarifications weren't necessary.

"How did it happen?" He rested his elbows on his knees and stared at her.

She wasn't looking at him anymore, she had her gaze fixed on one of the bare walls.

Even though the cabin had been refurbished it only held the basic items within...no extra décor or knickknacks people usually set around their homes.

"A game of hide and seek gone wrong." She looked at him. "I didn't know there were others out in the woods seeking besides the other Were-children playing with me."

Allowing her to work out how far she wanted to go with the story, he maintained his silence.

"We came here all the time during the summer months. Running and playing in the woods, we weren't allowed out this far. But rebellious as most youth, testing their limits, we skirted Den County's boundaries more than we should have. We were always in a group...we thought that would keep us safe." She lifted her drink to her lips, taking a fortifying sip.

Greta needed it.

He noticed the slight trembling of her hand. "You all should have been safe."

She shook her head. "It was Rorke's turn to count. He was inside and the rest of us took off into the woods. We were supposed to hide in the front only." She bit the side of her bottom lip as the heel of her right foot tapped repeatedly on the wood floor, making her knee bounce.

Purposely he kept his gaze on her face, using one of the few gentlemanly manners he had to not take a glimpse of her treasures as the edge of the shirt slipped up her thighs.

It caused his heart to ache to see her in distress. He should tell her to stop. Let her know she didn't have to continue if it was too painful. Even though he wanted her to share her story. "Gret—"

"I was trying to be clever. I figured if I ran to the back of the cabin and hid in the woods, when Rorke lighted from it to chase the others in the front I would go back around and sneak into the house. Then when the others came back in I'd be sitting inside smiling." She lifted the cup, drank deeply and hissed.

He was sure the hot liquid had burned her tongue.

Sitting her mug next to his, she balled her hands together in her lap. "I remember the sunlight sending rays through the tops of the trees. It was like running through a golden shower. I was laughing, holding my arms wide enjoying the beams of warmth that brushed my arms as I tilted my head back and ran blindly around the base of the trees. I couldn't resist shifting. I wanted to feel the light wind in my fur. Then…then—"

Her voice broke. He thought she was going to stop, but she lifted her gaze from the floor and met his.

There were tears hovering on the edge of her lower lids, filling her eyes with water.

He sucked in a breath imagining what was to come.

"I didn't even see the trap, just felt the heinous bite and the burning." She blinked and the river poured down her dark cheeks making them glisten like wet satin. "I—started to scream…tried to call out, but—but a hand clutched my muzzle."

"Blackberry, it's too painful...you don't have to go there." He slid to the edge of the seat, wanting to go to her, pull her into his arms and console her. It wasn't only for her sake, but his as well. Hearing her memories made his own come flooding into his mind. Memories he'd kept behind a fortress in his mind.

With a forceful shaking of her head, she continued, "I do! Because I should have smelled them, should have heard them. There were three of them. Men, dirty, stinky, lumbering men. The truck they tossed me into the back of wasn't even hidden. Evidently they had just laid the trap and were about to leave when I happened upon it. Like an idiot."

Unable to stay away from her, he moved and lowered himself beside her chair then rested a hand on her knee. "You were a cub, innocent and free. You had every right to feel safe in your world. Those men were schemers, corrupt." Even talking about the men he hunted filled his mouth with a sour taste.

"I was so scared. I didn't know if I was going to die or ever see my family again."

"I know." He did know. He knew that unmitigated fear that set in so deep into the core when one was found in the grips of pure evil as those men were.

One of her hands covered his as the other cupped his cheek. Soft warmth greeted him like a caress.

"Then, there you were." Her luminous gaze rested on his.

"There I was." There he had been for too long.

"You saved me in so many ways, Hansel." She softly whispered his name.

He turned his face into her palm and inhaled deeply. Her touch and scent were a comfort to his soul. "I was the one saved." He murmured against her skin.

"You renewed my fight." Reaching up, he brushed his fingers over the back of her hand as he met her eyes. "I refused to allow the events that I went through to happen to you. You were too precious to me from the first moment I saw you."

"When they tossed me in the cage."

"You shifted and my heart stopped. You were my kind, something I'd given up ever seeing again." His words sounded husky to his own ears.

"You healed me." Her fingers slid into his hair.

Staring at her, he wondered what it was about this female that made him feel and act outside of himself. It had been the same from the first moment he saw her bleeding in that cage.

Reaching down he encircled her left foot with his hand and raised it. Glancing down, he saw the puckered and thick skin around her ankle that made up the scar from the vicious teeth of the metal trap. His heart ached even now seeing it. If it had gone any deeper it would have severed her bone and possibly taken her foot. Bringing it to his mouth he placed his lips there, kissing her foot first then gliding his tongue over the markings as he'd done so many years ago. Some nights it felt as if an eternity had passed since Greta had run out of his life, others she seemed like a fantasy he'd conjured up to get through the worst days of his entrapment.

She gasped and her toes curled into his palm as he continued his worship of her ankle, thanking the Great Spirit she was safe.

"Hansel." Her hands in his hair slipped around until she cupped his chin and raised his head.

He glanced up at her.

"I'm fine. I'm o-kay." Her voice broke and there

were fresh tears shining in her ebony, golden-flaked eyes.

He rose to his knees as he trailed his free hand up the side of her thigh until he cupped her hip.

Gold began to saturate her eyes, leaving very little onyx remaining. Leaning in closer, he whispered, "I needed to know that for sure. Needed to touch you and know you were not only okay, but that you were real. Not a figment of my imagination, Blackberry."

"No more than you were mine."

Groaning, he pressed his lips to hers. Unable to resist tasting her. His tongue entered the warm recesses of her mouth and tasted the bitter bite of the coffee, the sweet hint of honey, the acidic bite of wine and the delectable flavor he'd yearned for all of his life—Greta.

She gave him passion for passion. No shyness. Fisting his hair, she sucked his tongue into her mouth drawing him deeper inside of her.

His bear growled. *Mine. Mine. Mine.*

Hansel agreed as the pressing need to claim her drove him. He was unsure how his life had been sustained over the years without her in it—he'd been half a person.

As he pulled his mouth away, he panted. He opened his lids and assessed her wondrous beauty in the hue of his mating need. Everything was painted with a golden brush.

"Greta...I didn't come here to make love to you...but I want you." Squeezing the full softness of her hip still in his hand, he continued, "However, if this is not something you desire then tell me. It would rip me apart but I will let you walk out the door and ensure you get back home...unravished."

Both of her hands were in his hair now and she used them to drag her nails along his scalp.

He shivered at the scratching sound and feel. The sensation made his mind think of other places he'd enjoy her nails playing along his skin. His cock for one. The hard member twitched in agreement.

"Blackberry." It was the only warning she was going to get. If she continued to caress him, he'd make the decision for her.

"Yes, I want this…I want you."

Moving her leg to the side, he settled between her parted thighs, his bear and male senses picked up on the musky spice of her need. He leaned in to capture her lips again.

"Wait!" She placed a trembling hand on his chest, keeping a small distance between them.

His brow tightened. "What is it?"

Licking her lips, her gaze skittered away from his for a moment. She took a breath that caused her chest to rise high. When her large almond-shaped eyes met his, he noted they were wider, as if she were hesitant or unsure about something.

"What?" He prompted her.

"I'm flying blind here." Her bottom lip rolled into her mouth.

He moved back. "Look, Greta, I would love to make you promises of forever. But, my life has a lot of questions over it and I still have unfinished business to take care of." He didn't want to hurt her but if she was looking for the Were-bear that would build a life with her in Den County he wasn't the one.

She shook her head. "I'm not looking for poetry and promises, Hansel. I'm barely figuring out the direction of my own life. I've never been with anyone before, but

I want this night to end with me in your arms."

The air in the room was sucked out. Every function in his body ceased and his mind went blank. Then in a blink everything started up again and clarity struck him. Greta, this beautiful, vivacious were-female was a virgin. And she was offering her innocence to him. He was the one quaking now. Did he want to take this responsibility?

In the Were community sex didn't hold any importance unless marking was exchanged. Other than that, it was just two Weres satisfying physical need.

If I do this, I can't bite her.

"Why me?"

Shrugging, she met his gaze squarely. "I don't know. I've never felt the heat of passion or even had my eyes show a twinge of gold for any other male. Maybe because until tonight I never stepped very far outside of my safety zone. However, you make me want to be free, dangerous, wild...even if for just one night." A single shoulder lifted and lowered. "So, why not you?"

He chuckled. "You have a way with words, Blackberry."

When her lips curled up in a smile, his world felt in line.

"Are you in, or would you like for me to tuck you in bed before I head back to my truck?" There was a twinkle of humor in her eyes.

"Oh, I'm game. When I get tucked in, you'll be in a tangle of sheets beside me."

She laughed. "Okay. Give me one moment, I need to do something first." Pushing him back she rose and walked to the corner of the cabin.

Enjoying the sway of her lush hips beneath his shirt,

he waited to see what she was doing.

She sat down in the single wooden chair beside a radio.

Earlier when he'd checked out the cabin he'd seen the CB but had not paid it much attention. Now, it and the woman before it fascinated him.

After punching in a number, for some station, she cupped the receiver and raised it to her mouth. There was a sound of static then it cleared. "This is Greta to Manni Armel."

She repeated it once more before a male voice came through.

"Greta, sweetheart? You still out at the lake?"

Hansel recognized the male's voice as the Were that had brought Greta into town and confronted him at the park with the group of men.

"Hi, papa-bear. No, I'm not at the lake anymore." She glanced at him. "I'm hanging out with a friend. I didn't want you and mama to worry."

"Ah, thanks. It was getting awful late and we were concerned."

"I'm alright. No need for you to wait up."

There was a pause. "Are you sure? With that rogue about to —"

"We won't, Greta. Be safe." A female voice came through the speaker.

He watched her bite into her lip as she restrained her laughter. "Thanks, mama-bear, I will."

Clearing the connection, she reattached the mouthpiece to the radio then stared at him. "Usually my mother is the worry wart. Strange that she seemed okay with me being out late."

"I'm sure they are extremely protective of you since you were taken."

She looked down at her hands in her lap. "Yes. That's something I needed for a long time."

"But not tonight?" He wanted to steer the conversation back to what was happening between them, not the horrific events of their past.

Her chin rose and the heat of her stare heated his blood from across the room. "No, not tonight."

After a sharp nod of understanding, he patted the chair cushion. "I believe we left off right here."

Smiling, she stood and took the steps across the glossy wood floor. "I think you are correct." She claimed her seat. "So, what were we about to do?"

"I'm better at showing than telling." Wedging himself between her thighs he pulled her to him and kissed her.

The kiss went on long as he held her close and they feasted on each other's mouth. They made love to one another orally, licking and sucking, nibbling and thrusting in and out of her lips.

Eventually he parted from her and pressed his forehead along hers as he took in large gulps of air.

She whimpered.

His body was on fire. With human women, he'd lusted after them but quickly his desire for them was doused. However, even at his peak of need, he'd never felt so bounded and connected to another the way he yearned for this were-female. Maybe because she was his kind. Maybe because of their history…he wasn't sure. All he knew was the feelings were scary but they were too thrilling and invigorating for him to stop.

"Are you okay, Hansel?" Her soft palm caressed the side of his face.

He chuckled. "Not sure."

"You want to stop?"

"Not on my life." He kissed her lips then her chin and down to the side of her neck. As his lips moved lower, he unbuttoned the shirt that hid her body from his view. He yearned to see her womanly curves beneath. Licking from her collarbone to the valley between her breasts. He drew that tight skin into his mouth.

"Hmm."

Smiling at her moan, he released the last button and parted the shirt until it fell at her sides. Awestruck by the sight of her gorgeous voluptuous body he just kneeled before her for a moment and took it all in.

"You are lovely." He brushed his knuckles lightly over her skin. It was dark and beautiful, and as soft and inviting as silk. The heat of her warmth greeted him as he caressed every valley and curve.

She started to sit up.

He pressed a hand to her belly. "Where are you going?"

"Nowhere." She laughed. "I was just going to take the shirt all the way off."

"Don't. Leave it." When the days and nights became long for him on the road, he wanted to remember the sight of her in his shirt. He'd never wash it again, so that he would be able to physically carry her scent with him.

"Okay." She relaxed back into position again.

As he took in the view of her nipples, he realized how appropriate the nickname he'd given her was. The tips of her breasts in their blackberry hue complimented the rich mahogany of her complexion. Blackberries had always been his favorite treat when he was a child. When he'd finally escaped captivity it had been the first thing he'd sought to eat. Now, he felt as if he'd been starved of his pleasure once again.

"You're very handsome yourself." Her thumb brushed his bottom lip.

He shook his head. "No, I'm too road weary for...beauty left me long ago." He meant that on so many levels. With such pain and misery as he had experienced in his youth, Greta had been the only thing of beauty that had existed in his life and even that he'd had to let go.

"That's not tru—"

Kissing her, he silenced her comment. He just wanted this night in her arms. A night to escape everything that haunted him for so long, even his own mental burdens.

He whispered against her lips, "Let me find solace in you."

There were a lot of questions still filling her gaze, but she nodded.

Taking what was offered to him, he bowed his head and took one of her taut peaks into his mouth. He drew on it hard. When she hissed in pain, he circled the tip with his tongue soothing it. His intent was not to hurt her at all, but he needed to share the intensity of his desire for her, with her.

Nipping and sucking one nipple after the other, he forced her passion to a higher level. Inhaling, he gathered her raw need into him, enjoying the dense scent of her arousal as it built. When he could not resist searching out the origin of her aroma any longer her gripped her hips and slid her forward until her ass balanced on the edge of the chair.

"Hansel."

"Trust me...I ne-ed this." His words were more of a growl than actual sentences.

Taking hold of her legs he placed one over each of the arms of the seat, spreading her wide. Beholding the scandalous view of her smooth, plump pussy, shining with her creamy arousal he licked his lips.

With his thumbs he parted her brown labia until the pink inner folds were revealed to him. "You may want to hold on, Blackberry."

She placed her hands on the sides of the chair with a look of curious excitement lighting up her features. He wasn't shocked that even as an innocent she knew what he was planning to do. Most likely she'd heard about the act from her female friends and had wondered about it. He couldn't hold back the pride that swelled his chest knowing that he was the one she was allowing to show her everything she'd fantasized about…and more.

Usually he didn't think about his depth of experience and how he'd acquired it, but tonight he was more than grateful for it. His aim was to please Greta in multiple ways.

Mine.

Not contradicting his bear, he bowed his head, barely touching the tip of his nose to the peak of her clit, and enjoyed the spicy wildflower scent of her pussy. Nothing on earth he'd ever come across smelled as good as this.

"Hansel?" Her voice trembled.

"Patience my sweet." He was sure moments like these were the minutia details that her friends didn't share. They were more intimate than the act itself. "A male always enjoys bathing himself in the scent of his female." He brushed her clit ever so lightly, but still remained in the same position—rested at the gate of an earthly heaven.

"But…" She hesitated. "I'm not yours."

He glanced up at her, but remained still. He watched her lick her lips, nervous.

"I-I mean, this is just for tonight. So, why go through all these preliminaries."

Her thighs quivered in his hands. He wondered if it was because she only wanted it to be for one night…or maybe like his bear, she wanted more. Either way, there was no place in his life right now for that kind of heavy discussion.

"You're right." He leaned back. "However, I want to do this night right with you or not at all." That was as close as he'd allow himself to declaring any emotions of how he felt about this lovely female before him. She deserved promises of tomorrow and forever, but until he had settled some things, he couldn't offer anyone that.

Mine.

No matter what his bear wanted.

"Okay."

His answer was a slow lick up between her labia.

"Oh…mmm"

He flattened his tongue, pressing it firmly to her sex and licked again but flicked her clit when he reached it.

Her thighs jerked in response.

Glancing up, he saw she watched him with enamored fascination.

After a quick wink at her, he gave all his focus to her divine pussy before him. The taste of her rivaled her scent, a sweet, pungent nectar that would be imprinted on his palate for the rest of his days.

Dipping his tongue inside the well, he pressed deep and stroked along the tightness of her walls. He looked forward to the moment she would surround his cock.

"Han-sel." She moaned and rotated against him.

Thrusting into her a few more times, he slipped away and suckled along the lips of her sex. They were full, smooth and plump from her aroused state. When he reached the stiff kernel of her pleasure, he circled it with his tongue, ensuring he swiped along the sensitive sides.

She cried out and bucked against him.

Oh, yes, his sweet Were-bear was highly sensitive. Enjoying that knowledge he continued to tease her.

"Ple-ase, ple-ase, Hansel..." she mumbled as if she wasn't exactly sure what to ask for.

However, he did. It was his plan to give it to her. He cupped her squirming ass tighter and lifted it up off the chair so that she was fully dependent on him for both her pleasure and her balance.

"As you wish." Setting his mouth onto her pussy, he drew her clit between his lips and alternated between sucking and flicking it. When she was shaking hard, and he knew her orgasm was near, he'd pull away and lick along her slit. He kept her on edge, wanting her pleasure to build so high she'd recall her first climax with fond memories once he was gone.

Once her head began to toss restlessly along the back of the seat and her nails had buried themselves deep into the fabric he knew she was more than ready. He gave her repeated swipes along her clit, brushing the tip and the left side where he'd discovered she was most sensitive. Relentlessly he plied her with precise attention until her dam broke and she was sailing along satisfaction river.

"Ahhhhh! Ahhhh! Ahhh! Ahh!"

Her body shook violently in his hands and she screamed.

But he didn't stop. He lapped up the cream coating her sex as he pushed her further. Lowering her to the seat, he pressed along the back of one of her thighs and pushed it against her bountiful breast, giving himself more room. All the while he continued to lick her pussy as his other hand stroked her quivering flesh then slipped his middle finger into her.

Warm and wet she greeted him. He pushed in and out, determined to take her to a second orgasm as he prepared her body to receive him.

Between the licks and finger fucking it didn't take Greta long to reach her pleasure again.

This time when her hoarse screams filled the cabin he guided in a second finger, working purposefully along her walls, trying to ensure that she would experience only a minimal amount of pain.

Thrusting her hips against him, she claimed all of her pleasure.

When her body calmed this time and her quivers became few and far between he removed his hand from between her thighs and kissed up her body until he reached her mouth. He hesitated, staring deep into eyes that he knew were a golden reflection of his own.

"Was it what you imagined it would be?"

"Better." She cupped his face in both her hands and brought his lips down to hers. She swiped the moisture of her orgasm from his lips then slipped inside. Her kiss was full of uninhibited passion.

He gave back to her in the same manner, sparring with her tongue in and out of their mouths.

They were both panting when she pushed him back.

His brows scrunched. "Why'd you stop?"

She placed her palms flat against his chest. "I don't plan to be a bystander in this night. I want just as much access to your body as I've given you to mine."

His bear growled.

He leaned in for a quick peck then smiled at her. "So, what is it you'd like next?"

"Your clothes off." Not waiting for him, she gripped the hem of his t-shirt and snatched it up and over his head.

Not wanting to hinder her, he lifted his arms.

Once his shirt was sailing across the room, she pointed. "Pants please."

Chuckling, he unlaced one biker boot and then the other. After a moment's pause to give a kiss and lick to her sex still on display, he rose before her. He toed out of his boots and kicked them aside as he took hold of his belt. Wasting little time he loosened it, then started unfastening his jeans.

She lowered her feet to the floor and sat up, his shirt still on her. "I love the show, but I want to join in." Her fingers took hold of his zipper and slid it over his hard cock.

He groaned as her hand brushed against him.

They both worked his jeans down his hips, but that's as far as they got when Greta gasped.

CHAPTER FIVE

"Oh, my..." Greta couldn't put more than two words together in her mind as she stared at the fascinating sight of the erect male before her. Hansel was the first male she'd seen. As a Were, they stripped most times before they shifted. Nudity wasn't anything they were ashamed or curious about. However, she'd never, ever witnessed a male aroused. Seen a cock stand out, hard and proud.

"If you keep staring at him, you're going give him a complex."

She glanced away from his shaft and saw the twinkle of humor lighting his golden gaze. Smiling, she teased back at him. "Would it sooth his ego if I did this?" Being led by instinct, she wrapped her hand around it and squeezed.

"Shit!" Hansel's eyes shut tight.

Doing it again and adding a stroke, she enjoyed the hiss that came out from between his gritting teeth. *This is going to be fun.*

"You may need to give me some pointers from here, Hansel. My knowledge in how to please you is very limited. I only have what I've gathered from secret whispers of my friends."

He opened his eyes and peered down at her. For a long moment, his intense gaze just held hers. "What is it that you desire, Blackberry?"

The deep, rough texture of his voice made her shiver and her sex ache.

"I want to taste you, as you did me." She was honest with him.

"Then do it." He fingered the wild, thick hair around ear. "You can't go wrong. Do what you're comfortable with."

With a short nod, she returned her gaze to the large, long cock before her. She wouldn't allow herself to ponder the mechanics of how it would fit inside of her sex, especially when the fingers he'd slipped inside of her earlier seemed more than enough. She gave herself a moment to familiarize herself with his length. Caressing him from the heavy sack at the base of his shaft, she then traced the ribbons of veins that ran up it to his plump crown.

"I love your touch…" He whispered.

Her chest swelled a little with pride and excitement. She didn't believe that she was Hansel's first sexual encounter, no way. A male didn't achieve the talent he'd exhibited between her thighs from instinct alone. He'd been too clever in getting her to not just one, but two orgasms. Now, she wanted to return the favor by bringing him pleasure.

"Good because your touch turned me inside out."

There was a bead of moisture at the small opening that beckoned her to taste it, him. She leaned forward and circled the wide head of his cock, discovering the ridges and dips, purposely avoiding that droplet. It amazed her how soft and hot his skin felt against her palm and her tongue. Shifting back, she pumped up and down his dick a few times.

"You're killing me." A shiver wracked his big, strong body as his hands flexed into fists at his side.

To see how she affected this great bear of a male excited her own lust. When she noticed the bead begin to race down the underside of his shaft toward her fingers, she bent down and caught it was the tip of her tongue then traced its path back to the top. She savored the briny essence of his arousal.

Without further hesitation she widened her lips and took him deep into her mouth. Even though she wasn't familiar with all of the mechanics of performing oral sex on a guy, she knew it wasn't called sucking for no reason. So she sucked. Thinking of her favorite honey and raspberry creamsicle she licked and sucked, drawing him in as far as she could comfortably take him. She didn't even attempt to try and get all of his large cock into her mouth. That would have been insane. Instead she allowed her mouth to work in concert with her hands as they stroked and squeezed the remainder.

"Fuck, Fuck...ahhh, Black-ber-ry." He cupped her face and joined the tempo of her oral play by thrusting between her hands and lips.

She added more effort to her manipulation, thinking about the alternating technique he'd used on her. Increasing her speed, she pushed him higher toward an orgasm. She sucked, circled and flicked along the tiny opening that had tightened.

His body was now trembling in her hands and his

words were more guttural than actual language.

Glancing up at him, she could see his head was tipped far back. She couldn't even see beyond his chin. But the veins raised in his neck and the tight grip he held on her hair spoke volumes of the intensity of his pleasure.

Slipping her hand down his length, she cupped the sack, now drawn so tight at the bottom of his cock it had practically disappeared. However, what she could grasp, she did and she fondled the two balls within.

"Shi-i-t…ohhhh, he-lllll, yes!" He roared as he bucked one last time into her mouth and climaxed.

Swallowing his hot thick, creamy release, she rejoiced at the fact she had been able to bring him there. His earthy, cashmere musk scent increased and surrounded her.

After one final groan, he stepped back and removed the rest of his clothing. Big, naked and proud, he stared down at her. "I don't want the memory of taking your innocence on the floor, which is where we're headed if you don't take that saucy ass of yours into the bedroom."

Slowly, she pushed up from the seat and stood before him. "Wow, I don't think more romantic words have ever been spoken between lovers." She winked at him.

"If you want romance, you've come to the wrong Were-bear. However, if you want to be fucked properly, I'm at your service."

With her full mating heat upon her, the last thing she or her bear wanted was a slow, gentle ride. "I'll take fucking…this time." Closing the gap between them, she palmed the back of his head and kissed him hard. Moving away, she left little space between their lips as she whispered, "Show me what you got, big bear."

He growled. Before she knew what was happening, he had her lifted up in his arms and her legs wrapped around his hips. "With pleasure."

Turning them toward the room he marched with fierce purpose, not stopping until there was a mattress beneath them.

She moaned and he settled over her. By his earlier words, she would have anticipated him just shoving into her, quick and hard. Instead, he kissed her, leisurely and gently, as if he were making love to her mouth.

Returning his kiss, she fingered the long strands of his silken hair. She wanted to imprint everything about this night and this Were-bear into her mind. He would be gone when day came, but he'd be forever in her heart.

That thought shocked her. However, she pushed it away, she'd analyze it later. Much later. If she allowed herself to dwell on hidden feelings toward Hansel, she would attach more meaning to this night. She couldn't afford that risk, to her mind or her heart. She needed to put them back on the path of mindless lust.

Palming his face between her hands, she pushed him back until she could meet his eyes. "Don't make me wait any longer....I want to feel you inside me. Now!"

A frown creased his forehead, but then cleared away. His features relaxed as he said, "You got it."

After a quick kiss on her lips, he shifted his body until she felt the head of his cock pressing against her sex.

Her breath caught.

"Don't tense up…look at me, Greta." He balanced his weight on one elbow beside her shoulder, as his other hand stroked her clit, sending her arousal up Pleasure Mountain again.

"I trust you." She trusted him not to hurt her physically, but even as she was prepared and ready for this giant leap into mature Were-bearhood, she still didn't trust the impact this night would have on her heart. *Will this really make a difference in who I am? Am I making a mistake? Should I stop this?* Thoughts rambled through her mind.

Just when she was set to bring it all to a halt, she gazed into his eyes. There was an emotion there, sincere and honest. She wasn't sure what Hansel felt about her, but there was something that connected the two of them that she could not explain.

Staring deep, she tried to see into his heart…his soul, but there was more than one wall that appeared to be blocking her. This Were was open to passion, but everything else within him was closed off.

Who are you, Hansel? Really?

"Stay with me, Greta." His thumb caressed her cheek as he slipped inside her, moving at a steady gradual pace.

She exhaled and gripped his shoulders tightly. "I'm here with you."

When he paused, the head of his cock pushing into the barrier of her innocence, she felt his body quivering against her own. Or maybe she was shaking enough for the both of them. She was apprehensive, but not afraid.

"Don't stop." Cupping the back of his head with one hand, she brought his mouth to hers and kissed him, pressing her tongue far between his lips and showing him what she wanted from him.

His hand moved from her clit and gripped her hip as he lunged forward, clearing the resistance and burrowing all way in—seated to the hilt.

He swallowed her scream and held her tight as she quaked and adjusted to the new, wondrous feeling of being impaled and stretched wide.

Vibrations tickled her lips as he groaned, but remained still.

Wanting to experience everything, she was the first to move. She rotated her hips. Heat shot from her sex up her spine. She broke the kiss. "Oh, my."

"It gets better." He chuckled and pulled out all the way, then with one solid stroke he was all the way in again.

"It does..." She arched up to him taking him deeper.

"Are you alright?" His lips were pressed to her ear.

She nodded, the fervent passion seemed to rob her of the ability to formulate words.

"Good." Hansel's thrusting became more forceful. He ground his hips against her causing the head of his shaft to graze along some secret spot along the top of her walls.

"Ohh...." Burying her nails into his shoulders, she locked her ankles at the small of his back and moved with him.

"Damn, you're so fucking wet and tight...."

She wanted to praise him as he was her, but she couldn't think, only feel. Satisfaction of this magnitude had never been a part of her life before. This experience of lovemaking...fucking, between a female and male was something she should not have forbidden herself over the years. What was it like between mates?

As that question rolled around in her mind, her body began to tremble from within her belly, her sex felt sensitive and alive at the same time. Every thrust of Hansel's cock seemed to drive her closer and closer to insanity. She wasn't sure if she could handle much more. This wasn't the same orgasm building as the two she had earlier by his mouth. No, this was different, something more….something *intense*.

Then it happened, her world exploded, the stars collided and the moon became one with the sun and nothing would ever be the same again.

Hansel's buff arms surrounded her and held her tight to him as he bucked against her and filled her with his heat, growling out his own completion.

Secure in his bear hug, she buried her nose along his neck and inhaled. She wanted to remember the feeling of being in his arms and his smell. Could there ever be anyone else for her?

Mine.

Her bear seemed to make a claim on Hansel, a claim she could not agree with. This was only for one night. Mutual desires fulfilled. Nothing more.

Easing back from her, he looked down. "You still doing okay, Blackberry?"

Smiling and feeling overwhelmed she exhaled before answering him. "I'm all good."

Pulling out, he pressed his cock back in. "You think you can go another round?"

She hissed before she could catch it, feeling the sting in her tender sex. "Yeah…um, I'm game." Sinking her teeth into her bottom lip, she tried not to wince as he slipped out.

He chuckled. "Sure, you are." Shaking his head, he untangled himself from her legs. "You don't have to be brave. Let's go for a shower and see if we can take away some of that ache before round two."

Taking the hand he offered her, she allowed him to pull her up from the bed. "What about the mating lust?" The golden tint over the world around her, was still a little hazy, not as bright as before, but evident nonetheless.

His brow crinkled, as if he were unsure. "It should keep." He took hold of her hips and stirred her body toward the bathroom

"Don't you know?" She padded along before him. Soon her feet greeted the cool tile floor. "I mean, I'm leaning on you for all your erotic knowledge," she teased.

"No." There was sharpness to his words and she could now see that his frown had gotten deeper, causing flecks of onyx to show in his golden gaze.

Stepping away, she turned and stared at him. She wasn't afraid, but she didn't care for his tone one bit.

He forced out a harsh breath and shoved his unruly, sex-tussled hair away from his face with a single hand. "I'm sorry, sweetheart. I didn't mean for it to come out like that." Setting his hands on his hips, he stared down at the floor. "It's never been like this for me before. So, so intense, all-consuming." He shook his head.

"I've always heard about the mating lust and assumed that it happened every time. A part of our Were sexual appetite."

Shrugging his shoulders he met her gaze. "Maybe. It's possible. In my past all my encounters have been with human women. I kept away from sleuths."

She was frowning now. "When you got away, didn't you return to your people?"

"No." Closing the distance between them, he nipped the side of her neck.

Shivering, she melted against him.

"Do you really want to talk right now? Because I have a few suggestions for what we can do with our mouths instead." He set kisses along her collarbone and then lowered himself until he could draw one of her nipples into his mouth.

Moaning, she held him to her. "Hm, we can talk later."

Circling her waist, he pulled her against him and lifted her up until her breasts were level with his face. Nuzzling her boobs he carried her into the shower.

"Um, don't we need some water?"

Tipping his head back, he winked. "I was planning to bathe you." Leaning in he circled the tight tip with his tongue.

She squirmed against him. "I'm sure."

Allowing her to slip down his body until her feet were steady on the shower floor, he reached out and turned on the nozzle of the shower.

"Ah!" She screamed as the icy water hit her back. Dancing away, she stuck out her bottom lip. "That is cold."

"I bet my original bathing suggestion is more desirable now," he taunted.

"Let's see how you like the cold spray." She shoved him back two steps.

Quickly he grabbed her waist and pulled her against him. "It's perfect now."

He claimed her mouth in a kiss, and all she could think was how right he was…this was just perfect.

~YH~

"Tell me about your experience at the evil circus,

Hansel." Greta lay curled along his side, her fingers idly drawing slow designs on his chest.

He caressed her hip with one hand, while his other rested under his head against the pillow. Continuing with the strokes to her warm, satiny skin he stayed quiet for long moments. The mating heat was subdued for the time being. It had taken hours and multiple positions between Greta's thighs, before he could even see clearly. He didn't regret one moment.

His bear growled within him, unsatisfied.

Hansel knew why. After he and Greta's shower session, when they'd ended up back in the bed with him inside of her, this time in a Were's favorite position, female on all fours before him, he had taken her deep and hard. Greta had participated just as vigorously, bouncing her plump ass back against his hips. His cock was hard and wet from her cream as he thrust into her tight pussy and everything had gone a rich shade of gold before him. The haze of the mating lust was so thick he couldn't see. However all his other senses had opened up fully. He could smell the potent bouquet of Greta's heat, the wood and polish of the cabin. His ears picked up every moan and whimper of the female tearing at the sheets before him and the night animals and insects in the forest around them. The most heightened was his sense of touch/feeling. It was not just that he could feel every nuance of texture of Greta's body where they touched or the air along his skin, but the baring of his gums as his canines lowered took most of his concentration. Not because it was happening for the first time while he was having sex, but more importantly because he had to fight them back and resist the urge to do what his bear had urged him to do—MARK GRETA.

He didn't and now his bear was angry and they were at odds.

Now, he was unsure about something else. This night brought more and more complexity to his life and emotions he didn't care for. He pondered for a few minutes just how much he wanted to share with Greta about his life. He wasn't the kind of person that opened up to anyone or made attachments. But, Greta was different, that he could admit to himself.

He chalked it up to their shared experience, she was a sister of tragedy to him, and left it at that.

She must have sensed his hesitance because she gazed up at him, balancing her chin on the back of her hand at the center of his chest.

"You don't have to tell me if it is too painful. I understand pain around that situation."

Rubbing her back, he gazed into the kind ebony eyes of the female that had grown to mean so much to him. Not just because of tonight or anything of their past. Just because she was Greta. "I don't mind sharing some things with you."

"Thank you." Her fingers curled into his chest and scratched along his skin as if trying to sooth him.

"I will tell you about the day of my escape."

"Whatever you're comfortable with."

He wasn't comfortable with any of it, but he would still take a small chip out of his wall for her. Moving the hand from behind his head, he wrapped it around her and pulled her closer to him. He refused to analyze the gesture as anything but that he liked her full, soft body against his own. Not because he needed her for emotional support.

"After I caused that distraction that helped you get away, the three men that ran the place kept a sharper watch on me." He stared up at the wooden slats that made up the arched ceiling.

"They didn't just chain me to a stake in the floor of the animal keep, but placed me in your cage. They told me that since I aided you in getting free I could take your place. My training time was doubled, as well as the length of time I performed for the audience they brought in for shows was extended. They were purposely exhausting me. Keeping me from considering my own escape I'm sure." Being in her cage and smelling her scent every night had caused him to long for her and his loneliness to feel insurmountable. However, he couldn't have kept her there with him. Greta had a family she needed to return to.

"But it didn't work."

"No. The more vicious they were to me and the harder they worked me the more I plotted and planned for my freedom." He gazed down at her and stroked the supple skin of her cheek. "What you don't know is that before you showed up, I had given up hope. I had nothing to live for...no family anymore. I was sore and emotionally empty. You gave me a purpose." Taking hold of her sides he dragged her up his body and kissed her.

It wasn't a kiss of passion, but one of thanks — soft and slow.

When the kiss ended, she settled back against his side. "I'm glad I could give you hope again. No one deserves to live out their days in that hell."

He thought about all the other animals, nonshifters, he had left there. It caused an ache of sadness in his chest. It was part of the reason he hunted them now.

"No one." She echoed. "How did you finally do it, if

they had you chained and caged."

"I waited until the perfect moment during my performance. They always removed my collar and links to put on one of those idiot ruffled collars around my neck before I entered the ring, so the humans that came to watch wouldn't see the chains. There was a point in the show where I would run in circles around Jackal, the ring master, and then they would turn on loud music and I was expected to stand up on my hind legs and move toward him to the beat—"

"As if you were dancing. I recall them trying to teach me that move even while my ankle was still tender and sore. I could never stay up long enough to complete the movements."

Hansel recalled those few attempts as well. He'd stepped before her, shielding her bear's body from the sharp bite of the tip of the whip, one of Damian the trainer's favorite tools.

"Well, when the music was loud and the tent was packed with people, I stopped myself on the farthest side of the ring waiting for the music to start. Once it did, I got up as I was supposed to, began to move in the rehearsed steps, but after a few I dropped back down. As soon as my front paws hit the sawdust-covered floor I started running toward the single opening that the people used to come and go."

"Didn't they come after you?"

"Yes. I but I ran toward the woods. I doubled back behind one of the worker trailers. There was the teenage boy that cleaned out the cages, he was about my size. I shifted to my human form and snuck inside to steal some clothes from him. By that time the crowd had also exited the tent and were running everywhere. Some headed to cars trying to escape the ferocious escaped bear. Others mingled around and still got on rides and bought food and souvenirs."

"That was a smart move to shift and blend in. Did you catch a ride from someone?"

"No. I didn't want the questions of where my parents were or how I'd gotten there. So, I just started walking down road. Two hours later, Damian and Bart, the accountant, came tearing down the road in the animal catcher truck. I thought they had me." He ran his hand along her spine.

She gasped. "Did they?"

He chuckled, recalling that moment. "Hell, no. They stopped and asked me if I'd just come from the Big Top and if I'd seen the runaway bear."

She laughed.

"I wanted to reach inside the truck and yank them both through the window and beat the shit out of them." Even now the heat of anger shook his core. He opened and closed his fists.

Greta took hold of one of his hands and lifted it to her mouth, kissing his knuckles until he relaxed some and opened it. She stroked the center of his palm with her thumb.

Her care and concern for him warmed every icy corner inside of him. It had been so long since someone else had worried or fussed over him, he didn't know how to respond to it, so he remained silent.

"I'm sure you did want to attack them. You had every right. What did you do?"

He sighed, pushing out frustration's poison energy. "Just looked them straight in the eye and said I hadn't seen it. They gave a sharp nod and sped away."

"What have you been doing since then?"

"Just wandering around the country trying to live

some semblance of a life." Uncomfortable with the conversation, he shifted her away from him and sat up. "I think it is time I get you back home safely."

Pushing into a seated position, she grabbed the edge of the sheet tangled on the bed and pulled it over her body—covering her nudity. "I don't need an escort, Hansel. I can take care of myself."

He had done that. Made her feel vulnerable and insecure all over again. He was a shit, but he couldn't help it. Life had thrown him too many curve balls he had to take care of before he was any good for himself or anyone else. If he stayed curled up in this bed beside her much longer opening up his heart and thoughts, he'd start to wish for things and a life that wasn't meant for him. He was a loner...experience had taught him a harsh lesson—that it was better not to feel for anyone or attach yourself because you could lose everything too easily. And the pain of that loss hurt like a motherfucker and he had barely survived it the first time, he couldn't risk it again.

For Greta.

Not even for Greta, he explained to his bear.

"I know you don't, but I won't be able to have any peace if I don't see for myself that you're alright."

"Fine." She climbed out of the bed and looked around the floor still clutching the sheet to her beautiful body.

Guessing what she needed, he got up and swiped his shirt from the floor and crossed the room. "Here you go."

Glancing at him, she saw the shirt he extended to her and took it. She quickly dropped the bedding and put it on, ensuring she buttoned every button. The fastening done up at her throat made her look more tense and uncomfortable.

"I'm ready." She started to turn, but he stopped her with a hand on her waist.

"Blackberry, thank you for this night." He waited until she met his gaze. "There has been very little joy in my life, but when there has it always seems to be brought by you." He cupped her face and stared into her ebony orbs. There were so many things he wanted to say, share, but he couldn't. Nor did he know how to. He was captured at such a young age that this was all foreign ground to him.

With one step, she closed the gap between them and set her lips softly against his. The kiss was closed mouth but more powerful than the hundreds they had exchanged throughout the night.

His heart beat fiercely in his chest and caused his gut to clench, ache.

She moved out of his arms. "This night will be one I will always remember fondly."

There was nothing left to be said and everything to say, instead he nodded.

"I'll wait for you outside." She walked away.

When he heard the soft click of the front door closing, he dropped to the bed and buried his head in his hands.

How can you walk away from her?

"I have to." He could feel the agitation of his bear. It wanted Greta. Wanted Hansel to claim her as his. However, he couldn't. What life could he offer her? A life on the road running down one lead after another was no way to live. No way to build a family.

He thought about what it would be like to have a family with Greta, but even the momentary consideration caused him pain in the deep recesses of his mind where memories of his lost family were stored. Shoving the thoughts away he stood quickly and grabbed his jeans from the floor. Greta was waiting for him and he needed to take care of her then get far away from her. It was for the best.

For who? His bear growled.

"Everyone."

When he got outside he saw her standing at the edge of the trees out of the arc of light from the porch. She was just as ready for their time together to end as he was.

Without a word he walked toward her and they fell into step together. He allowed her to lead the way.

Forty minutes later they arrived at a small clearing on the far side of the lake away from most of the cabins in the county. Her white truck was parked there.

Opening it up, she grabbed her clothes from inside and dressed in her jeans, blouse and shoes. "I feel like I should say something more than thank you." She handed him his shirt.

Pulling it to his nose he smelled it as he held her gaze. Wildflowers and rain — Greta.

Lowering the clothing, he wrapped an arm around her waist and drew her against him. Placing his lips along the shell of her ear, he allowed the heart of his bear to speak. "May tomorrow never come and tonight's end tarry so that I may live in this moment with you always."

"And I with you." She squeezed him to her.

He brushed his lips along her temple, then clutching his shirt he released her and walked away.

Moments later he heard her truck start up and the forest debris snapping beneath her tires as she drove away.

Even as his soul burned at the thought of parting from her, he knew it had to be done.

CHAPTER SIX

Shifting her truck into park in the driveway, she told herself for the one hundredth time not to think about Hansel. It had taken all of her strength and will power not to drive her truck back to the founders' cabin and race into his arms. Just to have him hold her one more time. However, what was the use, just to have him turn her away again. Remind her that there was no future for them? The hell of it all was that in her mind she knew that. Knew it just as clearly as Hansel made it.

It was her heart and her bear that she had to continue convincing.

Opening the door she slipped to the ground and assured herself that her feelings for Hansel were only because he was the first male she'd given her body to. The only one she'd allowed close to her heart. Now that she'd decided to start living her life, things were going to change for her. By this time next year she would hopefully be living in her own cabin with a mate and hopefully her first of many offspring.

Offspring. Her feet stumbled at the last step onto her parent's porch. She placed a hand on her stomach and thought about the feeling of Hansel's cub growing inside of her womb. She knew it wasn't even a possibility without three markings. But, she allowed the fantasy to play out just this once as she reached for the door.

"Glad you made it home safely."

Startled Greta jumped back and let out a low warning growl as she faced the darkened corner of the porch. One sniff and she picked up the scent of her father.

"You going to shift on your papa-bear?" Manni Armel rocked once in the chair he remained seated in.

Taking a breath, she relaxed. "Sorry, papa-bear." She placed a hand on her chest and felt her heart pounding. "I didn't see you there."

"Your bear senses on the fritz?" He chuckled.

She could see him clearly in the dark and even though he laughed, the humor didn't reach his eyes. They were dark and filled with concern.

"No. Just a lot on my mind and I wasn't paying attention."

He rose. "You should always know your surroundings, Greta."

What he said was the truth. Having lived the life that she lived because she got too forgone in her own mind was dangerous. She didn't fear being abducted again. She wasn't a small child. However, things weren't always safe and other things could happen and she needed to stay aware. "You're right. It won't happen again. Why are you still up?"

Stepping toward her, he placed a hand on her

shoulder. "I don't sleep until I know my daughter has come home safe. When you were taken years ago, I slept on this porch every night and prayed to the Great Spirit to return you to us. Then one day he did."

She moved into his embrace and welcomed the strength of her father's big strong arms. Not only because of the emotions surrounding her about that long ago time, but she also needed solace to deal with this night. Her feelings toward Hansel.

"I remember when I made it home you were here sitting on the steps, papa-bear. You were the best sight in the world to me." She squeezed tighter against him.

"You were that for me as well." He kissed the top of her head. "I just want the best for you, sweetheart."

Leaning back, she stared up into a face that resembled her own, just with more masculine features. "I'm alright. I've decided to really start being a part of my life instead of a bystander. So you no longer have to worry about me."

He squeezed her again then released her. "I will always worry about you. It's my job."

Smiling, she led the way into the house. "Okay, I can live with that."

"Good. Now, let me cut us a piece of your mother's peach cobbler she made for dessert." He walked toward the kitchen.

"Now, I'm pretty sure you had a nice big piece after dinner." She teased as she went to the cabinet for plates.

"What kind of father would I be if I allowed my daughter to eat alone?" He uncovered the pie that sat on the counter and grabbed a triangle-shaped spatula.

"Oh, one of the worst. You want some milk with it?" She handed him the plates.

"Yes." He cut the pie and removed the slices from the dish.

After pouring two glasses of milk she joined her father at the breakfast bar. The first bite of her mother's dessert was pure heaven. She allowed her eyes to close and just savored it. "Thanks, papa-bear, this was just what I needed."

"I'm glad I could be of service." He bumped his shoulder against hers.

They ate in silence then washed off their dishes.

"Get some rest." She raised up on her toes and kissed his cheek.

"You too, morning will be here soon enough and work is waiting for us both." He whispered as he walked down the hall and entered the first door to the room he shared with her mother.

Greta continued straight and went to hers at the end of the hall. Changing quickly into her pajamas, she slipped beneath the comforter on her bed. Over the last few minutes in her father's presence she'd done a good job of not thinking about the one person she needed to put out of her mind.

However, as her lids lowered Hansel's face was the last thing she saw and his name came out softly from her lips as sleep claimed her.

~YH~

Taking one final glance around the cabin, he made sure he hadn't left any of his meager belongings. He'd cleaned and straightened up and everything seemed as it had been the day before when the females had given him the key to the cabin. It was in his hand now and he pondered what he should do with it. He didn't want to go back into town to locate them to return it. He figured treating the place like a hotel would probably be best, and he should leave it on the table or under the mat.

Deciding on the mat out front, he picked up his bag and slung it over his shoulder.

A knock at the door surprised him.

Not only because the isolated cabin wasn't the kind of place where people would just drop by. But, it was just after nine in the morning, most Den residents he would assume would be at work by now.

His heart leaped in his chest as he crossed to the door hoping that maybe Greta had come back to him. To see him off of course.

"Good morning, Hansel."

He was stunned to see the females standing on the porch, however, he should not have been. They seemed to always show up at the right moment.

"Morning, Mrs. Rita, Mrs. Octavia, Mrs. Genma."

All three women's lips were turned up in high smiles.

"Hope you slept well." Octavia held out a wrapped item to him.

Taking it, he peeled back the white cloth and discovered a muffin inside.

"We figured you'd need something for breakfast." Rita placed a hand on his arm.

"That is one of Rita's award-winning muffins." Genma held out a tall sealed thermos to him.

It didn't take a genius to figure out it was most likely coffee. The muffin was already making his mouth water. He took the drink from her. "Thanks, ladies. You all didn't have to do this. But, I'm glad you came by so I can give you the key."

"Well, we didn't just stop by to deliver breakfast." Genma glanced at her fellow cohorts.

Suspicion began to crawl up his spine. Had they found out Greta had been here last night?

Reaching behind him, he pulled the door closed. He knew it was rude not to invite them in to sit down while they told them what was on their collective minds. However, he couldn't run the risk that they would pick up on Greta's scent that to him seemed to fill the small cabin.

"What other reason?" He popped the top on the thermos and inhaled the strong, sweet coffee, then sipped. It was hot but he didn't care, it was made exactly how he liked it—extra sweet.

There was another glance between them.

He continued to drink.

"Well, we don't want to hold you up from your travels." Octavia's gaze met his.

"As pressing as your own life probably is," Genma tossed in.

"There's a situation we hoped you would be able to help with. It's rather important." Rita's gaze was filled with hope.

For what, he wasn't sure. Maybe because she was Greta's mother, he felt drawn to the female. But, he couldn't allow his emotions to get any further engaged.

"Why don't you all tell me what it is I can do for you and I'll see if there is something I can do to assist?" He moved past them and sat down on the two steps at the edge of the porch, working on his delicious breakfast.

Like a line of school kids, the three females filed down the steps and stood before him once again.

"There's a problem….more like a situation," Genma kneeled before him. "Your assistance would be extremely helpful."

Octavia moved closer, moving to the side of the steps. "You see Rorke owns the furniture store in town. Normally, he has time to get all his production accomplished."

"But the orders now have gotten substantial with so many offspring on the way." Genma lowered her head, shaking it.

Rita took up the space beside him, sitting down and taking hold of his forearm gently. "We wish we didn't have to bother you, but his parent died when he was younger. He and his brother work the store together. But, his older brother's mate recently had triplets and he's had to be home helping." She placed a hand on his shoulder until he glanced over at her. "You see, this matter is urgent. It should only take a few days of your time, but weeks off Rorke's workload."

No. He just wanted to say the word, even if mentally. He thought about catching up to the mini carny circus. If he didn't follow his last lead he may lose them altogether. Besides, it was just furniture, not a life or death situation.

"Isn't there someone else in Den that can lend the Were a hand?" He pulled his gaze away from Rita's sincere gaze and finished off the last bite of his muffin. Hell, if they had promised him a basket of them for his trip he would have stayed a month.

"Normally, that would be the case. But, with the First Moon Festival coming up, all hands are occupied for one reason or another." Octavia placed a hand on his other shoulder.

"The First Moon Festival?"

"Yes. It's a few weeks away. It's one of two celebration events we have in Den County. At the end of the week-long festival there is a bear run for unmated Weres." Octavia smiled.

Genma glanced at Rita. "Do you think Greta will run in it this year?"

"I believe she mentioned it."

Hansel bit down hard on the inside of his cheek to stifle the growl from his bear threatening to rumble out. Lifting his drink he guzzled half of it and reveled in the burning. He needed something to take his mind off the idea of Greta running around before unmated were-males. It was on the tip of his tongue to ask for more details of the run, but it would just be torture for him to hear them, then recall them while he was far away chasing down the men that had murdered his family and stolen his youth.

"I don't know ladies." He passed Genma the empty mug and rose. "I really need to get on the road. There's a matter I need to attend to."

"Just spare us a few days, a week maybe." Rita stood. "It would mean a great deal to me. However, if you can't we will understand."

Octavia and Genma aligned themselves on each side of Rita.

Glancing from one face to the next, he battled within himself. His mind yelled at him to jump on his bike and hit the open road. However, his bear was on the other side of the divide, pushing him to stay — see Greta again.

He knew what he would do. However, he would stay far away from the enticing were-female. They had already said their goodbyes and his life didn't need the complications that came with being near Greta. He'd get the job done and hightail it out of the county.

Hansel knew it would be a daily fight for him with his bear, but he would stay away from her.

"Fine, I'll do it." He gripped the handle of the bag on his shoulder. "But, if Rorke was part of the group of men that wanted me out of Den, what makes you all believe he'd even want my help?"

"Genma and I stopped by his cabin last night after we heard." Octavia led the way to the driveway where their station wagon-style SUV was parked.

His bike couldn't be seen on the side of the cabin. He'd purposely hidden it last night.

"I radioed him this morning and let him know we would find him some help. He was very grateful for any assistance he said." Rita moved into step beside him.

"Trust us, he will take it, happily." Genma's face was filled with a bright joy.

"Happy? That's doubtful once he sees who you brought." He stopped in front of their vehicle.

Genma walked to the driver's side, Octavia claimed the front passenger seat while Rita opened the back door behind her.

"We will wait at the end of the drive for you to follow us there." Octavia called out, then slipped into her seat.

"I'd prefer not to cruise down Main Street if at all possible," he informed Genma.

She nodded. "Understandable. No need getting the males all riled up again. We'll show you the back route into town. Since the furniture warehouse sits at the back end of town it works out well." Genma got in, started up and then backed her car down the drive.

Shaking his head at his own decision to stay, he strutted up the side of the cabin to his Stateline parked at the back. He stored his things, then gunned the engine. It roared loud and fast. The sound always brought him comfort. It had been the first and only major purchase he'd made after working odd jobs for more than two years while he lived in a small, rundown one-room apartment.

He'd bought it from an old biker who collected them. The man had back surgery and didn't know when he'd be able to sit his rides again and was selling off most of them. Hansel had paid the man in cash all seven thousand he'd saved. The bike had needed a little work, from and accident and sitting around too long unattended. However, he and the man worked on it every night and two months later Hansel hit the road to a new destination until he'd hired on at a construction site and heard about a carnival that was coming to town. It turned out not to be a more legit one and not the one that had captured him. However, it put the lust of vengeance in his blood and he started on his path to locate the three men and see they paid.

Now he was allowing himself to be waylaid, but he wouldn't feel disgruntled about it. These ladies had provided a place for him to lay his head, which provided him with an opportunity to have a night with Greta that he would remember for the rest of his life.

Backing up until the nose of his ride was pointed down the drive, he headed toward the three females he would be following into town.

One week, that was all he'd spare.

He'd stay far from Greta and soon Den would be a speck in his side mirrors.

~YH~

A growl was his greeting when he pulled up behind the three ladies at the large warehouse at the end of Main Street. A big, bulky were-male was standing inside working on a piece of dark wood lying across a sawhorse. "What the hell are you still doing here?"

Hansel slowly got off his ride, not wanting to make any threatening move toward the agitated Were. Evidently Rorke was not going to be so welcoming of 'whatever help' he received.

Advancing toward the male standing underneath the open bay door, he held his hand out. "I'm Hansel."

Rorke's gaze lowered to his hand, but didn't take it.

"Rorke, I explained to you that I would bring you someone that could assist you with your backlog of orders." Rita patted the big male's shoulder. "Hansel was gracious enough to volunteer to lend a hand when he heard about your situation."

"Wasn't that wonderful and kind of him?" Octavia pressed her hands together before her chest as if she were thanking the Great Spirit.

"He even put aside his own plans to be here." Genma smiled and stepped beside Hansel, a show of her support.

"Well, he should just hop back on his motorcycle and hightail it out of here. Last thing I need is trouble."

Lowering his hand, Hansel shook his head. "I'm not here to bring any. But, if you have everything under control I'll leave you to it." He hooked his thumbs in the back pocket of his jeans and eyed Rorke.

Rorke stared back at him, his mental struggle evident in the bunched skin between his brows.

"Don't be foolish, Rorke." Rita pointed into the warehouse. "We can clearly see all that lumber you have piled up in there and we know your orders are toppling over themselves with the festival coming and all the offspring being born."

"Your parents raised you boys to be proud but not to have so much pride you'd be stupid." Octavia folded her arms under her breasts and tilted her head giving Rorke a stern look.

Dragging a hand through his short hair, Rorke appeared as if he were a young boy being called to task for his actions.

"I'm sure you don't want to disappoint your parent in the afterlife with the Great Spirit, now do you?" Rita placed a gentle hand on the side of Rorke's cheek.

Hansel couldn't help envying the maternal touch the other were-male received. Until he'd met these three ladies yesterday he didn't realize how much he missed the warm, comforting embrace of his mother and the steady, strong guidance of his father. It had been something else he kept hidden from himself not to feel the hurt of the loss.

He turned toward the woods in the distance behind the warehouse, not only to allow Rorke some privacy while he wrestled with his emotions and conscience, but also to get himself together. Standing there he took in a deep breath.

"What the hell, I'll do it. You ever work with a saw machine before?"

Facing the other male again, he saw that Rorke had his hand held out to him. Stepping forward he shook it. "My adult life has been filled with odd jobs. One of them was as a construction worker with a small company that built houses. So I'm more than familiar with woodwork."

Pulling his hand back, Rorke gave a sharp nod. "Then I'll run you through the nuances of furniture building. Shouldn't take you long to grasp it, it's just finer details and craftsmanship than a house."

"I'm ready when you are." Hansel declared.

"Well, since you males have a lot of work to do, we

will get out of your hair." Rita placed a kiss on Rorke's cheek and patted his shoulder.

The other two ladies did the same.

What shocked Hansel was when they made a beeline toward him. Each of them gave him a soft peck on the cheek before they headed to their car.

He fought the blush that warmed his heart and raced up to his face.

Rorke cleared his throat.

Hansel was grateful the sound broke the spell. He peered at the other Were and saw that Rorke was rubbing the back of his neck, appearing to be struggling with the onslaught of his own emotions.

"Let's get to work." Rorke led the way through the open bay.

"Definitely." Hansel followed, preferring to work with his hands rather than dealing with the emotions invading his heart.

CHAPTER SEVEN

"Are you going to eat that soup or play in it?"

Greta glanced up and looked into the concerned eyes of Ebony. She let her spoon go and it clanged against the side of the bowl. "I'm sorry. My mind is a little preoccupied."

"It's been that way for days now. I thought our trip to the lake had helped you put some things into perspective." It was Friday and they were having lunch at Gobi's Diner, their end-of-the-week treat. Normally Greta brought her lunch from home and ate it alone in the park, while Ebony took lunch with Dainton. Most likely feeding their lust somewhere because they always returned to the office glowing and giving each other teasing smiles.

"It did." *Until I ran into Hansel.*

"Well, there has to be more than work on your mind. If it is a mate, I heard the Bear Run will take care of that," Ebony teased.

It had been almost a week since she'd been with

Hansel and she couldn't get him out of her mind. The thought of the Run made her belly feel tight and her bear unsettled. She couldn't even imagine being kissed and loved by another bear. However, she needed to get her emotions together because it was just what she needed to do if she wanted to ever have a life. Besides she and Hansel hadn't exchanged even one bite so the feeling she had that they were connected was ridiculous. It was just because of their past, they were sort of siblings of tragedy—nothing more.

"Earth to Greta." Ebony snapped her fingers.

Eyeing the fingers in her face, then looking past them to her friend, Greta laughed. "It seems I can't keep my thoughts from straying."

"What's up? You can talk to me." Ebony picked up the second half of her smoked salmon wrap and bit into it.

"It's nothing. I think I'm just tired from the meetings surrounding the festival. Who would have known that being the honoree at the festival meant I was automatically placed on the planning committee." Greta leaned back against the booth.

"The other day you said it was interesting learning how everything came together."

"Don't get me wrong, it is. But, just makes my days a little long. You would think that since this has been going on since Den County put up its first General Store the festival would be a walk in the park. However, the ten committee members all have their own idea of what should be different this year from the last. How many booths there should be…yada-yada-yada."

Ebony laughed. "Oh, no. That would drive me insane. I think that's why I always worked better solo or in charge. I just need people to do what I tell them."

"Then you end up in Den in a three-deep office." Shaking her head, she smiled. "Poor, Ebony."

Tossing her napkin at her, Ebony grinned. "It is a change of life for me, but I enjoy it. We each have our corner to manage and it works. When we come together to decide on what outside companies to work with Dainton and I come to a quick agreement."

Greta rolled her eyes. "If that's how you see a two-hour discussion on the same points from two stubborn Were-bears you're right." She rubbed her chin. "Now that I think about it, the committee meetings are just like work."

"Keep it up and I'll take your dessert."

"I give, I give." Greta raised her hands up in the air. Ann Gobi made the best sherbet with chunks of fruit in it. It was what she looked forward to treating herself with all week.

"Figure as much." Ebony drank her tea.

Picking up her spoon, Greta ate her soup.

"Lidi, I need you when you have a second." Ann stepped around the counter holding a large to-go bag.

Lidi, a slim black female waitress, picked up her tip from a table, then made her way to Ann. "Yes?"

"I need you to run this food to Rorke over at the shop. He and Hansel have been working so hard at the warehouse they forget to eat. Octavia usually comes and gets it, but she's tied up."

Smiling, Lidi took the bag. "It would be my pleasure."

Ann couldn't have said Hansel.

The attractive, svelte waitress quickly untied her apron and passed it to Ann as a large smile graced her lips.

She was sure the female was all too happy to take a lunch sack to a sexy were-male. Greta's bear went on alert.

"Whoa, why are you growling?" Ebony whispered as she looked around the diner. "Are we under attack?"

Leaning in, Greta asked, "Did you hear who Ann said was working with Rorke?"

Ebony shook her head. "I wasn't paying attention. Should I have been?"

"No, no. It's probably not even important." Greta felt agitated. She tapped her thumb restlessly against the table warring with what she should do if Hansel was still in town.

A warm hand covered hers, stilling her movement.

Greta looked up into the concerned gaze of her friend.

"It has to be something, you look like you're going to crawl out of your skin. For a Were that's not saying much, except I'm not talking about you shifting." Ebony removed her hand. "So, talk to me."

For a moment, Greta wanted to say it was nothing but she did need to talk a little about it. "I think Hansel is still in town."

"Mr. Sexy Biker Bear from your past?" Ebony's eyes lit up with intrigue.

"Yes." Greta sighed. "It's none of my business why he's still here, but the last time I saw him he was clear about leaving town."

"And you're a little hurt that he's been here all this time but hasn't come to see you."

Burying her face in her hands, she groaned. "I shouldn't be." She looked at Ebony. "Hansel's life is his own. We don't have any ties to each other."

"Just a complicated tragic past that the two of you experienced in some form together." Ebony's gaze softened. "I'd find it hard not to feel some kind of bond with a male that was an important part of my life."

"If it wasn't for Hansel helping me escape, I never would have made it back to my family."

"Well, take it from someone who has never had a family. That's something to be grateful for and have a special place in my heart for the person who made it happen."

Greta knew Ebony was correct. However, things between her and Hansel were a little more complicated than that, especially since they had sex. Something she would not have done if she'd known he planned to hang around in Den.

Liar. Her bear contradicted.

"So, what are you going to do? Sit here or find out why your Were-bear is in town?"

"He's not my anything." Greta picked up her water and drank, feeling unsure of herself.

"Dessert ladies?" Minni, their waitress, came with her tray and collected their lunch dishes.

"I'll have two orders of apple crisps with extra honey glaze to go," Ebony never looked away from Greta.

Understanding her friend's message, Greta dug into her purse and pulled out enough money for both lunches and tip and placed it on the table. "Nothing for me." She scooted to the end of the bench. "I may be a little late returning from lunch."

"I'll let Dainton know. I'm sure the dessert will keep away any questions he'd ask." Ebony winked at her.

"Thank you." Greta covered her friend's hand on the table. She wished that she could communicate more about what was going on, but Greta wasn't even sure herself.

"Anytime."

Greta left the diner.

~YH~

"She's attractive and definitely has a thing for you."

"I guess." Rorke glanced out the front of the warehouse window as the bright orange SUV pulled away. Lidi, a waitress from Gobi's, had just left after bringing them lunch.

The female had stood watching Rorke eat the first few bites of his thick sandwich as she attempted to get him involved in conversations from how many cradles he had to make to if he was excited about the festival. Rorke had given her one- or two-word responses. Not pressing him further, she had given Rorke a wide smile, then told them both to enjoy their lunch.

Not ready to eat, Hansel had set his to the side, planning to have it for dinner later. The females in town were too kind to them. Making sure they had breakfast early in the morning when they started and a big lunch to keep them going. Hansel wasn't only not used to so much attention, but also to eating so hearty.

"You guess?" Hansel eyed the other male. "Only thing that would have made her actions more clear would be if she had stripped naked before you."

That got a rise out of the Were. Glancing up Rorke's mouth tilted in a crooked smile that all males understood.

Chuckling, Hansel shook his head and finished carving out the last corner on the side of the cabinet. "Maybe you ought to consider chasing her during that Bear Run thing you all have coming up."

Rorke sighed. "Not planning to participate this

year." He took a large bite out of the second half of his sandwich.

"Why not? You're about my age. In this county, isn't this when you all settle down with a mate and start popping out multiple offspring?"

"Yes, but as soon as my brother is back to work and we can hire a permanent worker, I plan to take off on my wandering time."

Hansel frowned. "What's that?"

"It's what you get to do every day." Rorke picked up his drink and took a healthy sip from his straw. He lowered the plastic cup back to the stack of lumber where he sat. "Travel the country, see what is out there and experience life beyond our boundaries. Normally it is something Weres do their twentieth year, but we lost our parents then and it just was never the right time. But, I can't see myself settling down with any female until I get this gnawing out of my gut that pushes me to go."

"I understand." Only thing about it was the last few days he'd remained his gut was urging him to claim a mate and put down roots. He didn't know if it was the generosity of the Weres here and how they cared for each other or something else.

Someone else.

Purposely he ignored bear as he'd kept away from the one person he desired to see.

Allowing the conversation to end, Hansel placed the cabinet onto a flat dolly and rolled it out to the back loading dock. The day was unseasonably warm and he needed to be outside and feeling it on his skin. Taking off his shirt, he tossed it to the side and grabbed a handful of sandpaper. Running his hand along the furniture, he couldn't help admiring his work.

Knowing that this piece and several others he'd put together would be placed in a home for years and possibly generations to come did something to his heart.

It tightened in his chest and made it a little difficult for him to breathe. He barely recalled what his bedroom looked like at his home with his parents. He recalled model airplanes, cars and ships he and his father had assembled together. But, his furniture escaped him. He fought against the overwhelming sadness as he realized how much of his parents and his early life he was forgetting.

His exhale sounded more like a groan, but he swallowed the sorrowful emotions down and focused on his work. In a few more days they should have Rorke's backlog to a manageable point and Hansel would continue on his way.

Setting the stack of rough paper on top of the cabinet, he kept one sheet and squatted beside it, sanding the intricate pattern he'd just finished carving out.

Hansel inhaled deeply. He took in every note of the wildflowers and raindrops that let him know Greta was close by.

"What are you still doing in Den?"

The melodic, raspy seduction of her voice caused his head to spin with more than one image of the last time he'd seen her. How many times he'd buried his cock inside of her.

His bear was on full alert.

Rising to his full height, he allowed his gaze to rest on her as a screen of gold haze settled before his eyes. She was all business, dressed in a black lace-sleeved dress. The openings gave him a peek at the tempting brown skin of her arms that he desired to trail his fingers against again. The dark blue dress wasn't tight, but still complimented her full-figure, giving a hint of her ample breasts and round hips. It ended at the center of her knees. Her legs were bare but her feet were covered in some sort of ankle high booty heels. Allowing his gaze to rise back to her face, he was taken in by her round face framed by the ebony length of her hair.

Was it possible that she was more beautiful than she had been just days ago.

"Are you going to answer me?" She licked her lips as if she were feeling uncomfortable under his heated stare.

"Just here to lend a hand." He clutched his hands, keeping himself from reaching for her. The gritty sandpaper pressed into his palm and gave him something to hone in on, something other than Greta.

"Didn't you think I deserved to know you were still here?"

"Do you care? I thought you got what you wanted that night. Nothing more."

"I'm not saying...um, that I wanted more. Just—" She cut off her own words, seeming to struggle with what she wanted to say. One hand fidgeted with a sleeve of her dress as her feet rocked on the narrow heels of her boots as her eyes roamed over his torso.

Her gaze followed a bead of sweat that rolled from the dip at the base of his throat down the center of his chest from his steady work in the sun. When it was caught and absorbed in the waistband of his jeans he heard her breath catch.

"Something you see you want, Blackberry?"

Her lids shot up and she pierced him with a hard

look. She glanced over his shoulder, looking toward the inside of the warehouse. She stepped closer to him and whispered, "Don't call me that."

Shit. Her scent seemed to have elevated, there was a hint of spicy weaved through it now. She was just as aroused as he was.

He moved in closer to her, just enough to see her pupils constrict with desire but didn't touch her. "Sorry, I enjoy the sound of it. Especially since every time I say it, I remember the color of your nipples and how their hardness feels against my tongue."

Greta's chest began to rise and fall. "Han-sel..."

The soft, vibrato of his name rolling over her tongue was his undoing.

Mine.

"Come with me." He tossed down the sandpaper, not giving a damn where it floated to. Taking hold of Greta's arm he pulled her along in step with his strides. Thank goodness her legs were long, because she could keep up without double-timing it.

"What are you doing? Where are you taking me? Why are you dragging me around?"

Even as her questions tumbled from her mouth one after the other, Hansel continued on his path into the woods.

She was curious, but he noticed she never once tried to pull her arm away or stop their progress.

When the dense forest behind the warehouse surrounded them he came to a halt and released her arm. "Why are you here, Greta?"

She stumbled away, catching herself with one hand against the trunk of one of thousands of amazing Redwoods that were the home to Den County.

He did have a moment of conscience as he looked

down at those sexy mini boot things she was wearing and how impractical they were for walking in the woods. It wasn't enough guilt to take her back out. He needed privacy with her.

"What? I told you. I found out you'd been hiding out in town so—"

Laughter ripped from his gut. Folding his arms over his chest, he eyed her. "Working at a warehouse in town does not constitute hiding out. Try again."

Balling her fists she stared back at him. "Look, I just came over here to see why you're still in my town. But, frankly I don't even care what you—"

Moving away from the tree, she started to brush past him and walk away.

Catching her at the waist, he halted her progress.

She twisted her body and grabbed his forearm as if still attempting to flee, but her nails were digging in, holding on, not pushing him away. "Let me go!"

Her tone was filled with passion and the vehemence of her command came out as a breathy moan.

"Blackberry…I want the truth," he growled as he pressed his lips to her ear and held her against his chest.

"Hansel…I told—"

Jerking her hard against him, he flexed his fingers on her hip. "The truth." He kept his voice barely above a whisper, knowing with her acute Were hearing she heard him clearly.

A whimper escaped her lips. "I—I—I…"

"I can smell your heat." He gripped the fabric of her dress and inched it up her thighs. "Tell me you came over here because you had to see me." Higher the material lifted. "Say you couldn't get me out of your mind over the last few days." He pulled up higher.

"I shouldn't." Her hands clutched at the sides of the tree before them.

"You should. Don't fight it, Greta. I can't. I've thought about nothing but you. It practically kills me not to see you out every day…every night." He slipped both his hands beneath her dress, making her take a wide stance to accommodate his touch as he squeezed and stroked her sex through her soaked lace panties.

She pressed her ass back against his hard dick, grinding into him as her head tilted back onto his shoulder. "Oh…Hansel. This is madness."

A rough chuckle came out, even though he didn't find any humor in the situation. But, he agreed with her, this was madness. He shouldn't feel this way toward her. As if she were a part of him somehow. He should have been able to satisfy his lust and move on like he did with other females.

"How golden is your sight, Blackberry?" The mating lust was so dense he could barely see, flying blind he went but touch, smell and sound.

He slipped a finger under both edges of her panties and pressed along the sides of her clit.

Bucking against him, her body shook. She began to arch and grind her sex along his nefarious touch.

Holding still he let her pleasure herself with him.

It didn't take long before she had her thighs parted wide and was fucking his fingers with vigorous pumps of her hips.

The multiple moans and short catches of her breath were sending his desire into overdrive, but he held onto it. He enjoyed Greta being so free with her passion. It was impossible for him not to imagine her over the last few nights fantasizing about him while she lay alone in her bed, touching herself and reaching climax with his name on her lips.

"Let go, sweetheart." He nipped her ear gently. His gumline was tingling was his bear attempting to bring out his canines. Hansel struggled against it. That would be wise, he told himself.

"Ah-ah-ah-ah-ah-ah-ah-ahhhhhhhhhhh!" She cried out as her orgasm overtook her.

As her body shuddered in ecstasy, he grabbed the sides of her panties and shoved them down her legs to the forest floor.

She kicked them away as he rose and tore at the belt and fastenings of his jeans. Once his cock was free of the restraining material he took hold of it. Pumped it once, twice and a third time...priming himself for the wet glove of Greta's pussy.

He pushed her dress high above her waist leaving the mahogany silk of her round, plump ass bared to him. Bending down he licked each globe then rose and palmed one of her supple thighs and lifted it up, giving himself room between them.

"This is going be one rough ride, baby." With no other warning he guided himself to the mouth of her sex and thrust in strong and deep. Taking hold of her hip, he didn't temper the pace of his glide as he'd done during their first night together. Oh, no, he was showing Greta the raw, bold and violent need of his passion — his desire for her. He gave it to her hard, over and over again. The sound of him pumping into her wet sex and the slapping of flesh echoed through the forest and mingled with their groans.

His emotion where she was concerned had become one of 'no-holds-barred'. In a sense he knew it had always been that way since the first moment she had shifted inside that hideous cage. It hadn't been sexual back then, but his bear and everything inside of him had leaped to protect her, shield her.

Make her mine. He couldn't blame that thought on his bear, it was all him.

"Oh, yes! Hansel, I'm....so close. I ne-e-ed more of you."

She was popping her hips back, taking everything he had to give her and demanding more. Her claws were out and her nails were imbedded deep in the bark of the tree.

The sight of her bear claws unsheathed and the sound of her passion-filled voice, begging and pleading with him to satisfy her on a deeper level — Were-style

Still holding her thigh in one hand, he moved his other from her hip up her body until he was sliding it along her arm. He linked his fingers through hers, needing the intimacy of the connection.

No longer able to hold back, he unleashed his bear, giving it liberty to take him and Greta beyond the superficial level of pleasure. In a swift move, he released her leg, dragged the collar of her dress wide and below the curve of her shoulder as he sank his teeth into the firm flesh at the end of the slope of her neck.

Mine.

Greta's scream of fulfillment caused birds to take flight from the trees.

His growl of passion was harsh and loud as he seated himself home at the mouth of her womb and climaxed.

Shivers of satisfaction raced along his spine as he slowly became aware of everything at once. Assuaged with guilt, he removed his teeth from her, licked over the opening and stumbled back.

"Hansel…oh, no…no, no, no…"

Fuck! What have I done? He yanked his pants up his hips, then pulled them together as he stared at the woman before him.

"Yes, what *have* you done?" She turned as she put her dress to rights, her gaze landed on him as she shot daggers at him.

"Why didn't you stay away? You shouldn't have come here." He shoved his hands into his hair wanting to scream, yell, tear something apart, but instead he sank his teeth into his bottom lip trying to keep his cool, in an uncool situation. *This wasn't what I intended.*

"You! What you intended." She charged at him, not stopping until she was a foot away as she shook with anger, a she-bear full of righteous indignation. *Ugh, males. Always thinking everything is about them.*

"I know it is not just about me," he growled. "I've got important things that I *still* need to do. Between you…this county….I keep putting them on hold."

"I'm trying to have a life finally. Which you clearly stated doesn't include you."

Lowering his head and staring at the forest floor, he sighed. I want it to include me. *Oh, Blackberry if I could promise you tomorrow I'd give you the moon forever.*

Knowing that doesn't make this any easier. "I had plans to participate in the Bear Run. Finally get a mate…start a family." Her voice hitched and wobbled. *What weremale will seek me out now?*

Two things caused his soul to shatter, the sound of Greta crying and his bear whining inside of him at the thought of his mate with someone else. He looked up at her, gazing upon her profile as she stared into the forest. Seeing her unsure of herself as she stood clutching her collar tight over the place where he'd marked her.

I'd seek you.

A laugh broke from her lips. "You…yeah, right. Don't tease me, Hansel, this day is bad enou—"

Lightening of understanding struck them both simultaneously.

She faced him as she took several cautious steps away as if she was afraid to make any sudden moves.

He was feeling just as anxious and unsettled as he remained frozen in place, his feet stuck as if weighed down with lead.

"Please tell me you said that…with your voice….out of your mouth," she pleaded.

"Said what?" He couldn't put words to anything right now, he was also too unsettled in his core. All he could do was hope she was talking about the last words he *actually* spoke. "What did you hear me say, Greta?"

She licked her lips and fingered her hair behind her ear as if she wasn't sure what to do with herself.

"What did you hear?" Finally able to get his body to move, he took a step toward her.

Shaking her head, she didn't stop her retreat until her back was pressed against the tree they had just had sex against.

"Tell me!" Birds scattered and small woodland animals scurried away at his shout. He wasn't angry at Greta, more at the universe….definitely pissed at himself for allowing his bear to take the lead and bite her. What should have been mark one.

"I'd seek you. Damn it!" She yelled back, slamming her hands hard against his chest.

The impact caused him to titter back some but he

still held his place. "I never spoke those words, Greta."

Her eyes filled with tears. "How is that possible? Every Were knows that mind-linking doesn't take place until the second bite." She shut her eyes.

"Something must be wrong."

There wasn't a hint of gold in her eyes when she looked at him again. "Did you at any time the other night allow your teeth to break my skin?"

"No." He folded his arms over his chest.

"Think Hansel. Maybe you thought it was insignificant, a small scrape."

"Hell, no. I was careful. Do you think I want to be in this situation?"

Wrong words.

A single tear dropped from one eye and rolled down her cheek.

His gaze followed it, his heart ached. He wished things could be different.

He reached for her. "Greta, I'm—"

She lifted her hands, warding him off. "Trust me, I know where you stand on this." Pushing off the tree, she walked further into the woods."

Fuck! Fuck! He quickly halted his rant, remembering she could hear his thoughts.

"We have to think. This has to be a fluke." She stopped, resting her hands on her hip.

He could hear the different theories she was tossing around in her mind as she attempted to sort out why they were at the second level of bonding. Allowing her her mental space, he returned to the night they were together and ran every moment through his mind. He came up empty time and again.

"Greta, I'm at a loss. At no time the other night did I come across any wounds or cuts on your skin that I licked—transferring my serum into you."

"Maybe the Den elder Weres can help us figure this out." She turned. Her face was tight with stress and worry. She took a few steps toward him. Maybe because of her mental exhaustion the hitch in her step appeared a little more pronounced than usual.

At that moment his bear brought the old image up of how they met. Hansel recalled Greta shifting to her human form in that small filthy cage. The fear and pain on her face as she stared down at the deep lacerations on her left ankle. Her face had contorted as she got ready to scream, cry out.

He'd been shocked to see another Were. The other animals and bears the vicious trio had brought in were always just animals, none shifters. Seeing her upset and the agony she showed, he'd done something he hadn't done since he lost his parents, he shifted. Taking human form he rushed to her, grateful that the chain holding him was long enough for him to reach her cage. He kneeled down close to her and shushed her.

The memory of her gazing upon him with hope-filled eyes still made his heart swell even now. He'd wanted to be her savior, in whatever capacity he could. Freeing her was not in his control, but healing the grotesque wound was.

"I healed you."

Her brows tightened. "What?"

Pointing at her ankle, he repeated it. "I healed you. Your first night at the carny circus."

She rotated her left foot in her short boot. "That can't be it. It's possible to lick someone and not release your serum into your saliva. It's basic Were-bear first aid."

"I was young and inexperienced. I wasn't thinking.

I just wanted to help you. Heal you. Share my strength with you in a horrible situation." He tilted his head back and stared up at the dappling sunlight between the trees.

"It all makes sense now."

"What does?" Lowering his head, he met her gaze.

"How you located me."

"I wasn't trying to find you, Blackberry. I was headed somewhere else, when I pulled off to rest and took a little walk through the forest." He shoved his hands into his pocket. That wasn't completely true, he was more drawn through the forest than out for a nature hike.

"I know. But, you still saw us that day at the stream during the salmon catch. You roared." She moved to him. Not touching him, but close enough he could feel her heat.

"A Were-male picked you up in his arms."

"Even from that distance I knew it was me." She reached out and touched the end of his long hair, where it lay against his chest.

"I know it was you." He inhaled deeply, taking in her scent. He'd never tire of smelling wildflowers and rain showers, that earthy scent that was Greta. Lifting his hand, he covered the back of hers, holding it against him.

She sighed and slipped it away as she stepped back appearing contrite as a shadow entered her onyx eyes. "With one mark I could have still found someone else. A Were ready to settle down with me."

Stop fucking saying that.

"Why? Are you going to declare yourself to me, Hansel?" She raised her arms up at her side and allowed them to fall back against her thighs with a loud slap. "Maybe you planned to drop to your knees right now and place the final bite along the side of my pussy."

He reared back.

A harsh laugh came from her. "I thought not."

Turning away from her, he took steps that widened the gulf between them, not just physically but emotionally as well. "You don't understand—"

It was her sharp intake of air that stopped his sentence and swung his body back around to her.

The horrified expression on her face shocked him. Then he knew what it was that she had seen, his back.

"Oh, Great Spirit..." she reached out a hand and grabbed his shoulder attempting to force him back around'

When that didn't work, she tried to move around to get behind him. "Hansel." She gave him an incredulous stare, her dark eyelids stretched wide.

"Leave it alone."

"What happened to your back?"

He sliced a hand through the air and stepped back from her. "Just leave it alone."

"I will not. Tell me what happened to you. How did you come by all those scars?" She rested a hand over her heart.

"It doesn't matter." He continued to move back.

She kept advancing until she had him pressed against a tree. "Hansel, with everything else that is happening between us right now, just talk to me, please."

The last thing he wanted to do was to relive his hellish existence. However, something inside of him ached, desired to share the burden with someone. *She* was the closest thing he had to a family. If not Greta then who?

"I know somehow they did this. Those men from the circus." Closing the distance between them she touched his shoulder, urging him to turn.

Letting out a heavy sigh he shifted, displaying the physical evidence of his harsh life.

Slowly and one scar at a time she traced each mark from his shoulders down to his lower back. Her touch was painful to endure, not because she was pressing down or hurting him physically, but emotionally the gentle brushing of her fingers brought back every memory to his mind.

"There are so many of them. A few of them are close to your kidneys. If they had been deeper they could have killed you." She kept caressing them over and over again, like a painter with a brush trying to bring to life every detail.

Bowing his head, he stood still and allowed her touch to do what time could not—heal him.

"When they first captured me I was a wild one."

"How old were you?"

He glanced over his shoulder and met her gaze. "Maybe six winters."

"Practically a baby."

Shrugging he, said, "I guess in some ways."

"You had to be terrified. I know I was when they got me."

"I was afraid, but I was angry and violent. I tried hard to attack anyone who came near my cage. I wanted my family, my life back." He stared before him, out into the distance. He could see the warehouse and thought about his work there this week. Rorke must be wondering where he went.

"Where is your family?" She came around him and

blocked his vision of everything but her. "Why didn't you go back to them when you finally got away?"

"The vicious trio killed them the day they took me." She embraced him.

There wasn't anything sexual about her hold, it was one of comfort and support, as if she were trying to absorb his pain of loss. Leaning back, she gazed into his face. "How did it happen?"

Pulling her arms down, he took hold of one of her hands and began to walk with her toward the warehouse as he spoke. "My father was always strong, protective and enjoyed giving in to my stepmother and me. My birth mother died when I was two winters. However, I was really close to my stepmother. She was sweet, kind and had the best smile." It had been so long since he'd talked about his family, it felt as if he were telling someone else's story. He recalled more about his stepmother than he did his real mother. He recalled Mindy, a beautiful dark-skinned black were-female had a way of squatting down before him when she talked to him and would curl her finger beneath his chin. It always tickled and made him laugh.

Greta remained silent as if she were allowing him time to gather his thoughts and talk at his own pace.

"My stepmother was pregnant. In the final stages if I recall correctly. She wanted to go hiking one last time before the baby came and she began her confinement." He linked his fingers through hers and stopped at the edge of the woods. "So, we drove out to the woods not too far from Yosemite National Park. I recall my father wanted to keep away from the campers out there so we hiked around the more secluded areas. We all shifted and were running through the woods one second and the next thing I know there were these three men in our path." His chest was tight and it was hard for him to take in large amounts of air.

Squeezing his hand, she urged him on. "I know it's painful to talk about, but it helped me when I shared my story with you at the cabin."

She was right, but it didn't stop him from wanting to keep it all buried inside. He pulled away from her and lowered himself to his haunches and picked up a fallen pinecone, pressing the pointed edges into his thumb. He wanted to focus on something other than the pain in his heart.

"My father saw them first. He let out a roar to scare them off. For most humans that was enough to get them away. Not these guys. Two of them had guns while the other held a trap they must have been getting ready to set. When they advanced toward us, my father growled and ran toward them." He closed his fist and the dry brown pinecone crumbled under the pressure.

"One shot. It was load. I didn't even know what it was since I'd never heard anything like it before. But my father dropped to the ground almost instantly. Mindy, my stepmom and I rushed to him and I saw the blood pouring out of his head. It was like being in a nightmare." Opening his fingers he allowed the fragments to fall from his hand to the forest floor.

"My stepmother whimpered and roared, she moved her body before mine in an attempt to shield me. That fucking blast happened two more times. It was like everything happened in slow motion. Mindy slumped over my father's body. Her breathing was raspy and she was shaking."

"Were you hit?" Her voice was soft, as if she was didn't want to intrude on his memories.

"No. My stepmother took both bullets. They grabbed me from her under her paw were she was still trying to protect me." The ache in his heart was so intense at the loss of his family he dropped to one knee. He couldn't breathe and for a moment everything around him vanished into whiteness.

Soothing warmth surrounded him. Glancing over he saw Greta kneeling beside him her face soaked from her tears. "I'm so sorry about your family."

Cupping her face, he swiped away the wetness with his thumb. No one had ever cried for him or shared in his pain. "I not only lost my parents but my unborn sister as well."

She pulled him into her embrace.

He held her tight against him and buried his face in her neck. He used her scent to help him center himself.

"I'm glad you are okay."

"Evidently, my family walked into their trap even before they had it set. I was what they wanted. Being with them I learned it was easier for them to train young animals to perform. I put up a fight in honor of my parents for some time. Damian had a poker and a whip he was fond of using. He used it on me so many times in the day my wounds never were able to heal fully." Moving back, he stared down at his hands and thought about the moment that he would be able to place them around Damian's neck. "Months into my captivity I asked myself what I was fighting for. They were hurting me just enough to keep me in line, but not to kill me. With my family gone I had no one. Then I just gave up hope and gave in."

"Your sleuth didn't come looking for you?"

He shrugged. "We weren't really part of one. Not one like Den. I recall other shifters being in our neighborhood but we were integrated into human society."

"That seems so odd to me."

Standing up, he helped her to her feet. "I'm sure. Besides my family there wasn't really anyone else in my life."

"What did you do after you got away?"

"Odd jobs and travelled from place to place."

"Aren't you tired of it? Haven't you ever wanted something more permanent?" She folded her arms beneath her breasts and met his gaze.

If there was anyone he wanted to promise forever, it was Greta. However, he had lived his adult life in pursuit of the men who had killed his family and he wasn't sure if he could let that go. "I don't know. Maybe."

"I'm not trying to make you do something you don't want to do. But, we still have a problem between us."

She was right. "How do you want to handle this?"

"Not sure. There has to be some solution to this."

He led her back out of the woods to her vehicle parked at the side of the warehouse. "I'll be around until Rorke's orders are stable. How about dinner tonight? Maybe we can figure something out?"

Her hand fiddled with the handle of the driver side door of her truck, unsure. "Okay. I'll radio you when I get off."

Nodding, he watched her get behind the wheel. She gave him a small smile as she backed out.

Things had not turned out at all as he had planned, but he couldn't find it within himself to feel disappointed in the situation he was caught in. No matter how it turned out, he wasn't in it alone. Greta was in it too.

CHAPTER EIGHT

"Papa-bear, glad I caught you." Greta got off work early so she could get home and talk to her parents.

Her father was just sitting in his after-work lounger, in a few minutes he would have been settled into his before-dinner nap.

"Hi, Greta. You're home early."

She set her purse onto an end table and took up a center spot on the couch. "I wanted to talk to you and mama."

"That sounds serious." He leaned his big chair back but he didn't pop the footrest up.

"It's more important than serious." She knew she was downplaying a major issue between her and Hansel, but until they came to terms with what all of this meant and a way out of it, she wanted to keep that close to her chest.

"So, what is it?"

"I want to talk to you both together."

"Rita dear, can you come in here please?" Her father

shouted over the back of his chair.

"What is it, Manni? I thought you were going to take you daily na—" Her mother came in drying her hands on a towel and smiled when she saw her. "Hello, honeybear, when did you get home?"

"Just now." Greta got up and hugged her mother.

Her mother's brows were pinched. "Is something wrong?"

"Things are fine. I just wanted to talk to you and papa about something." She led her mother to the couch.

They both sat, her mother at the end closer to her father, and Greta reclaiming her seat in the center.

"You got our attention, let's hear what's on your mind." Her father folded his hands in his lap.

Her mother stared at her.

"I want to ask a favor of you both and I really need your support in something, papa-bear." Greta had never spoken to her parents about a male before, not even when she was a teenager, she felt a little out of her league and nervous.

"Whatever it is, Greta, you can talk to us." Her mother placed her hand on top of hers then squeezed before she removed it.

"The first thing is I would like to invite someone over to the house for dinner."

Rita and Manni looked at each other, then back at her.

Her father's gaze was filled with light and wonder. "That's no problem. Can I assume it is a male?"

"Yes." Greta answered.

"When? I want to make sure I have the things to make my special salmon casserole." Her mother's face was practically beaming.

She swallowed. "Tonight."

"Tonight?" Her mother's voice rose as she pressed a hand to her chest, shocked. "I've already started dinner. I don't have time to run into town to the Berrystand Market."

"I know it is short notice and all, but this is really important to me."

"Who is it?" Her father's brows were pinched, she knew he was running through all of the available males in town.

Licking her lips, Greta took a breath and let it out quickly. "Hansel."

"What!" The chair her father was in sprang forward as her father stabbed at the control button. "I thought that scoundrel had taken himself across the county line days ago." He stood up, grumbling under his breath.

"Papa-bear..."

"Manni dear, let's not get all worked up before we hear her out." Her mother was relatively calm, appearing like the complete opposite of her father.

Greta assumed that it was because unlike her father, her mother knew a little more about Hansel's remaining in town then even she did. She didn't put much past her mother and her friends. The older women of the community just allowed the males to think they were running things. What Greta really wanted to know was if her mother knew about Hansel working with Rorke why she hadn't said something to her.

"Darling, is there something going on between you and this drifter?" Her mother offered her a kind, supportive smile.

She glanced from her mother to her father, who still sported a scowl, and back to her mother. "Honestly, I don't know. I'm not even sure if anything more than what was between us in the past is possible. We are on two very different plains of life." The words she shared were true. The rest of the day at work when she wasn't thinking about the hot, passionate sex they shared in the woods then she was mulling over the ways they were different in their personal goals.

How could two people who were so different have anything special together? She asked herself for the umpteenth time.

"So, what's this past you keep hinting at? You ready to share that with us yet?" Her father's arms were folded over his chest, still as broad and wide as she recalled it being when she was a child and would lean against while he held her in his arms.

"Not really, but..." Her words drifted away as she stared down at her hands linked on her knees.

"Oh, sweetheart." Her mother's voice was low, but heavy with hurt. "I've never wanted to push you. Respecting your desire not to have to relive the apparent nightmare you went through." She sighed. "However, I just wished—n"

"You trusted us enough to let us in." Her father returned to his seat and placed a hand on her shoulder. When she looked over at him he continued, his features more relaxed than they were moments before. "That you would allow us to share in your pain. Now that this Hansel fellow is here and connected to that nightmare I think it is important we know. Especially if you want us to open up our home to him."

"You're right, papa-bear." She leaned against the back cushion and rested her head as she stared up at the ceiling, then just started talking. She didn't analyze any of the words that came out of her mouth, just allowed them to spill, one after another, occasionally tumbling over each other.

When she was done the room echoed with grim silence. She was afraid to look at her parents, unsure of whether she would see pity on their faces. That was what she had wanted to avoid since she had returned and people started asking questions about what happened to her, where she was, how she got captured. There wasn't anything she left out from the trap outside the cabin to Hansel distracting them while she got away. She knew that if she shared the horror of her incarceration at the circus, people who look at her with pity in their eyes because she was some unfortunate soul.

She wasn't. Thanks to Hansel she was a survivor.

Finally, she lowered her gaze and met both of their eyes. At some point they must have leaned closer to her, because they were practically head-to-head. If the moment wasn't so serious she would have laughed at how they appeared—like congenital twins joined at the temple.

She did feel better to see their gazes were bright-- her father's with pride, her mother's with relief.

Greta felt the swell of her heart as it filled with love.

"Sweetheart, we are so proud of you. To be so strong, courageous and determined at such a young age. It's outstanding. I'm honored to be your papa." He pulled her up and into an embrace.

Her throat felt tight and strained from the flood of emotions.

A short whimper came from her mother, but Rita kept the tears at bay as she took Greta's hand and held it cocooned between hers. "I can't tell you how many nights your father and I have lain in bed and discussed the burden that was practically visible on your shoulders. How it grieved us that you would not talk to us. Then there were all those nightmares for months when you got back. I would just lay beside you and hold you all night just to try to keep them at bay."

"I remember." Greta recalled how much she hated sunsets because the terror would come soon.

"Now I know who this Hansel was you would mumble about in your sleep. It was the only time you were at peace through the night."

"What?" She pulled away from her father's arms and stared at her mother. "You never told me that."

"Me either."

Her mother simply shrugged and stood up. "Not knowing the situation I didn't want to bring up something that may have made things worse for you." After a pat to her hand, her mother stood up.

Greta didn't know what to say. In a way, her silence had probably caused more of a strain than if she had just let it all out. Dealt with it.

"Well, I have cooking to get done and you have a were-male to radio I'm sure."

"I do." Standing, Greta shook her head as she thought about the wonder of her parents. "I'll come give you a hand after I shower and change, mama."

"Great." Her mother headed toward the kitchen. "Get your nap in, Manni dear. The last thing Greta's young male needs to do is meet a grumpy bear."

Bending down, Greta kissed her father other the brow, keeping him from seeing her smile at her mother's words.

Reclining back in his chair, he grumbled, "I'm not sure how you Armel females think a male is supposed to get any winks in with all this information and

'Guess Who's Coming to Dinner' issue tossed into my lap."

"I'm sure you'll figure it out, dear." Her mother rounded the corner.

"I love you, papa-bear." Greta touched his shoulder.

He patted her hand, then held it as he glanced up at her. "Same here, sweetheart. No matter what you can always come to your mama and me. Remember that."

Nodding, Greta walked away.

When she woke up that morning, if someone would have told her that all of these events would have transpired before nightfall and that it would end with Hansel being in her family's house breaking bread with her father, she'd have called them a foolish liar.

Turned out she was the fool.

She entered her room and realized she was glad about it.

~YH~

"Hansel."

Hansel stared down at the hand of the big bear of a male standing on the porch. He had no doubt of two things: one, Manni Armel was waiting on him and two, even though his hair had a lot of gray in it, this male would give him a good fight if he felt Greta was being treated wrong.

Approaching the older male with respect, Hansel grasped the hand offered. "Mr. Armel. Thanks for allowing me to share dinner with your family."

The shake was firm, giving a show of strength, but Hansel didn't pick up any threat in his touch. He was grateful for that.

"You'll one day learn Hansel that in a male's household he doesn't get much say once his mate makes a decision about something." Manni pulled his hand away.

"I hope to be fortunate enough to experience that one day." Hansel felt those words deep in his heart. Maybe because he was before the father of the female he truly would love to have in his life on a more permanent basis. However, things in his mind hadn't changed much since he'd parted ways with Greta earlier. So, he wasn't here to make any promises. Just get to know her and her family better with the time he was given.

One corner of Manni's lips tilted in a smile, barely. "Well, Rita and Greta have been working hard on dinner and I'm sure they are wearing the hardwood floor out while we're standing out here." Stepping back, he opened the door.

Taking the older male's kindness in allowing him to enter first, Hansel took the four steps two at a time and went inside. Sure enough, Greta was standing in the middle of the living room with her hands knotted before her body. Nervously, she looked from him to her father, then rested her gaze on him again. "Hello."

She had changed her clothes from earlier. She now wore jeans and a buttoned down white shirt, appearing more casual and relaxed in her home setting. "Hi, Blackberry."

Her eyes shied away as she bowed her head and glanced at the floor.

He was positive that if her mahogany skin could have held a blush, her cheeks would have been flooded with a red tint now.

"Well, Hansel, it is wonderful to see you again." Rita drew his attention as she moved from the entryway that he assumed led to the kitchen. The older female, with her striking dark skinned looks, short natural hair and almond-shaped eyes was a breath of fresh air as she moved toward him.

He met her half way and returned the hug she offered. Being with Rita always filled the hole in his heart that was an emptiness of missing his mother. "I feel the same."

"Again?" Should I be concerned young were-male for you stealing my wife away instead of your intentions toward my daughter?" Manni grumbled.

However, when Hansel turned and looked at the male he could see there was a brightness of humor that lit up his eyes. This male was confident of his mate's love and knew he had nothing to worry about.

"I wouldn't have a chance." Hansel smiled and gave him a nod.

Lowering his arms from around Rita, Hansel then moved to the female he really wanted in his arms. When he got to her, he didn't trust himself to do more than place a light kiss on her cheek. "Thank you for the invite."

"You're welcome. I'm sure you're hungry and lunch has worn off."

Lunch had barely been able to compete with her ferocious appetite after the lusty activity he shared with Greta. He kept those words to himself but allowed the heat of the memory to fill his eyes.

Greta clearly picked up on his thoughts. *Hansel, I'd like to get through dinner with my parents without embarrassing myself.*

Promise me a walk in the woods afterwards.

Maybe. Depends on how you behave. "Follow me to the dining room." She led the way behind her parents through the archway with what appeared to be a little extra sway to her luscious hips.

His bear released a low growl.

They crossed the kitchen to a back room with a large bay window that caught the small bend in the lake a ways off from the cabin.

"Genma, she lives next door and her living room has a better view of the lake. There's a lovely dock that stretches over the water from behind her cabin too."

"Sounds wonderful." He glanced from the view to Greta. *Make that a walk by the lake, Blackberry. I'd love to see your body in the moonlight.*

This is not *behaving.*

"Have a seat." Manni gestured from the head of the table toward a chair at one of the sides of the cheery wood four-person table.

"Thanks." Hansel waited until Greta and Rita settled into their chairs. "Everything looks and smells wonderful."

"I hope you enjoy roasted chicken, succotash and herb butter couscous." Rita beamed from the opposite end of the table from her mate.

"I've never been picky. But have found it an honor whenever I can enjoy a home cooked meal." Hansel took the platter of sliced meat Rita passed to him. He added a few slices to his plate then offered it to Manni.

"Well eat all you'd like. But save room because Greta made a blackberry cobbler for dessert." Rita handed him the vegetables next.

Blindly he took the bowl as he glanced across the table to Greta as she finished scooping herself couscous.

He waited until her ebony eyes met his. "Blackberries are my favorite."

Keep it up, Hansel, and you're going to lose your walk and your dessert.

Oh, I plan to have both *my desserts.* This woman was an addiction to him. He warned himself to be careful, there wasn't room in his life for promises and she deserved more than empty ones.

Greta kept her thoughts silent but Hansel didn't miss the slight tremor in her hand as she passed the dish to her mother.

"Ahem."

Hansel glanced at Greta's father hearing the older male clearing his throat.

With an arched eyebrow Manni shifted his head from left to right as he stared at Greta and Hansel.

The Were was perceptive, Hansel didn't doubt the male had more than a few questions on his mind.

"I hear you're helping out Rorke at Ursine Furniture." Manni set the last dish down in the center of the table after he served himself.

Picking up his fork, Hansel nodded. "Yes, sir. Rorke and his family have a great business. It felt good to put my hands to work."

"My papa always said a were-males not anything without an honest day's work." Manni lifted a chunk of meat to his mouth.

"Your father must have been a wise Were." Hansel reached for his iced tea and enjoyed the sweet honey and orange combination as he drank.

"He was. How about your own father. What's your relationship like with him."

Greta gasped. "Papa-bear, maybe we should discuss something—"

"I'm sure Greta probably told you both where we met. Well, I lost both my parents and an unborn sister the day I was captured."

Manni's face twisted in disgust.

"Oh, my. The loss you must feel." Rita covered his hand.

He glanced at her and saw the tears filling her eyes. "Mrs. Armel it was immense, when it happened and years that followed I wanted nothing more than to die along with my family if I could not have them back. Then the Great Spirit brought someone into my life that gave me hope. A renewed inspiration to live." Still holding the older female's hand, he shifted his gaze to capture her daughter's across the table. "It wasn't the best situation that brought Greta into my world, but I'm grateful just the same."

"We are grateful that you helped her return to us." Manni's voice drew everyone's gaze down to his end of the table. "Her mother and I felt…lost, simply shells of our former selves. I will be forever in your debt."

Hansel shook his head as he leaned back in his chair. "No…no, you're not."

"Sacrificing yourself for me." Greta held his gaze.

I will always protect you. "I just did what any Were would have done for another," he said out loud.

"Maybe, but we are still honored to have you here in our home. And in town for however long you will be staying." Rita smiled.

The conversation moved to the preparation for the First Moon Festival and other happenings around town. Hansel enjoyed the easy banter between Greta's parents and the love around the table they all had for each other. Even though their comradery made him miss his own family, it felt good to be a part of this one, this night.

~YH~

"Your parents are great."

"Even my papa-bear?" Greta teased as they walked

slowly down the dock over the lake after dinner and dessert.

Hansel chuckled. "Yes. After he warmed up to me."

Greta bumped her shoulder to his as they continued on. "Papa can be a bit stern and stubborn at times. However, I hope you know he meant what he said about his gratitude."

Placing a hand at her waist, he stopped her before they reached the end. "I don't need it. You did more for me showing up in my life than I did for you. Remember that." He brushed her hair back over her shoulder.

"Okay. I will not mention it again." Her heart hadn't stopped fluttering from the moment he'd entered her family home. Now, being so near to him made it feel like it would beat out of her chest. "Hansel..." She slipped her arms up around his shoulders. "I know I don't have the right to ask for more than you're prepared—"

He cupped her hips, then drew her body against his. "You can always ask me anything."

She still hesitated. She enjoyed his warmth and strength as she stared out at the water and admired the reflection of the moon on it as she gathered her thoughts.

"Blackberry." He palmed her ass and brought her closer to him. "Look at me."

Meeting his eyes, she saw not only the sparkles of gold in his ebony orbs, but something else, some deeper emotion. Afraid to look further, she waited. Not wanting to see more there than might really be.

"I don't know what my future will hold. Or even where I will end up." His sigh was heavy as he rested his forehead against hers.

She took in a breath and held it.

"Hell, there is somewhere else I really should be right now, tonight." His head lifted and he met her gaze again. "But, nothing else feels as important as whatever is going on between us right now."

Letting the breath out slowly, she fingered the long, thick waves that hung over the collar of his shirt. "What are you saying?"

Instead of answering, he fit her body into the notch of his, leaving no space between them and kissed her. It was hard, deep and full of need as if he were searching for something that could only be found in her.

Capturing his thick tongue as it slid into her mouth, she suckled it and returned his kiss, passion for passion.

Both of them were breathless by the time they pulled apart.

"I don't want you to explore what is between us."

"Are you sure Hansel? I don't want to start putting all my energy and hope in a relationship between us only to have you get that urge inside of you again. Next thing I know you're on your motorcycle and hitting the road."

"I understand. Tonight I was thinking maybe it's time I stop chasing ghosts and start living."

"Okay."

"Okay?" He squeezed her ass.

She giggled and then felt a little silly for letting such a frivolous sound come out.

"You're beautiful." He placed his palm along her cheek. "Everything about you fascinates me."

"I feel the same about you." She pressed her breasts against his chest.

"Flirt."

"I'm learning." She'd never allowed another male close enough to her to even want to flirt. Now here was Hansel. "Let's sit."

They moved the last few steps to the end of the dock and Hansel sat first, tugging her hand.

When she started to settle down beside him he surprised her by pulling her into his lap. "Ah!" Quickly, she straddled his hips and locked her ankles behind his back. "Don't you dare drop me." She struck his shoulder with an open hand.

"Never." His hands were at the small of her back, the only thing keeping her from falling back into the water.

Sitting in such a precarious way, her ass and most of her body hovering over the lake with this male's arms secure around her made her feel alive. Hansel did that to her, made her feel free and adventurous, ready to jump out of her self-imposed shell and take on the world.

"What you do to me." She held his gaze hoping he understood all she was saying to him.

He pressed up against her, the hard evidence of his cock brushed her sex. "I'm hoping it is the same thing you do to me." He wiggled his eyebrows.

She laughed. "You are incorrigible." Her words didn't stop her from grinding her aching pussy against his shaft, teasing them both through their clothing.

Hansel groaned and held her firm against him. "Why did you choose to wear jeans on this night instead of another one of your sexy skirts?" He kissed along the side of her neck.

Tilting her head to the side to give him more access to one of her many sensitive areas, she whispered, "I'm pretty fast at getting out of them."

Pulling the side of her collar away, he used his tongue to draw a design on her shoulder. "You can?" He met her gaze. "Prove it."

"Agree to swim with me and I will show you."

He winked at her. "You're on." Taking hold of her waist, he moved her to the side, fast. He leaped up to his feet, then held his hand out to her.

Claiming it, she allowed him to assist her to her feet. In recorded time they were both stripped down to bare skin and standing side by side with their toes hanging over the edge of the last wooden slat. "You ready?"

"This will be the first late night swim I've ever had."

"Really? We do this a lot in Den." Shocked she glanced at him.

"Yup." He took hold of her hand. "Not much frivolity in my life."

"Well, let's start to change that." Jumping, she tugged his hand and pulled him into the water with her.

The icy water that surrounded her was invigorating, but it did nothing to her body compared to the male in the lake with her.

They broke through the surface together. "I thought the idea was to jump into the water not get yanked in."

Treading water, she smiled at him. He looked gorgeous in the moonlight with his hair slicked back and his golden eyes showing boldly in his pale complexion. "Maybe, but what's the fun in that."

"I'll show you fun." He shoved a large wave of water at her.

Screeching as she got splashed, she swam away purposely kicking water at him.

"Don't make me come after you," he teased.

"I dare you." She gave him a brief glance as she rotated onto her back and glided fast through the water.

The chase was on.

A lot of splashing echoed around her, however, it was a few moments before she realized she was the only one making the sound. Stopping she looked back at the last spot she'd seen Hansel, expecting to see him swimming toward her. But, he was nowhere to be found.

Then he was there. Coming up from beneath her, taking hold of her waist as he brought them both up out of the lake.

She laughed and wiggled against his hold, but he didn't let her go. "You cheat!"

"Hey, you never said how I was supposed to catch you."

"Semantics." She stroked her hands along his back, feeling every old wound on his back along the way as she enjoyed his naked form against hers.

His kicking was keeping them afloat as he propelled them to the bank. "You want to know something else I've never done before?"

"What's that?" She bumped against his chest and felt her nipples tighten harder.

"Made love in the moonlight in a lake." He planted his feet into the lakebed and held her. Gliding his hands from her waist to her ass, he pressed her to him.

She parted her thighs and wrapped her legs around him. The surface of the water floated around their waist. "Then I suggest we mark this one off both of our bucket lists." Lowering her lips to meet his, she slipped her hand between their bodies and took hold of his long, thick cock.

Guiding it into her, she sighed in his mouth as she felt the stretching of her pussy around him.

A growl rumbled in his chest as he thrust in the rest of the way.

Mine.

She didn't see the need in arguing with her bear as she was taken to one pleasurable height after another in the arms of the were-male she was falling in love with.

It was the truth, she had tried to fight it, but the fact remained she was in love with Hansel.

CHAPTER NINE

"Oh, my word, I can't believe you've never played football before." Greta tossed the ball to Theo, the quarterback on her team. It was a Saturday afternoon and a group of them had gotten together for a game.

"I've seen it played on TV and maybe passed a game or two during the summer of children leagues but I guess you have to have friends to be invited to play." Hansel shrugged as he moved closer into the huddle with the other people of their team.

"Well, you have pretty good hands for a person who has never played. You could have gone pro." Rorke commented.

"Yeah, and as soon as some corner slams his body into mine and pisses me off can't you see the newspaper headlines? 'Bear Ends Up Running Wild Through Stadium Terrorizes Players'."

The eleven members of their team all broke out in laughter.

Seeing Hansel smiling and having a good time with

her friends and community warmed her heart. She had been getting that same wondrous feeling for the last two weeks since they'd started hanging out together.

Besides work and her Festival Committee responsibilities, Greta spent all her time with Hansel. Even at night she slept at the Founder's Cabin with him and went to work from there with him following behind her truck on his motorcycle. He always gave her a final wave when he passed her job to head to the warehouse.

She could get used to a life with Hansel. Easily.

Monday the First Moon Festival would kick off and Rorke brother, whose wife had delivered the triplets last week, would be returning to work by the end of the week. She wasn't sure what the changes would mean to Hansel but she was willing to speak with some of the businesses in town to get him another job so he could stay in the county. Tonight she had planned to cook him dinner, instead of going to Grub's restaurant or eating with her parents like they usually did because the cabin's kitchen was very small. It wasn't really conducive to doing more than small quick meals.

After they ate she would open the dialogue of them making their relationship permanent and him staying on. Her body wanted his third bite so bad at times she ached in her soul for the ultimate connection to him. Being his one and only mate.

"You got that Greta?"

"What?" She blinked and stared from Theo to the faces of her other teammates moving out of the huddle. Evidently she had missed something that she was supposed to do.

Sports, just like all competition with Were's, was a

serious thing. And with the current score tied at twenty-seven all, their next play could win the game.

As they all started getting in position on the line of scrimmage facing off with Cord's team, she rushed and spoke to Hansel who was on the opposite end of the line.

What am I supposed to be doing?
Listening.

She growled when she glanced down at him and caught him winking at her.

Funny. Besides that.

"Blue Fifty-Nine. Hike!" Theo called out.

Todd, playing center, shot the ball back to him.

Run to the end zone as fast as you can.

Hearing Hansel's words as he took off and tried to avoid Gordon who was manning him, Greta growled fiercely as she ran. She shoved and pushed Lidi, Cord's safety guarding her, and ran to beyond the first five yards where Lidi couldn't touch her again until she had the ball. Greta ran with all her might, heading toward the two trees that represented the goal post she continued to check over her shoulder at Theo, wondering when he would send a bullet her way.

Then she saw the ball release from his hand but instead of it spiraling in her direction it went to Hansel. She was the distraction, set up to fake out the other team.

In awe she watched Hansel dash away from Gordon with a burst of speed, beating him by three steps as he caught the ball that dropped in over his shoulders.

Hansel cuddled it tight against his side and completed the four steps that took him into the end zone.

"Yay!" She screamed, leaping up and down with

excitement. With all the players on Theo's team she rushed toward game winner.

She was gathered up in Hansel's arms and kissed on the side of her neck as everyone patted him on the back.

Pressing closer to him, not caring about his sweat or her own, it made her feel bashful to have him show his affection for her before other people. Generally his affection was saved for private moments.

She hoped this meant that he was considering things for them moving to the next stage as well.

They all shook hands with Cord's team.

"How about I treat the team to some strawberry ice?" Theo offered.

Everyone agreed and headed from the field with the other team, walking toward Main Street.

People were everywhere setting up booths for the festival and decorating floats for the parade that would kick it off on Monday.

"Excuse us!"

The group's attention was pulled by a woman calling out with a loud screeching voice form a cream-colored Winnebago with green detail down the side.

Greta could feel the tension and hear the murmurs of the other Were's around her. Den residents didn't like outsiders and humans were the worst in town. If they even sensed something was off or different in Den they could bring more attention to their county. The last thing they wanted was more strangers nosing around and asking questions, possibly discovering that shifters existed.

Cord broke from the pack and walked to the passenger side of the vehicle to the pale-skinned white woman with faded red hair. "You all lost?"

With a large smile and wide eyes she glanced over to the middle-aged man with dark hair driving. Returning her gaze to Cord, she said, "Why yes we are. We're from Idaho. We were looking for an event we heard about, but I think we got turned around. Our GPS lost signal and with nothing but long roads and trees around this area isn't easy."

"An event?" Cord folded his arms over his broad chest as he eyed them. "You all are a bit far from home."

The woman's giggle was high, pitchy. "True. However, we home school our kids and believe education should be experienced in life not four walls."

Her husband was nodding his head, causing his long stringy hair two sway around his face.

Greta could see the children, three of them, peeking from between the seats and pointing at different things they saw through the front window.

A good example of just why they closed off the town during the festival. Tomorrow the barriers would be put into place. After this, Cord may order them to be set up tonight.

"Where are you all trying to get to?" Cord's voice was tight, urgent.

Distracted by her kids chatter she glanced around. "What do you all have going on here? Is it a carnival? Maybe we could hang around and have some fun—m"

"I'm sure you all would like to get on the road and get to your destination. You all have traveled so far as it is." He demanded as he cut the woman off and ignored her question.

"Oh, yes, yes. My kids have never seen a wild animal circus...kind of a freak-show like." She was pulling several papers down from the dashboard as she spoke.

Hansel's body tensed beside hers as he moved in a few steps toward Cord.

Greta, like most of the people, was more interested in getting rid of the family. She wasn't really paying much attention to what the woman was saying. However, when Hansel kept moving closer an uncomfortable feeling began at the base of her spine and crawled upward.

Hansel?

Hansel didn't respond.

Cord placed a hand on the door. "What's the town you're looking—"

"Ah, here it is!" She held the tan flyer up. "Circus of the Wild."

Even from her distance she could see tigers, bears on hind legs with ruffled collars and decorated horses with a rider.

Hansel reached over Cord and snatched the paper from the woman's hands.

"Well." The woman pulled her hand back and placed it against her chest, shocked by Hansel's rudeness. "You can have that one if you like, we have another one. We picked them up at a convenience store when we crossed over from Nevada."

Cord frowned at Hansel but addressed the woman. "What's the address on your other sheet?"

Residents had stopped working and were observing the strangers and the situation. Greta knew everyone was analyzing whether they would need to assist in any sort of way, by attacking or hiding things. Werebears of Den stuck together.

Lifting another flyer from her pile she gave Cord the name of the town.

"I know where that is. The county is about a couple hours down the road. It is the next town." Cord gave them directions that would lead them onto a road far away from Den, then a direct route straight into the next town.

As the Mayor of Den County did his job getting rid of the interlopers, she weaved her way through the crowd and went to Hansel's side.

The family finally waved as Cord and Theo directed the people and traffic out of their way so that the driver could make a wide U-turn. Soon they were driving out of town.

"How about those strawberry ices?" Theo tried to return the focus back to where they had all left off before the visitors' arrival.

She slipped her hand around Hansel's bicep. His muscle was tight with tension. "Hansel—"

"I have to go." He still hadn't taken his gaze off the flyer, now crumbled at the side by one of his hands. His jaw flexed as he started in the direction he'd parked his motorcycle instead of to the ice cream shop.

Still holding on to him, she applied pressure as she stood firm and yanked on his arm.

Jolted some, he stopped and glanced back at her. There was a red tint to his eyes, making them appear more burgundy than black.

She removed her hand from his arm.

Hansel blinked once, twice, three times before his gaze cleared and she could tell he was seeing her. That he finally recognized her.

"Where are you going?" She truly knew she didn't need to ask. The name of that horrid spectacle was just as ingrained in her mind as Hansel's. However, the question she was asking was deeper than a mere physical destination.

"Greta, this is it." He lifted the paper, now fully crumbled in his fist and shook it. His eyes were bright, a frightening excited tone entered his voice. "It's a sign. Information to help me locate them has come back around. I thought it was lost with my delay here."

"Your delay?"

He shoved his hands through his hair, frustrated as if he struggled to find the right words. "You know what I mean. They don't stay long in one place, you know that. So, when I stayed to help out I knew it was a sure thing those men had already packed up and moved on to another town."

She shook her head, even as the members of the two teams that had not already dispersed after the strangers had left began to gather around them. "You don't even believe in signs or fate." Or us evidently. "Don't you think it's time you let it go? If you don't they are still controlling your life."

"They're not controlling a damn thing about me anymore," Hansel spoke through a tight jaw. "I *choose* to hunt them. You should understand."

"What's going on?" Rorke stepped out of the group and moved closer to them.

Fear gripped her heart and caused her eyes to burn with unshed tears. "I understand the hatred for them, believe me. But, the thirst for vengeance is something that only you have. *I* want a life." *I thought you wanted that too.*

He closed his eyes and stood there before her taking in a deep breath. When he stared at her there was an emotion filling his gaze. She didn't even allow it to give her any hope.

I do. "I do...it's just I *need* to see this through or it will haunt me forever."

"Greta, let us help you two with whatever is happening here." Rorke tried again.

She ignored the big male beside her. "You do what you feel you *need* to do. I'll do the same." Turning away she started walking.

"Greta…I'll be back. I promise."

She paused. Glancing over her shoulder, she allowed every bit of her hurt, anger and emotions to fill her gaze as she stared at him. "Save your promise. When you finish with your quest just get on your bike and move on to another town, no life." Finished she strutted through town with her head held high, even though the pain in her gut was overwhelming. She wouldn't let anyone see her beat. No, she would save that until she got home in the privacy of her own room.

~YH~

"Greta!"

Hansel watched the woman he loved continue to walk away.

"You going to tell me what's got you and Greta so riled up and at odds?" Rorke stood before him, his hands planted on his sides.

Hansel groaned. "I need to talk to her. Make her understand but I don't have the time."

"Generally people make time for what is important to them. She important to you?"

"Hell, yes!" Hansel growled and leaned his head back. He was torn in two. He stared up at the cloudless sky but he held no answers for him. Lowering his head, he glanced at the were-male he had grown to call friend. "But right now there is something I need to do."

"What's that?"

Hansel held his fist out to him and opened it.

Rorke removed the crumpled paper and straightened it out. "I saw you snatch the flyer from that woman, this where they're headed?"

"Yes."

"What does it have to do with you?" Rorke looked from the paper depicting the ridiculous costumes Jackal and Damian liked to dress animals up in.

Besides Greta and her family, he hadn't shared his life or experience with anyone. But, he had grown to not only like Rorke but trust him as well. "You all know about Greta being taken when she was younger."

"And thankfully she made it back to us."

"Yeah." Hansel nodded recalling the ache in his soul the day she escaped, but he knew she had a family she needed to return to. "Well, these are the ones that had her...had us."

Frowning, Rorke stared at him. "So this is where you and Greta know each other from?"

Greta had told him that she hadn't shared any of her experience with anyone until recently and that was only to her parents. Hansel felt it was time that Den knew both their stories, instead of holding it away as if it were something to be ashamed of.

Dainton, Cord, Theo, Gordon and a few other males circled around them.

"That's right. I was already there. Had been there for a few years. They killed my family and took me. Just to train me to be one of their circus attractions," he pointed to the bear on the flyer. "Their idea of training was with whips and pokers until you submitted, learned and got it right."

"Shit! Well that explains the scars all over your back. You must have been really young." Rorke shook his head.

Hansel shrugged. He knew that Rorke had probably seen the markings on his back while he was working with him, but the male had respected his privacy at the time and never asked. Another reason he thought of this Were as a friend.

"I was much younger when I was taken than Greta's age when she arrived." Hansel let out a heavy sigh. "I knew that if I didn't belong there, she really didn't. The first night she got there, she told me about you all. About the town she was from. She had to get away otherwise they would have destroyed her spirit as they had done mine. Meeting Greta renewed it."

"So what do you plan to do?"

He looked toward the direction Greta had gone. She was no longer in sight. He refocused on the males around him. "I have to finish this. If I don't, these men will continue to hurt animals and possibly other Weres in the name of entertainment and money."

"Then we're with you." Dainton placed a hand on his shoulder.

"You don't have to do that." Hansel stared at Greta's cousin and business partner. He hadn't spent as much time with Dainton as Rorke, only a dinner at Greta's parent's home where Dainton and Ebony had joined them.

From Greta he was aware that even though Ebony and Dainton loved each other they had not completed the final mate mark. Greta explained to him that Ebony wanted to have her first shift before she allowed Dainton to commit himself to her permanently. The dark skinned woman reminded him of someone, was an outsider like him. When he had first met her, he swore he'd seen her somewhere before, but he could never place his finger on it.

"On behalf of my cousin, and you, these asses need to be stopped." Dainton looked around at the other Weres surrounding them. "Who's with us?"

Hansel was amazed at how fast the circle closed around them as everyone stepped up. He gave a sharp nod of thanks. His throat felt a little tight. He'd fought every battle in his life alone and to know that these Were-bears had his back in this situation left him speechless for a moment. Hansel cleared his throat. "We're going to need a plan."

"Meet at my office in twenty." Sheriff Smokey ordered. "I'll pass the word around and see who else is in."

"Do we need such a big group? There's only three men in charge of the operation." Hansel met the Sheriff's gaze.

"That may be, but we'll need help getting those animals taken somewhere safe. If they have been in captivity and trained we can't just let them out in the wild."

"I can use the phone in your office, Sheriff and see if I can track down the zookeeper at Sacramento Zoo," Gordon offered. "It's not as large as San Diego but I'm sure they would probably appreciate some animals with a little special ability. And the animals will be safe and treated well."

"I guess I hadn't thought much beyond getting back at the men who were responsible for killing my family and imprisoning me and Greta," Hansel admitted.

"Well, that's what a sleuth can do for you." Rorke patted him on shoulder.

"I'm starting to realize that." Hansel slapped his friend on the back.

The group split in two, some of them headed with Hansel and Rorke toward the lawman's office, while a few went with the Sheriff to round up others.

Hansel couldn't deny the excitement racing through his blood like fire, he was finally going to have his day of vengeance. The only shadow of it was where all of this would leave him and Greta when it was over. If there would even be anything left for them.

He had to believe there would be.

~YH~

"Greta, I don't think you have thought this through."

Glancing at her friend, Greta took a seat as she handed Ebony a glass of tea. "You keep saying that."

She and Ebony sat on the back porch of her family's cabin. Ebony had refused to allow Greta to ride home alone when she came storming away from the group that had played football and went to the office where she had parked her truck before the game.

Not really a sports person, Ebony was one of the bystanders cheering everyone on. Greta didn't even realize the other female had followed her until she climbed into her truck and the passenger door opened and Ebony got in.

"Because it's true. You and Hansel have something really special. I saw that a few nights ago at dinner here."

"Had something." Greta stared off into the woods. "I don't know about you, but I don't like knowing a male's feelings for me come second to his need for violence...revenge."

"These men injured you and took you away from your family. From what I know they did the same to him." Ebony placed a hand on her knee.

She looked to the side at her friend. "But, it's over. We are free. What if they capture him again or hurt hi—?"

"Ah, that's what it is. You're afraid something will happen to Hansel." Ebony squeezed her knee then removed her hand.

A blink made Greta realize that she was crying as twin tears dripped from her eyes and ran down her cheeks. "I guess so. He was out of my life once...I am not sure if I can survive it again."

"That was to protect you then. Besides, he's bigger and tougher now than the boy they captured and the teenage male he was when he escaped. You have to trust him to deal with this and come back to you." Ebony lifted her tea and drank.

Staring down into the amber liquid in her glass, she wondered out loud. "To what?"

"Excuse me?"

Greta sipped her tea and let her mind roam for a moment.

"What are talking about? He'll come back for love and a life with you."

She set her glass on the wicker table before them. "For how long, Ebony?" Greta rose and walked to the railing. "What could I offer a were-male who has lived on the fringes of society. Chasing excitement and challenge as often as the wind changes direction. Soon this staid life that we live in Den County wouldn't hold him. Hansel would get bored and desire to leave." She shook her head and focused on the bounty of Redwoods that were *home* to her. "Why would I want to set myself up for such heartache?"

Ebony appeared beside her. "How could you not? You love him...you told me you're already mind linking with him. I don't think you have much of a choice."

Facing her friend, Greta said, "I do. It won't be easy, but at the Bear Run if I find another male willing to give me all three marks right then it can break the connection I have with Hansel. I can have a life that's secure."

As she shook her head, Ebony sighed. "Don't do that to yourself. Don't do it to Hansel."

"It's already done here," she tapped her temple. "Soon it will be he-r-e," Greta placed a trembling hand over her heart.

"Oh…Greta." Ebony stepped forward and pulled her into an embrace.

For a few minutes Ebony allowed the tears to fall unhindered. She mourned the loss of a mate she yearned for and the fading dream of a life she imagined with Hansel.

Greta took a deep breath. She pulled herself together and stepped away. "Enough sadness." With one hand she swiped at the tear streaks on her face. "It is time to focus our attention on something else."

"What's that?" Ebony used the back of her hand to wipe her own eyes.

"Your shifting?"

"What?" Ebony reared back, then moved away. "I can't shift. Trust me I've tried." A shadow of sadness clouded her eyes.

"Yes you have…alone." Greta put a gentle hand on her arm until Ebony met her gaze. "Now, it's time you let someone help you, Miss I-can-do-all-things-alone." Greta shook her head and stripped out of the jeans, t-shirt and sweatpants she'd played football in. "You're just as stubborn as Hansel."

"Cause he has to deal with you and your new-found charismatic view on life." Ebony bumped against her and teased.

Greta stuck her tongue out at her then leaped over the railing, landing perfectly on her feet. "Stop stalling and get your ass down here."

With a growl, Ebony removed her clothes and jumped the rail. "I'm here. Now what?" She fingered the gray lock at the front of her hair and placed it behind her ear.

Seeing the nervous gesture of her friend, Greta spoke calmly. "Shifting doesn't only happen in the body, it takes place in the heart first then the mind."

Placing her hands on her hips, Ebony cocked her head to the side. "I'm not sure I understand what you mean."

"Do you feel your bear inside of you?" Greta placed a hand over her belly where she felt a fluttering of her own bear shifting around restlessly.

Ebony's hands clenched and unclenched. "Yes."

"How does it make you feel?"

"Strange…odd." Ebony licked her lips. "But—"

"But what?" She pushed.

"But not alone. In my life, I've always felt alone until Dainton, Den and…" she placed a hand over her stomach. "My bear."

Greta smiled. "Good. We love you, and you know Dainton loves you. More important than that…your bear is a part of you. You all must be one. You have to allow it the freedom to share in all things you feel, do, love and let it protect you when it's needed."

"How do I do that?" There was a sound of desperation evident in Ebony's words. "When unlike you and Dainton I only discovered months back how different I really was to everyone else around me." She used one hand to rub her arm as she stared off in the distance.

"I'm sure it had to be hard." Greta whispered, not wanting to hinder the emotions Ebony was so evidently struggling with.

"You don't know the half of it." Ebony looked at her, her eyes filled with troubled clouds and sadness. "Being in the foster care system, you feel so alone. Always. For me it wasn't like some of the other kids whose parents, even deadbeat ones, came to see them or finally got them back. I knew no one was coming for me."

"Dainton told me about you being in foster care until you ran away and lived on the streets."

"And how I stole someone else's identity?" A broken, emotionless laugh came out.

Greta shrugged. "But later you made it right."

Ebony nodded.

"What happened to your family?"

"My parents died." Ebony's voice was flat, as if she'd spent years detaching herself from the loss. "A social worker had left me in her office one day. I went through my file and saw the first one. They were shot in the woods. Found naked. Some campers realized that my mother, barely alive, was pregnant. They cut me out of her."

"They saved you." Greta offered her a smile.

"There were many nights after being beaten, starved or just cold on the streets I wished that they had let me die along with them."

"No, Ebony." Greta hugged her friend, not discouraged or put off by the fact they were both nude. As shifters, nudity didn't faze them on any level. "The

Great Spirit gave you a chance at life. Your parents would have wanted that."

"Now I realize that." The pulled away from each other and Ebony took in a shuddering breath. "Funny enough, when I read the file back then I thought my parents were some weird, hippie-types. It wasn't until I found out who I was and came to Den and saw this," she waved her hands between them. "How often people are naked because they are going to shift or shifted back that I realized they were probably in bear form and out for a walk." Ebony smiled.

Greta laughed. "True."

Taking a deep breath, Ebony held her hands out at her side. "Tell me how I get this bear to come out."

"Your bear is you." Greta gave it to her straight.

Her friend frowned. "Okay."

"You have to envision what you look like."

Ebony's lids lowered.

"The things you can smell, see and taste." Greta continued to coax her. "Feel the wind in your fur and the sound of the forest coming alive around you like you've never imagined."

Her friend's body began to tremble, a shimmer vibrated around the edges of her body--evidence of a shift beginning to take place.

Greta understood that once Ebony got the shift down, the transition would be smoother and practically unnoticeable.

"Ahhh! It hurts!" Ebony cried out.

"Breathe. Don't fight yourself, Ebony. Let the change happen," she encouraged. "Show your true self."

Then it happened. One second Ebony's chest was rising high as she struggled to take in a deep breath, then a dark brown bear with a silver Mohawk at the crown of her head was before her.

"Oh, my." Greta laughed and clapped. "You are one magnificent beauty."

A roar erupted through the forest.

"I'm glad you agree. Now let's do some running and I'll take you to my favorite back scratching tree." Greta shifted before her next breath was complete.

Leading the way, she shared in the joy of her friend and her new ability. Even as a part of her heart was light with joy for Ebony, most of it was filled with the pain of her life before her without Hansel in it.

CHAPTER TEN

"Which trailers belong to the carny bastards?" Rorke stood next to him at the edge of the woods that surrounded the open land where the traveling circus and carnival had set up.

It appeared to be an old farm, possibly a past cornfield Hansel imagined by the size of it.

After two hours of watching and waiting, the place was quiet now. Even the Ferris Wheel was still. Every customer that had been there a couple hours before paying to see the attractions and attempting to win prizes from the rigged games from the small town a few miles away had gone home. In the distance, Hansel could see a few RV's, Winnebago and trailers camped out for the night. He wondered if the small family that had stopped in Den had made it. If they had *enjoyed* the event.

Hansel swallowed down the sour taste in his mouth. "The red with the gold embroidery around it belongs to Jackal, the ringmaster." He pointed to the one beside it. "That green one with the black pin stripes is Bart, he's the money man." He shifted his gaze past the brown and green drab trailers toward the trailer before the dingy white tent where they hid the cages and stalls of the animals. "That black one is Damian," this time he spit the acidic taste that flooded his mouth onto the ground. "He's mine."

"Should we split up?" Cord asked.

Peering around through the dark, Hansel met the gaze of all fifteen males and females that had traveled with him from Den. He was overwhelmed by the support and grateful to have them with him to take these men down. No matter how much he had wanted to, he knew that he would not be able to do this alone. Not and ensure the animals were cared for and he got out alive. Before he reconnected with Greta he hadn't cared about his life, but he wanted to return back to her — even more than he wanted these men to pay.

"Yes. But, we only need two teams," he informed them.

"Why only two?" Dainton frowned as he looked from one trailer to the next.

"Because at this time, all three men will be in Bart's trailer counting up the funds turned in at the entrance, games and concessions. They'll work until around midnight to divide up the money for pay in the morning and secure the majority of it in the safe built into Bart's trailer."

"So, one team to go with you and the other to the animal tent?" Dainton clarified.

"Dainton and Rorke with me. Gordon, if you and Theo can take care of the rescue with everyone else I'd appreciate it." Hansel directed.

"We're on it, on your go," Theo declared.

Gordon nodded.

Hansel felt his body tighten, and his bear clawing at him to get out. However he reined him in for now. "Let's do this."

They split. The group of twelve male and female Weres that came with them from Den moved silently toward the animal tent as he and his two friends hustled toward the green trailer. After the carnival was closed down for the night, all the lights were turned off leaving the area cloaked in darkness. This was perfect to keep their movement hidden in the shadows.

Most of the workers were in the worker tent where they would eat and drink the night away. Already he could hear the distance grumblings, swearing and laughter from the group he remembered becoming extremely loud as the night wore on. Even though most of the people that worked the freak show hated the three men in charge, it was their livelihood, so Hansel wanted to make this all happen quickly. So, they could keep from having to harm anyone that felt *obligated* to step in to assist.

Outside the trailer door they stopped, listened.

"That motherfucker operating the ring toss better not be cheatin' us. Look at this damn total he brought in." That high pitched, nasally whine Hansel recognized as Bart's.

"I'll make his ass take an assistant. We send someone to keep a count of what is coming in, make sure things is on the up and up." Jackal's gravelly voice rang out.

"If he's pocketin' cash money, I'll get it out of him. Put his ass in Simba's cage." Damian cackled, deep and rough. "Show the rest of 'em, don't be shittin' around with our funds."

"That would be a show these small town folks would pay to see." Jackal, always considering the next big event spoke. "Maybe it's something we can think about adding to the show schedule."

Their harsh, loud laughter vibrated the walls of the trailer.

Hansel's jaw flexed as he tightened his grip on the door handle and gave a sharp nod to Dainton and Rorke. Ripping the door open, Hansel vaulted up the stairs, then entered the trailer.

"What the fuck!" Jackal rose.

Bart started raking all the dollars and coins across the table toward him and shoving fistfuls of it down his shirt.

"Your fuckin' asses better not be thinkin' of robbin' us." Damian pulled his ever-present whip off his hip.

Hansel could practically see the trainer's mind processing how he could fight off not just one big male, but three. Hansel knew all three of them made an impressive sight as their height and size filled up the trailer.

"Oh, that's not why I'm here." Hansel allowed his red, hazed gaze to roam from one male to the other.

"Why don't you tell us, who the fuck you are then get the hell out." Jackal stepped forward, still dressed in his white ruffled shirt and black pants. Only thing he'd taken off was the red and gold embroidered coat, which was draped over the back of the chair he'd vacated.

"I'm sure you all wouldn't know my name if I told you, because I'm a little different than the last time you saw me."

Damian scowled and stared at him, attempting to place his face.

"Did you used to work for us?" Bart asked, still trying to hide the money. "You thinkin' we owe you money?"

"If that's it…I don't give back pay." Jackal declared, shifting his gaze from Hansel to the two males behind him.

"Oh, I'm here for pay, but I plan to claim it from you guys' hide."

"The fuck if you will." Damian released the whip with a snap.

Dainton and Rorke growled behind him.

Hansel took a step forward, his fists balled. He couldn't wait for the moment he would take that braided leather and wrap it around the trainer's throat.

"Hold on a second, gents. Can before it gets hairy in here. Can I know my charges?" Jackal smirked.

Without taking his gaze off Damian, Hansel spoke. "As many animals as you all capture and snatch away, I'm sure my story isn't any different. It wouldn't stand out to you. But, just in case you recall the cub you picked up in Yosemite after shooting a male and female bear…that would be me."

"What?" Bart squeaked.

"That's impossible," Jackal declared as if his words were the end all to be all of life. "You can't be Douglas the Dancing Bear."

Hansel fucking hated that moniker.

"That shit ain't even possible," Damian sneered, then rolled his bottom lip and licked it.

A tick Hansel was familiar with. It usually came before he threw his whip or shoved his iron poker into the back of an animal.

"I don't know what fuckin' game ya'll runnin', but it ends here." Damian popped his whip.

Hansel grabbed the tail of it, ignoring the sting of the tail striking his forearm as he launched himself at the trainer. As his fist connected with Damian's jaw, he heard the telltale sound of fabric ripping, then an ear-piercing roar—one of his friend had shifted.

Bart screamed and leaped away from the table to run into the back, most likely trying to hide.

Exchanging one punch after another with Damian, who fought back maliciously, Hansel glimpsed Rorke out of the corner of his eye leaping across the short card table after Bart. Answering the question who had shifted—Dainton.

He couldn't concern himself with the fights going on around him, battling Damian would take all of his attention. The man may not be as big as he was now, but Damian was evil to the core and that made him fight dirty and lethal.

Taking the return punch Damian landed against his jaw, Hansel easily recovered, barely feeling a sting and kicked the man in the chest. Damian went sailing back, striking his side against a chest along the side of the trailer.

"Ah, you son of a bitch." Damian gripped his side and kept his body bent over.

When Hansel went to him to finish him off, he found himself leaping out of the way of a knife Damian had pulled out. Hansel was grateful for fast reflexes as he avoided every slash the trainer made through the air toward him.

Damian struggled to his feet and advanced on him with a fierce downward swipe. A move that, if Hansel hadn't countered it, would have sliced his chest open diagonally. But, Hansel waited for that perfect moment. As Damian's hand came out and across him through a hard left at his forearm. He wasn't sure which was louder, the sound of the bone breaking, the trainer's blood curdling scream or the clattering of the knife to the hard floor.

After Damian dropped to his knees grunting and holding his awkwardly bent arms, Hansel picked up the whip and moved behind the vile man.

"This is for my stepmother, not a bitch." He wound the length over and over again around Damian's neck as he spoke. "My father, a great male. For my unborn sister." Hansel pulled the ends tight. "And Greta, the small female bear you injured in your trap."

Hansel's body trembled with rage he'd held pent up for years. He clutched the leather so tightly his hands burned, but he didn't care. Everything around him was painted a dark red in his sight. It appeared as if blood coated the trailer.

Damian was purple and swollen as he made gagging sounds as he grabbed and clawed at his own throat, attempting to remove the choker.

"Hansel, stop." Someone spoke to him in a strong but calm voice.

However, he still pulled on the whip, his biceps flexing, blugging. "Damian deserves to die like so many other Weres and animals this sadistic man has killed mercilessly."

"He does." Dainton stepped before him, not touching him or helping Damian. "But, do you want that to be by your hands?"

"Yes!" Hansel wanted to recall this moment for the rest of his life knowing that Damian would not harm anyone else.

"No you don't, Hansel." Rorke stood beside Hansel and placed a steady firm hand on his shoulder. "That would make you just like him. A murderer. You're not a murderer."

"He kille—" Hansel's voice broke as the emotions of anger and sadness waged within him. "My family and hurt Greta."

Damian's body was starting to twitch and buck, as the man fought for the last grips of life.

"He will get his due one day. Just don't let it him taint the rest of your life with his evil and cruelty," Dainton declared. "Let him go, Hansel."

His jaw flexed as he looked from one friend's calm, determined features to the next. What they said was true. If he were a lone Were still he would only have himself to deal with, but going back to Greta he would have to tell her about the death and she already wanted him to walk away from the vengeance. He didn't want to imagine how she would feel about him taking someone's life. Even someone that deserved to lose it.

He released the ends of the whip and shoved Damian forward and out of his way.

With his last shreds of life, the trainer coughed as he hastened to remove his own weapon of cruelty from around his neck.

The room went from blood red to a pale pink as Hansel's fighting haze began to clear. He glanced around and saw Jackal against one wall, beaten and battered and gripping his stomach as he coughed up blood.

Hansel looked at Rorke.

Rorke shrugged. "He's not dead."

Glancing around, he looked for Bart, but didn't see him. He headed toward the back of the trailer.

"Where are you going, Hansel?" Rorke grabbed his

arm.

"Looking for Bart."

"I didn't kill him either." Dainton declared.

Chuckling, Hansel shook his head. "I didn't think you did. I need to ensure one last thing before I go."

Rorke let him go.

Continuing around the overturned table and the floor that was littered with money and debris, Hansel passed the single bathroom and walked the short hall until he got to the small bedroom. That's where he found Bart, half under the bed face down. Hansel noticed that the bottom half of one pant leg was ripped and there was blood dripping from teeth marks in the banker's calf.

Gripping the man by the belt of his jeans, he dragged him out.

Bart groaned and whimpered.

Ignoring his sounds of fear and pain, Hansel turned him over and saw the claw marks over the man's shoulder.

The carny accountant's face was twisted in agony, but he kept his eyes squeezed shut as if he feared seeing something else coming his way.

With the man's shirt in shreds it made it easy for Hansel to find what he searched for. Reaching out, he grabbed the safe key away from the rivers of blood streaming from the cuts. Snatching the thick chain hard, Hansel smiled at the sound of it snapping.

Opening his eyes, Bart made a feeble attempt at reaching for the key with his good arm. "No…wait. My money!"

Hansel kept it away and rose to his feet. "You're the cheat and the thief, Bart. You've just as much blood and debt on your hands as Damian and Jackal."

Disregarding the man's pleading, Hansel went back to the front. Rorke and Dainton, now dressed in black custom pants that he'd removed from Jackal, stood like twin pillars by the door.

"Let's go."

They all filed out of the trailer.

The workers were gathered in a large crowd outside of the trailer. Most likely hearing the commotion and waiting to see what was going on. However, just as Hansel figured, none of them cared enough about the owners to enter the trailer and intervene.

"Hey, what going on?" An old man, who looked relatively familiar, stepped forward from the pack of people.

If he wasn't mistaken this man had snuck the animals treats on occasion when he mucked out the stalls. "Seymour…right?"

He rubbed his hands down his filthy jeans. "Uh, yeah."

Tossing him the key, Hansel said, "That's to the safe. Take everyone inside and get all you've been due over the years. Don't leave a penny behind."

Seymour's eyes stretched wide and lit with joy as he gazed at the key.

The people around them murmured with excitement.

"I don't know who you are, but thanks." Seymour smile.

Holding the man's gaze, Hansel said, "You'll thank me by all of you finding new avenues of employment, legit circuses if you've a mind to continue in the business. This one has been permanently closed down."

"You got it." A woman called out.

Giving them a nod, Hansel headed with his friends to the long trailer filled with various caged animals loaded and ready.

Approaching Theo who stood by the driver side door, Hansel shook his hand. "You all work fast."

"We can say the same about you three." Theo teased.

"What the fuck are you wearing, Dainton?" Gordon walked with a group of Weres.

Dainton shrugged. "My clothes got ruined so I took what was available to me."

Theo laughed. "Just couldn't keep from shifting could you?"

"Hey, those bastard's had my cousin…I only did what I felt was right." Dainton smiled.

"Understandable." Gordon faced Hansel. "My contact at the zoo is waiting on these animals, so I best head out."

"I'll ride down. Follow you." Turning to face everyone with clear vision, Hansel's chest filled with pride. "I don't know how to say thank—"

"Then don't." Rorke cut him off. "I told you, you're a part of a sleuth. It's what we do."

Keeping his words to himself, Hansel patted Rorke on the back.

It took them less than thirty minutes to return to their vehicles hidden in a clearing through the woods, to say good-bye and for Hansel to return on his Stateline to follow Gordon down to Sacramento.

He and his bear were anxious to return to Greta and make things right, but he knew that he had to close off all the open doors in his life before he could commit to her and a life in Den.

After he completed the job with the zoo, there was

one last thing he had to do. Something he'd put off for too long.

CHAPTER ELEVEN

"Greta, are you sure you want to do this?" her cousin Dainton walked over to where she stood at the hood of her truck as they waited for all the other participants to arrive.

Pressing her elbows against the warm hood of her truck, she stared into the thick forest that led to the river about two miles away. It was the place of the Bear Run. Taking a deep breath she faked a wide smile that she truly didn't feel. "Yes, I'm going to do this."

"What about Hanse—"

She shot a look at Ebony whose car was parked next to hers, cutting her friends words off. "If Hansel was going to come back, he would have been back. Both the parade and the festival went on without him." That wasn't completely true.

Even though she had told him don't bother to return, in her heart she had hoped that he would. At least come back and try and show her he was okay. However, the rest of the group had come back, even

Gordon drove into Den the following afternoon after taking the animals to the vets at the zoo. But, no Hansel.

"I'm sure there's a reason. A good reason." Dainton couldn't even finish his sentence without shaking his head, evidently unsure of his own words.

"See. You can't even pull that off." Greta pushed away from her truck and began to remove her heels as she noticed the clearing was packed full of vehicles and the Run would begin soon. Like a fool she had bought a pretty dress and had dolled herself all up, trying not to give up hope that she hadn't meant a damn thing to Hansel. Not really.

"What did Rorke say to you when he stopped by your house?" Ebony moved closer to her.

Greta focused on the menial task of placing her shoes on top of the hood. It was those words that had made her hope. Hope that maybe her foolish, hastily spoken words hadn't forced the male she loved away. Looking over her shoulder, she met the steady gazes of Ebony and Dainton. "Rorke said that Hansel would be back. That there was something he needed to do first."

"See." Dainton declared placing a hand on her shoulder. "Just don't do this."

"Please." Ebony's eyes and voice were both pleading.

However, Greta couldn't give in. Not again. "A week. I've waited a week. No more. Not when there are Were males who have had no problem letting me know over the last few days they are willing to overlook my two marks and still give me all three tonight."

Her heart throbbed, as well as her shoulder and ankle—Hansel's markings. Greta's bear wasn't too happy about her decision. It shifted restlessly inside her core.

Lenny Gobi chose that moment to wave at her from his dark blue SUV as he pulled in and parked.

Greta offered him a smile and swallowed, attempting to rid herself of the ill feeling.

"Not feeling well?" Dainton taunted.

She shot a look at her cousin's smart remark. If she didn't love him so much she would wipe that smirk off his face with a knuckle sandwich. "Discomfort in the beginning is to be expected since I have two marks. It will pass." She spoke the last three words through gritted teeth.

"You hope."

Rolling her eyes at her cousin, she was glad when the First Frost Festival MC, Jack Ruxpin, the owner of Fill and Fix It mechanic shop, stepped into the center of the clearing.

"Unmated Weres are you ready?" Jack called out, his voice loud and full of bass.

Roars, cheers and lust-heavy pheromones filled the clearing.

Dainton and Ebony returned to their cars. Greta continued undressing, keeping silent as she fought the thoughts and concerns running through her mind.

Standing nude and unashamed, she waited for the announcement.

"Go get your mates!" Jack commanded.

Males and females ran and shifted mid-step as they dashed into the woods ready for the chase and being chased. As she moved toward the edge of the woods she saw her cousin give her a nod as he lounged nonchalantly against the hood of his truck. Ebony had already taken her bear form and raced off.

Even from her distance to him, Greta could see the calm patience of his face and the joy in his gaze. He'd waited a long time for this moment. Dainton would finally be able to place the third mark on Ebony and claim her as his mate completely.

She envied their happiness of having the person you love yours for eternity. Resolute, she shifted and took off into the woods. Immediately she scented several males within her vicinity, but she didn't give head to them and continued her journey through the lush foliage. Even though she and Lenny had an understanding, she wasn't in pursuit of him. Not just yet. She was enjoying just the freedom of the run. If he happened upon her at some point, fine, but part of the fun was eluding the male that pursued you. It wasn't supposed to be an easy catch.

Although she passed by more than a couple Weres already entwined in passionate embrace.

As her paws dug deep into the dirt as she ran, her ears picked up on a sound that didn't seem to fit the surrounding. It was a roaring noise. However, not one of any animal.

Her bear paused. She sniffed, not picking up on anything different. Straining her ears, she listened more intently.

The distinct resonance became louder, grew closer. Her heart quickened as she realized why the reverberation was so familiar, it was a motorcycle engine.

There was no need for her to wonder who would go against the rules of not bringing a vehicle into the woods during the run, because only one Were she knew was that bold to disregard decorum. Hansel.

Without pondering her actions she took off, in the

opposite direction. Her heart was pounding out of control. She could barely breathe as she struggled with her bear that wanted to turn back. Locked in on the male that had marked her twice, but she forced her beast to keep moving.

Then he was there, before her.

Her paws skidded along the underbrush as she came to a hasty stop mid-flight. Back peddling to create distance between her and the big male and his ride.

It was practically evil for a male to look that good. He and his bike fit perfectly together, as one. He wore his normal style of jeans and leather riding boots, but instead of his jacket and t-shirt he sported a white tank. His thick, dark brown hair was wind-blown, only adding to his damn good looks. She wanted to shift and bury her hands in it and mess it up even more—remind herself of its silky texture.

Still straddling his running motorcycle he stared at her. Not moving, just keeping his magnetic gaze on her.

The woods became overwhelmingly filled with the earthy, erotic scent of cashmere. The intense smell caused her body to tremble and things around her to become tinged with gold. A whimper of need began to roll up her bear's throat.

"Grr." She forced her bear to growl and snarl, flashing all canines. No way was Hansel just going to show up like he'd gone to the market for honey and returned.

"What are you doing here, Greta?"

Digging her claws in the dirt, she scratched around—a warning. Watch out, an attack is imminent. Of course she would have to force her bear to even consider harming Hansel, but she could still exhibit the threat. Hopefully that would be enough and he'd go away.

After he killed the motor of his ride, he swung his leg off the back and stood tall and broad before her.

I know you heard me.

She closed her eyes and turned her head, trying to ignore the thought he shot into her mind.

"What are you doing here? I sent Rorke back with a message for you. I doubt he forgot to pass it on." His sexy, mouthwatering strut brought him closer.

"Grrrrr…" She moved back, one paw at a time as she kept her gaze on him. Greta didn't consider it as retreating, more like self-preservation. It would be detrimental to her for him to be within reach. She snapped at him.

"You want to bite me, Blackberry?" Low and sultry his words came out. "Mark me as yours?"

Who speaks to a bear like that? Damn. She kept that thought locked in a private corner of her mind.

He pulled his shirt over his head and tossed it back to his motorcycle. "I won't stop you. Isn't that what this Bear Run is all about?" After he unfastened the top two buttons of his jeans, tempting her with the glimpse of his lower abdomen, he squatted down before her.

Leave me alone, Hansel.

"Why? So, you can allow some other male…the opportunity to mark you?" A red spark flashed in his gaze and his words came out slow, methodical. "Fuck, no." He cupped her chin, his fingers giving a light scratch to the under jaw of her bear, gentle even though his words were harsh.

Her bear closed its eyes, then stretched its muzzle forward enjoying the touch and begging for more.

Greta shifted. Quickly she rose to her feet. "Go back to wherever it is you came from."

She disregarded the fact that his hand was still hovering mid-air from where seconds ago he had been petting her bear. It was now hip level to her. No matter how hard she tried, her mind flashed an image of what was close to his hand that she would enjoy him 'scratching an itch'. She stepped back.

He rose. Resuming his full height before her, she saw the golden flecks in his eyes. No one had to tell her that he'd caught a glimpse of her thoughts.

The smirk on his lips declared it clearly.

"There was something I had to do."

"You were gone for a week." She folded her arms under her breasts, inadvertently lifting her bosom higher.

Admiring them, then taking in all of her nude form, he inhaled loudly. *You're beautiful.*

Keep your eyes on my face.

His gaze made a slow crawl along her form, when they finally met hers they were so gold that the onyx color was now flecks.

"I can smell your desire, Greta. Intense. Heady. Beckoning. Wildflowers *wet* after a rain."

More wetness flooded her sex at his words.

"Grr." A low-timbre growl came from him.

"Why did you bother to come back?" She asked trying to keep the focus on the conversation and not on her lust.

"There was never an intention not to return. Even though you told me that. But you wanted me back, didn't you?"

Rolling her lip in she bit into it as she glanced away, staring into the night and trying to block out the whimpers and passionate sounds echoing through the woods. "What I wanted was for you to stay." She met his gaze, allowing him to see her hurt.

He moved closer, but didn't touch her. "I had to see dispensing with Damian and the others. I couldn't allow that heinous place to continue. Could you?" Reaching out, he brushed his thumb along her shoulder and down her forearm.

"We could have called the authorities. Told them what was going on and let them do *their* job."

Cupping her arm, he shook his head. "Oh, no. During my time with them, I'd seen inspectors and investigators come through. Jackal was a master at deception. He could con the officials and make the single-ring circus appear on the up and up. I couldn't run the risk of that."

She dragged her hands through her hair. Confusion between her mind and her thoughts frustrated her. "Fine. Yes. I get it." Shaking her head, she met his gaze. "But, that's this time. What will be next, Hansel?"

"Nothing. I swear." He pulled her against him, then cupped her face.

Her heart thumped hard in her chest. "Don't just tell me what you think I want to hear. Because there are were-males in these woods ready to prove it to me."

"Only. If. They. Are. Looking. To. Die." The metallic in his eyes flashed red.

The fierce possession in his tone tightened her lungs and made her body tingle. Still, she shoved away from him and faced the trees behind her. "You can't go around killing as a way to solve all of your problems."

"I've never killed anyone, Blackberry." The heat of his body warmed her back as he stepped to her. "Although I was close to it. I *wanted* to. But, Dainton and Rorke kept my conscious clear of that guilt." He took hold of her waist and drew her against him.

"I got your message from Rorke." She remained ridged, even though everything within her wanted to lean back against his chest. "But what was it this time you *had* to do?" Turning around she met his gaze. "Any Were I mate with for life I have to know they are here for the long haul. Why didn't you come back to m-e?" Her voice broke. She felt the ache of his rejection and absence tenfold all over again.

His hands flexed at her waist. "I had to close the final door in my past."

"Who was she?" Her sight became blurry. She blinked and the tears she'd held in over the week fell. This had been one of her fears. Even though Hansel had told her he didn't do commitments and all of his other relationships had been fleeting, him loving someone else had been one of the thoughts tormenting her mind.

"They?"

Stepping out of his arms, she placed her hands on her hip. "How many females were you involved with?"

His brow dropped in a frown. "My family, Greta. I went back to the Yosemite area."

"Oh." She felt like shit. She'd let her own fears and insecurities get the best of her.

"All of the years since my freedom I never went back. It was like this place on a map I just kept circling around, but never ventured to it." He dragged his hands down his face, then exhaled harshly. "I couldn't do it. I don't know if it was fear of returning there or the overwhelming sense of loss I was afraid of…but I kept away."

"I'm sorry, Hansel." She could not only feel the energy of his grief, but hear the jagged, rambled thoughts in his mind. For the first time since he'd shown up she reached out to him. She cupped his squared jaw-line. "Why now?"

"You." He slipped his arms around her.

"Me? I don't understand."

"I wanted to be the male you need. In order for that to happen I had to face not just the men that took everything from me, but all my demons. My name is Hansel Haskin."

"Haskin? So, you do have a last name?"

"Yes. For years, I couldn't identify myself with it because it hurt too much. Bring up memories of my lost family." His hands pressed at her lower back, settling her against him.

Only Hansel could turn her body on and make her feel safe and protected at the same time.

"Understandable. How did it go?"

He sighed. "It was hard when I first got to the site where my family died. But, it became easier. I felt like they were there with me for a moment then gone and able to find their rest."

She rested her head in the curve of his neck. "I'm glad you went. That you got to reconcile your past."

"Yes. Now, I need to reconcile with my future." His hand glided up and caressed the length of her spine.

Does that have anything to do with me?

It has everything to do with you, Blackberry.

"I missed you calling me that." She peered up into his face, seeing the same passion she was feeling reflected there.

"I missed seeing them." His other hand palmed one of her breasts, then flicked a thumb over her nipple as he winked.

"If that's true, prove it." She taunted him, shifting back and forth she grazed his sculpted chest with her nipples.

"My pleasure." Lowering his head, he set his lips on hers.

She met his kiss. Claiming every moment that she'd lost with them being apart. Reveling in the taste of him, she slipped her tongue into his mouth.

A growl vibrated along her palate as he deepened the kiss. Burying his hands in her hair, he palmed her head and ravaged her.

Fisting his hair, she dispensed her own share of ardent desire.

Stems of a bush rustled.

~YH~

"Grrrrrrr!" He broke away from Greta and shoved her behind him as his body went on alert at the sound of the intruder on their reunion.

A light brown bear came through the foliage and rose to hind legs issuing his threat to Hansel.

"Lenny?" Greta stepped around him and addressed the bear dancing around before them.

The Were shifted, becoming a male with short blond hair. "Greta, what's going on?"

"Hansel returned." She gestured toward him, as if those two words should clarify whatever this other male had been planning.

"I'll fight him for you, if that's what you want." Lenny, similar in height to Hansel, puffed his chest out.

Without a pause, Hansel stepped forward to answer his challenge. He spread his arms out wide from his side. "Say when?"

The other male's fists balled and he began to

advance.

"Hey! Enough macho shit." She stepped between them and placed a hand on the center of both their chests as she glanced from one male to the other.

"Look, Greta, if this vagabond Were, isn't smart enough to know what he has in you, I do." Lenny leaned in.

Hansel released another growl. His bear was itching to get out and show this male he had no chance with his mate.

Mine. His bear declared.

Meeting his gaze for a brief moment, she allowed Hansel to see her matching emotions for him.

She shoved Lenny back. "That's for me to decide, Lenny." She turned to the encroaching Were. "I appreciate you stepping up and agreeing to mate with me today." Letting out a heavy sigh, she held his gaze. "However, I know now that it wouldn't have been fair to you."

"Because he came back?" Lenny asked.

"Because I love, Hansel." She took hold of Lenny's hands as she spoke with a voice soft, kind. "You deserve better than a mate who longs for someone else. You're a great Were, so go find a female that can appreciate that."

After he leaned down, he brushed his lips over her cheek.

He didn't like the other were-male touching any part of Greta, not one bit.

"Thanks for your honesty." Lenny glanced past her and met his gaze. "You better do right by her."

Feeling no need to respond, Hansel folded his arms over his chest and held eye contact with the other were-male.

Soon Lenny shifted and was gone.

Shaking her head, Greta faced him. "Males."

"Mate."

She rolled her eyes, but there was a smile on her lips. "We'll see how this night goes. I'm still one bite shy of that."

"That's just what I was getting to, before our interruption." He kissed her, then slipped his hand into hers and walked toward his bike.

"Were you now?" She stood next to his bike.

"Give me a second to remove the rest of my clothes and I'll prove it to you."

He enjoyed seeing the shimmy that shook her body as her gaze turned gold once again.

Making quick work of his jeans and boots, he stood before her and let her look her fill. He didn't even attempt to hide the stiff evidence of his arousal. Just as the heightened scent of her body let him know her desire for him, he wanted the same revealed to her.

Her lovely brown skin made the golden glow of her eyes more captivating as she took in his form from his head to his feet.

Pausing there she smiled.

"Why are you smiling?"

She glanced up as she leaned back with her palms flat on the leather seat of his ride. "I like your feet. They look strong, masculine…they're sexy."

Shaking his head, he denied her words. "Male's feet aren't sexy, they're functional." He stepped forward and cornered her against his bike, lacing his fingers with hers.

"Trust me, Hansel, everything about you is sexy. You should hear what the were-females of Den whisper about you when you walk into a room."

Leaning in, he kissed her mouth then dragged his lips up along her cheek to her ear and whispered, "I only care about one female's opinion of me." He nuzzled the shell with his nose.

"Who's that?" She wrapped one leg around his and slid it up until the heel of her foot was grazing the sensitive skin behind his knee.

He let lose a low growl.

"The Were I love."

The beating of her heart was like a small drum through her chest and against his where they were touching.

"Me-e?" Her breathy question came out, hesitant and unsure.

Angling his upper body back so that he could stare into her eyes, so that he could ensure she understood him. No misleading. "I love you, Greta Blackberry Armel."

"You do?" There was a quickening to her breathing.

"Everything about you. Your kindness, your sweet spirit, your relationship with your parents, how you care for your friends even more than yourself. I even love how shy you can be at times." Each thing he spoke about her was punctuated by nips along her chin to the sides of her breasts.

Hansel?

"Yes, sweetheart."

"I love you too. But, I really, really would like to make this mate thing official before I burst into flames from desire."

A hard chuckle erupted from his chest. The laughter turned to groans when he embraced her and kissed her deeply.

There were two things that he loved, Greta and his

motorcycle. He'd had more fantasies than he could count about enjoying them both at the same time. Grasping her hips, he lifted her and set her on the bike.

Pulling her mouth from his, she frowned. "What are you doing?"

"Trust me." He winked at her.

She gave him a suspicious stare, but she didn't stop him.

Assisting her to lounge back against the passenger seat, he placed one of her feet flat on the hard cover of the gas tank keeping her knee bent. Her other foot he rested on the board at the bottom of the bike. He allowed his gaze to travel slowly along her body, admiring her position. She looked wild, free and open to whatever pleasure he had in store for her. "You do look good enough to eat."

"Prove it." Her response was bold and saucy as she placed her hand at the center of his chest and dragged it down to his dick and gripped it.

He growled and pressed along her soft palm twice before he removed her hand. "I'll need all my focus for this."

Pushing her bottom lip out, she pouted, but her eyes were still lit with joy.

Lowering to his knees, he licked both of her nipples then glided his tongue down past her navel and over the round supple area of her belly.

She trembled. "Hansel…"

Keep saying my name. "I want the entire group in the forest to know you're mine."

Setting her palm along his jaw she smiled down at him.

Encouraged, he placed a hand on the inside of her thighs, keeping her open at the perfect angle. He inhaled deeply and drew her spicy/sweet aroma into his lungs and filled his senses with her essence. Through his golden haze he beheld the slick, swollen, shiny pussy before him. Bowing his head, he licked slowly around her clit, taking in the elixir of her cream, a balm to his soul.

Greta bucked against his mouth as she began to moan.

Continuing his oral play, he pulled her clit into his mouth and suckled it. Wanting to heighten her pleasure, he pressed two fingers into her warm, silk-like pussy. He pushed in all the way scissoring them along her walls. His body quivered with the need to be inside of her.

Not yet, he told himself. There was something that needed to be done first.

Parting her thighs wider, she rotated her hips and joined the rhythm of his hand and tongue.

In and out, he stroked her, over and around he flicked as she rode up and down his fingers.

"Oh, Han-sel...babe, oh..." she was panting and whimpering as her climax built.

The bike rocked beneath her.

Having no desire to see her end up on the ground, he wrapped an arm around her waist to hold her in place, keep her steady.

As her body started to shake and shivers raced through her, he increased the intensity of his fondling.

"Han-...Ahhhhhhh!"

While her orgasm overtook her, he continued to finger her pussy as he shifted his mouth to the side just a few millimeters away and allowed his canines to extend as he opened his jaw and sank his teeth into her femur artery, allowing his essence to blend into the flow of her blood stream. The only place the third and final mark could happen.

~YH~

"It's done isn't it?"

Hansel's tongue swirled over the bite he'd just put on her upper thigh.

Her body hummed. The low growl of her bear that rolled up her throat and out her mouth sounded more like a purr, she smiled. She stared down into the wonderful loving eyes of the Were she had given her heart to, without regret. Watching him as he rose, she studied him for a response to her rhetorical question.

There wasn't truly a need for her question. She could feel the shift happening in her body, a connection with her mate weaving into her DNA, changing her. Yet, she remained the same. But better. Now that she had Hansel.

"Yes, mate." He leaned toward her, holding her gaze.

Mine.

She loved hearing his bear claim her with that single word. Rising up, she lowered her top leg to the backside of the motorcycle, then slipped her hand behind his head and drew him closer. She kissed him. Tasting herself on his tongue she moaned. She was just as much a part of him as he was of her.

This is forever.

We are forever. At some point during the kiss, he took a seat before her.

Sighing, she leaned away from his scrumptious mouth, barely leaving a breath of space between them. Moving her had between them, she flicked the nail of her thumb over the tip of his cock.

He grunted and gave her a quick hard kiss.

"I do believe that only one of us got pleasure during that last round." She smiled. "You seem to prefer taking care of me first."

"What can I say, I thrive on pleasuring you." He winked and licked his lips.

"How about we fix that?" She slipped along the leather until she was straddling him as he straddled the front seat of the bike.

"I like the way you think, dirty Were." Wrapping his arm around her hips he pulled her closer.

With her hand still between their bodies, she gripped his cock tighter. Using the muscles of her thighs she rose up enough to press him against the opening of her sex. She lowered and felt the wondrous sensation of her mate filling her, stretching her walls.

He thrust upwards to meet her, not stopping until her pussy was kissing the base of his dick.

"Let me love you, Hansel." She ground her hips and squeezed her walls around his thick length.

As he groaned, he palmed one of her breasts and whispered, "You already do, Blackberry."

She buried her hands in his long hair. "I'll spend the rest of our life to ensure you don't forget it."

"Let's get to it."

Right there in the middle of the forest, she rode him fast and hard, taking them both to ecstasy as her heart soared. Years ago she thought she'd returned home, but it took this moment for her to realize it was simply the Redwood Forest, Den County, just a place without Hansel — her mate.

EPILOGUE

"So this is how you all close the festival?" He stood at the park, beside Greta among all of Den County's residents—young and old.

Greta grinned up at him, snuggling against his side. "Yup. It allows us to be together as a sleuth, congratulate and recognize all the new Were pairs."

Stroking her back, he returned her smile. He'd lost count of the places and times in the forest they had made love. What he did recall was his bear waking up with her bear curled against him. Her scent, warmth and fur mingled with his. It was something he looked forward to for the rest of their lives.

"It's nice. Greta Haskin."

"I love the sound of that." She kissed his cheek. Glancing around, she peered at the people milling about and offering one congratulations after another.

"Welcome to our family, Hansel."

Turning at the deep baritone, Hansel saw Manni Armel standing behind him. Rita stood with her husband, but broke away to pull her daughter into a hug.

Hansel's chest swelled at the warm greeting he witnessed from the older were-male. "Thank you. I'll take care of her and protect Greta with my life." He held his hand out.

"I know you will." Manni claimed it, but dragged him close for a quick embrace and fierce pat on the back.

The gesture choked Hansel up. It made him miss his father at that moment. Douglas Haskin would never be forgotten.

"Oh, Hansel. You've made me so happy and proud to have you mated to my daughter." Greta's mother hugged him and kissed him on both cheeks.

"Thank you," he whispered. Hansel was sure that Greta and her father with their keen Were hearing had heard him. However, he was hoping Rita picked up on the meaning of his message.

She stepped back and winked at him, then stepped back to her husband's side. "From a type of brother and sister of tragedy to mates. The Great Spirit always has a plan."

The perceptive older female had gotten the hint. It wasn't until he had been away during that week that he realized all of the events an opportunities Rita, Genma and Olivia had provided and orchestrated to keep him in Den and around Greta. He wasn't sure how she decided that he and Greta were meant to be together, but he didn't care. It had all worked out.

"So, what do you plan to do now that you live in Den? Besides finding a location for a cabin for you and my daughter. A little bigger than the founders place." Manni asked.

"I'm hoping he'll agree to stay on with my brother at the furniture factory while I'm away. And permanently after that." Rorke answered as he stepped up beside Hansel and placed a hand on his shoulder.

Honored at the offer, Hansel gave his friend a sharp nod. "I thought you'd never ask after all that backbreaking work you had me doing for weeks," he teased.

Rorke laughed. "You handled it all like a pro. We'll be proud to have you as part of the team."

"You got it." Hansel shook hands with Rorke. He wished the best for his friend on his wandering time. Knowing what it was like to feel empty and out of sorts, he truly hoped his friend found what he was looking for to get his life started.

More people came and went, there was a band playing and food offered. Hansel glanced around and was happy to see Dainton and Ebony smiling and cozied up with each other, a mated pair, finally.

Dainton met his gaze and gave him a nod.

Hansel returned it.

The children of the town were running around presenting the females of each new mate with flowers. A little female gave purple tulips to Greta.

He observed a little boy moving shyly to Ebony offering her a bouquet of blue roses.

Ebony kneeled down before the little male and spoke softly to him. She reached out and curled a single finger beneath his chin as she tilted his head up, then smile at him.

Hansel's heart stopped as he witnessed the gesture.

The young, towheaded male blushed three shades of pink at whatever Ebony said to him.

However, Hansel was no longer interested in the

bashful youth. No. His gaze was locked on Ebony.

It's not possible.

What mate? Greta tensed at his side.

He began to cross the field, then stopped. "I have to be imagining things. Too much excitement and reconciling emotions."

"What?" Greta looked at him and glanced around, as if attempting to track his gaze.

Shaking his head slowly, he murmured again, "It's just *not* possible."

Cupping his face, she brought his gaze down to hers. "Mate, if you don't tell me what is happening I can't help you figure out whatever it is that has you twisted in knots. I can feel it."

It was true. They were one, linked not only by mind but they shared heightened emotions as well.

"Look at Ebony."

Greta's brows pinched in a frown but she turned and glanced in the direction of her cousin and friend. "Okay?"

"You see how she's kneeling, speaking to that little cub with her finger curled beneath his chin?"

"Yes." She gazed up at him again.

"My…my stepmother used to do the same thing to me. That same gesture. Even the side tilt of Ebony's head." His throat felt tight, emotions were building inside of him.

She rubbed his arm. "I'm sure seeing it has brought up memories. Happy ones I hope."

"It's not that." He exhaled. "I don't know how it's possible. It doesn't seem likely at all…"

"But," she urged.

"I think Ebony is related to my stepmother somehow."

With intense, dark eyes, Greta starred up at him. "Hansel—"

"I know." He shoved a hand through his hair. "You don't have to tell me it is crazy or that I'm reaching. I'm telling myself that every second."

Stepping close to him, she linked the fingers of one of her hands with his. "I wasn't going to say that. I just remembered what Ebony shared with me a week ago about her parents."

"Who were they?" He tried to control the anxiety in his voice but was finding it difficult with the new revelation. Especially if it was possible he could have some family, even if distant and by marriage.

Greta glanced over to Ebony and then returned to him. "She doesn't know." She squeezed his hand. "I didn't think anything of it, but she said she discovered in her social services file that her mother and father were shot out in the woods."

It was his turn to frown—confused at the similarities of their pasts. "How old was she?"

He noted the workings of his mate's throat muscles as she swallowed.

"She wasn't born yet."

"What?" Lurching back, he pulled his hand from hers. He felt like he was coming out of his skin. "Help me understand that."

Licking her lips, Greta continued, "Some campers came upon the incident and realized that her mother was pregnant and barely alive. They cut Ebony out. They were naked with no identification."

Everything around Hansel went black then white, before his vision balanced back out. As his sight cleared, he found himself unable to pull his gaze away from Ebony as she rose beside Dainton and hugged the

Were-bear.

Hansel started to cross to her, but was stopped.

Before you go charging over there, Hansel, with your belief...think about it for a moment. It could all be a coincidence. You and Ebony are very different.

He understood why she spoke those words mentally, to keep him from being embarrassed and others from hearing if it was all a mistake.

However, he knew it wasn't. Smiling down at his mate, he claimed both of her hands and allowed her to see and feel the joy filling him up inside.

"I know it seems farfetched, but maybe it will help you piece it together if you know that my stepmother was a beautiful, intelligent, kind, dark-skinned were-female. Unlike my birth mother who was just as pale as my father and I." He leaned down and kissed her. "I guess I get my taste in females from my papa-bear."

Nodding, she grinned at him. "I guess you do."

Keeping hold of one of her hands, he walked with purpose toward Ebony and Dainton. He not only had a mate, but he had family of his own.

"I'm glad to see congratulations are in order, cousin." Dainton hugged Greta when they arrived before them and shook Hansel's hand.

After the greeting was passed, Hansel took a breath. Then another one. Not sure how to say the words rolling through his mind.

Greta stroked along his palm of the hand she still held. Her supportive gesture calmed him.

"Ebony, I'd like to introduce myself."

Ebony's eyebrows rose, then she looked from him to Greta and finally toward her mate.

Dainton shrugged.

When the pretty mocha-skinned female with the

gray streak in her hair, similar to their father's, met his gaze again he went on.

"I'm Hansel Haskin and I'm your brother."

"What?" Dainton and Ebony both responded simultaneously.

Hansel drew confidence from Greta, slipping her arm around his waist. He began to explain the situation around his parents' death. Why they were in the woods outside of Yosemite. How and why they were killed.

Ebony first listened as her features relaxed with curiosity lighting her gaze. It soon turned to sadness, then hope as her eyes filled up with water and tears began to run along her cheeks as she listened. Dainton held Ebony close.

"I thought you were dead with them. I didn't know the campers had performed a laymen's C-section." He held his hand out and waited.

His sister slipped her hand into his.

"From the moment I met you, you were familiar to me, but I didn't understand why. But, when I saw you with the little guy just a few moments ago I knew. You're the spitting image of your mother in looks and mannerisms. Except that gray streak you inherited from our father."

"Dainton, could it really be?" Ebony gazed at her mate for confirmation.

Staring at her lovingly, Dainton assured her, "It sounds like it."

Hesitant, Ebony stepped toward him. "I have a brother…family."

Pulling her into a fierce hug, Hansel held her. His sister. Over her shoulder he saw his mate wiping tears from her eyes as she leaned against her cousin and observed them.

It amazed him how empty his life had been and now he had love in abundance, he was no longer alone. Things would be different for him from here on out.

I love you, Blackberry.
I love you, mate.

Curious about Dainton and Ebony? Want to read their story and discover where they started?

Continue to Book 3 of the erotic shifter fairy tale, Scrooge's Bear…

SCROOGE'S BEAR

Erotic Shifter Fairy Tale 3

Yvette Hines

CHAPTER ONE

Cloves and apricots. The scent drew him from the lobby of the elite hotel into the bar. He'd just completed a dinner meeting with a new fertilizer supplier and was on his way toward the front door when the delicate sweet and warm woodsy blend tickled his nose and tightened his core.

Where is it coming from? His bear nudged him on. It was late and he really needed to begin the three-hour drive back to Den County. However, he moved one step after another in the direction his animal nature guided him. Crossing the threshold of the bar he was bombarded by the multiple colognes and perfumes of the many women and men milling around. It was a Tuesday night, he doubted it normally was so packed with people, however, it was Christmas Eve. He assumed most were in town visiting family or on their own getaway, possibly part of an office holiday party. He supposed for most Sacramento was a great place to be for Christmas, but not for a Were-bear like him. He and his kind enjoyed quiet time hibernating in their cabins with their family.

Even with all the other scents swirling through the air, the clove and apricot overpowered them all. Glancing around the room, he searched for the source disregarding one woman after another as they huddled around in groups at tables or on the dance floor swinging their hips before men to upbeat holiday tunes. Then his gaze glided over a woman sitting alone in a corner booth, far away from the source of music and revelry. A chestnut-brown-skinned Black woman, dressed in a dark emerald-green pantsuit, as she were attempting to pay homage to the holiday, but not. Her hair was long. He didn't know how long since she had it pulled back in a bun. A classic, elegant and professional look. She was on her cell phone, but he could tell she was searching for someone by the shifting of her gaze as she inspected and rejected one man after another.

Was she meeting someone, or just hoping to catch someone?

The growl that rumbled low in his chest shocked him. It wasn't like him to be territorial over a female. He didn't lack for female companionship. Since he traveled in and out of the county conducting various business ventures, he met more than his share, and enjoyed them.

She shifted slightly in her seat and turned her head toward the door and met his gaze. And he was practically rocked back on his heels by the impact of the contact. What seized his breath in his chest was the vibrant gold tinge on the peripheral of his vision. Shit.

Damn. Heat bloomed in his core and began to spread out through his body.

Fuck. The hair on the nape of his neck began to rise.

The last thing he needed was to go feral in a group of non-shifters and wind up on the eleven o'clock news as a special report. That would bring unwanted attention to his community. They lived under the radar and liked it that way. It was probably best for him to execute an about-face and hightail it back up to Den.

However, he'd never been one to do exactly what was expected of him. A wild card among his friends and family, he danced to his own beat too often. And if this business trip opened the door for him to get a little hot sheet action, he was all for it.

Knowing he took a risk, he moved forward—in part because he wanted to, but more importantly, because he had to.

Holding her gaze he moved toward her. His vision became more of a tunnel and his hearing distinguished between the music and other people and zeroed in on all things of the woman before him—her slight elevated breathing and heart beat.

It wasn't beating in full excitement or arousal mode but it was definitely headed there.

As he drew closer, he noticed other things like the wide strip of gray hair that blended into the dark locks being held back. Also the tension at the corners of her mouth, making her appear to be a woman who didn't smile often.

Arriving at the table beside her, he held his hand out. "Hello, I'm Dainton."

~YH~

Ebony stared down at the hand offered to her—a strong, large, wide hand. The question of whether or not she should take it never crossed her mind. It wasn't that she was some germaphobe. But, taking heed of her reaction to him since she'd spotted him at the door, she wasn't taking any chance.

She'd never been one of those women who believed the hype of Hollywood movies where the girl got a million butterflies in her stomach at the sight of a handsome man and dreamed of romance. She categorized them with the fools that had faith in Santa Claus. Even with the experiences of her past haunting her, she still found herself unable to slow down the quick pace of her heart, which had increased with every step he had taken toward her.

Tonight must be the night of firsts, since she'd never utilized the service of an escort, but here she sat with one towering over her in what must be six-five plus of "oh my god" maleness. Where did people find men so striking and imposing? The man could have had a career in the NFL. Or been some corporate tycoon. She'd been around more than her share in the business field and none of them wore a suit like this man. At his astounding height and girth, he had to have them tailor made. With what she was paying the service for his company, they could afford it easily.

Still aware that he waited for her to accept his proffered hand, she spoke into the phone. "Nikki, I'll call you tomorrow."

"You better," her best friend began. "I want every detail."

"You know that is not my style."

"Hey, with my husband in Afghanistan working for the last seven months and having to live vicariously through your hot, high-dollar adventure, you're going to tell me about it with every T and I that was performed dotted and crossed. You got that, Ebony Scrooge?"

Ebony felt the corners of her mouth twitch a little. She only had one friend in the world, and that was Nikki. Over the years, it had been hard for her to connect with people and believe that they would stick around for her. However, Nikki Tiglen had borrowed a pen from her during freshmen orientation at the state college and been in her life since then. "Fine, I'll see what I can do."

Laughing, Nikki said, "You better. Take care of yourself. You need this."

With her escort standing so close, Ebony wasn't in a position to question or comment to her best friend. It had been Nikki's idea to contact the service as a sort of liberation and celebration of starting a new life for Ebony. She had allowed Nikki to convince her that restarting her life by revitalizing her nonexistent sex life was the key. Ebony wasn't sure if she was convinced.

The man drew his hand away and slipped both of them into the pockets of his slacks, disturbing the lay of his coat.

"I guess. Talk to you later."

"Nightie Night." Nikki's sing-song words came through the line moments before the call was ended.

While she took a moment to drop her cell phone into her purse, Ebony gathered her thoughts and tried to use the seconds to take a deep breath. Big mistake.

The man had the most alluring cologne she'd ever smelled—a robust woodsy scent with a hint of cinnamon. Just the small whiff made her toes curl in her shoes and created a strong desire to lean in and bury her face in the curve of his neck.

Clearing her throat she looked up at him. "Please sit. I don't relish having a crick in my neck when I wake up in the morning."

As he lowered himself to the booth seat across from her, she noted the frown on his face at her tone. She purposely maintained a crisp and direct speech, the same she'd used for years at the investment firm. A job she held no more. However, she wanted this giant of a man to know she'd hired him and to her it was business — sex — but business.

He maneuvered his bulk into the booth, settling across from her. Once he was situated, squeezed into what appeared to be a tight space for him, she felt the heat of his knees on the outside of hers. Maybe because she was a tall woman, and he was a huge man, their legs met in the center below the table. It felt intimate with her knees pressed together between his. She crossed her ankles and pulled her feet back, trying to give herself a little space, even if it didn't change much.

Staring across the table, she was seized by the intensity of his gaze on her. She swallowed a few times, finding it difficult to have those unique eyes on her. His eyes were so dark they were black, which was impossible since no one technically had black eyes. However, the other fascinating part was that it appeared that his irises were tinged at the edges as if traced by a gold thread.

"My name is Ebony. There's no need for last names since we will not be acquainted for very long." Licking her lips she swallowed again. She needed to take control of this evening. She was the one paying for him to be here. "I'm glad to see that the service believes in punctuality. I hope they've also trained you all to follow instructions of the client. To the letter."

His brows bunched together over the bridge of his nose. "Trained me? Is that right? Like a bear in a circus or something?"

Was it her imagination or did this man appear a little bristly. "Well, I would not have used those terms."

Linking his hands together on top of the table, he leaned back against his side of the booth and slid down a little further causing his knees to now reach the sides of her thighs.

Damn. Ebony felt trapped. There was nowhere for her to scoot to so that she could escape the heat radiating from his body and crawling up her legs to the apex of her thighs. Pressing her hips down into the bench seat she stifled the ache that was growing there. She knew that sexual attraction to this man was a plus and would aid in what she needed to do with him tonight. However, it was the power of it that shook her inside.

"Look. I don't want this to start off on the wrong path. Before we head upstairs—"

"Upstairs?" A single eyebrow rose.

Biting the inside of her cheek she kept herself from rolling her eyes. Why was he acting like a mockingbird? As if he was clueless to what was going to happen. Maybe it was their cover so they wouldn't seem like prostitutes. However, no one was really fooled by what the real purpose of an escort service was. Even though Lady Salista had made Ebony sign an agreement that she was only expecting company and companionship for the evening and that she was not paying for anything sexual. After the eContract was signed, Lady Salista called her and said if anything physical happened between her and the escort it was mutual agreement between Ebony and the escort. But a nice tip was expected to the escort for the contractual service.

Ebony clearly understood the meaning of that to be 'pay the man for the sex so it doesn't get traced back to her company'. Ebony wondered if this was how the NY Madam hoped to keep her name clean.

"This is supposed to be a meeting over drinks." She definitely needed one. Lifting her hand she started to wave a waitress over. "What would you like to drink? Bourbon, wine, beer…"

"Nothing." Reaching up, he pulled her hand down. "I'm more interested in our discussion about upstairs."

She couldn't keep her eyes off his hand covering hers. It was sheer will that kept her from pulling her hand from beneath his much larger one. It was as if her hand was encased in a heating kiln. A feeling began to spread through her body, itchy, tingling…chills, she couldn't put her mind to describe it accurately because it was something she'd never experienced before.

The contact between them gave her thoughts of the two of them bare, curled around each other in the forest. Her lungs began to squeeze and release rapidly as if some invisible fist was working them, leaving her feeling more breathless than when she ran ten miles daily on the treadmill.

"Umm…um…" She wanted her lips to form the words move your hand, but her voice seemed stuck in her throat for the second time that night. The urge surfaced to grab her purse and coat and walk out of the bar, not stopping until she was sealed in her car racing down the road to nowhere, anywhere but here feeling discombobulated and unlike herself.

Thankfully he moved his hand.

Raising her gaze as she filled her lungs with an excessive amount of air, she looked at him and wondered if he had sensed her discomfort. She shook that thought away.

Pulling her hand beneath the table and covering it with the other, she rubbed it slowly trying to stop the wicked sensation.

"Miss, did you need something."

Ebony snapped her head toward the waitress who arrived at the table. Evidently the young black woman must have caught her signal anyway.

The waitress looked between Ebony and Dainton as if trying to assess if there was a problem.

"Yes. Water, please."

The server set a small white napkin with the name of the hotel bar and logo on the bottom corner in front of Ebony. "You, sir."

Looking back at her escort, she saw that he had not even glanced in the direction of the young woman standing next to their table.

Are his eyes more gold? Impossible.

"Nothing. I have everything I need already."

Tapping the table with her long acrylic nails, the worker said, "I'll be right back."

Not willing to waste anymore time of the night, Ebony began to enlighten her "date." "Were you briefed about my expectations?"

"I'd rather hear from you what you want...desire tonight," he said without missing a beat.

Lifting her chin, she gave him one of the stares she'd perfected in her many years of being a department head, the kind that had always clearly shown those on her staff that she was disappointed that they hadn't fully researched something before they presented it to her. "I would have hoped that there was some sort of required briefing before the scheduled meeting.

Evidently I was wrong. Let me explain my request and requirements for this evening."

Unlike her staff, this giant of a man didn't appear to be fazed one iota by her frosty glare.

The fact he didn't cower before her sent a frission of heat along her spine. No other man had stood up to her. The main reason she had been without male companionship for too many years for her to count. What woman wanted a man in her bed who couldn't give back as good as he got?

Licking her lips, she reminded herself that this man was not an option any further than sex. One night. This was not a long-term set up. So a growing admiration for him was for naught—worthless.

The waitress silently set down the tumbler of ice water and moved away.

"I will give it to you straight and short. I'm looking for something beyond drinks tonight, company. Of the physical kind."

Still silent, he did nothing but tilt his head, a testament that he understood her meaning.

She went on. "I know per my contract with Lady Salista's agency, the service you agreed to isn't physical in nature. That if we are both mutually attracted to each other anything that progresses beyond the assigned date is exclusively between us. Are we both on the same page so far?"

"Definitely. The attraction between us is strong and powerful." His eyes seemed to brighten even more.

Ignoring them, she reached for her water and sipped from it several times. She was feeling so heated she would have preferred to tip it back and finish it off in one gulp or pour it over herself. But she resisted.

She set the glass back on the table, but kept her

hand around it, absorbing its coolness.

"I've rented a room in this hotel for the night. However, I think what I need shouldn't take more than an hour."

"Really?"

The fire coming from his gaze made her nipples draw up and the seat of her panties become drenched. This man most likely had no problem giving it to a woman good all night long. Things she had only heard about from her friends. Her past experiences were dismal at best. In her youth all the men were jackrabbits in the bedroom but little pleasure for her. Her desire for this night was for a great mind-blowing orgasm, she just hoped for what she had to pay for this man he could deliver. After that, she would put him out, shower, sleep, and be on her merry way to somewhere in the morning.

Being a corporate nomad didn't sit well with her.

"Yes. I need release. Nothing long and drawn out. Once I've had enough it is over." She felt she needed to be clear with him. "There are rules."

"I'm sure." One corner of his mouth curled up.

"Are you laughing at me?" she bristled. Did he see her as some hopeless thirty-four year old that couldn't cut it in the real dating world? Maybe that was partly true, she was hopeless when it came to a date, but that was only because her career had come to mean everything to her. Now she was ass out.

"I'd never laugh at a beautiful woman who's honest about her sexual needs." This time a smile stretched all the way across his mouth but there was warmth in his eyes, damping the heat just a little.

She hadn't missed that he'd called her beautiful. Men in her life before hadn't given her compliments like that, too afraid of sexual harassment. Not to mention she hadn't been interested in what they thought of her looks but her ability to do a damn good job.

"Tell me. How does a sexy, drop dead gorgeous woman find herself alone for the holiday and in need of paid companionship?"

Clearing her throat, she pushed away the hum of joy at his approval. "Christmas, Easter, Groundhog Day...all just another day on the calendar to me." It was the truth. In her life holidays came around just to remind those less fortunate of what they were truly missing out on. Bah Humbug. "Furthermore, there will be no need of flattery. We both know this is a short business arrangement."

"Okay." He nodded. "What are your other rules?"

"No kissing. No trying to restrain me, I prefer to be on top. No naughty, wild antics or kinky stuff. I just want it done. I'd like to climax once...twice if you can manage it." She doubted she'd get in more than one. No man had ever made her come more than once in an encounter.

Stoic for more than a minute, he sat there staring at her without breaking eye contact. She found it hard to read his thoughts, know how he felt about all that she said.

Finally, he broke his silence. "When do we start?" His voice seemed rough, like claws dragged along the side of a tree—rich, rough, and scratchy.

The visual image that accompanied the thought made her spine tingle and a bead of sweat roll between her breasts. *How did something like that turn me on?*

Tightening her hand around the glass, she lifted it again and drank, giving herself some time. This was the moment where the snow stuck. She had to decide unequivocally to take the plunge.

"Now."

He rose. She never would have figured as squished as he'd appeared in the booth that he would be able to move with such speed and be standing beside her once again with his hand held out to her.

With him standing so close, her body reacted. Every hair on her body stood up on ends. The sensation was unexpected and odd, making her skin feel foreign and alive. The urge to find a tree and rub up against it arrested it. Grabbing her glass instead of his hand, she finished off the water and wished she had ordered something stronger.

Shoving out of the seat she circumvented his hand, not sure if she was ready to let him touch her yet, then headed toward the door. "This way." She spoke to him over her shoulder, but didn't pause in stride to see if he followed her.

I'm in charge. I'm in charge.

Even as she repeated those words to herself, she didn't feel in charge. Maybe when she boldly completed the request form or when she spoke to Lady Salista on the phone and told her what she wanted. However, once big, tall and fierce stepped up to her table with his dark, intense, liquid gold gaze...control evaded her grasp. But, she would be damned if she allowed herself to exhibit that to him. No way. She was a virtuoso at commanding people to do what she wanted. It was how she'd succeeded so well in business at such a young age. At thirty she had become the youngest deputy CEO at her old company. And wherever she ended up next she'd do greater things.

Right now, she was going to take her pleasure from

a bear of a man and then walk away.

CHAPTER TWO

Dainton watched her sashay away. He wasn't in the least put off by her prickly exterior. He'd met porcupines in the woods that were more approachable than Ebony. However, it was her hard as a frozen Lake Michigan persona that made him desire her more — want to see her melt in his arms.

He's sensitive ears had picked up on the exchange of conversation between her and another woman who spoke to her as if she were a sister or best friend.

Ebony Scrooge was a woman with a story. One he doubted she would be willing to share with him. A man she considered her one night stand. Correction, her male escort. That thought brought a frown to his face as he followed her hasty steps through the crowd partying in the bar toward the door.

What would make a hot as hell woman need to hire someone to have sex with her? Sex, for sure. If Ebony had not been forthcoming with anything else about this night it was that she had paid some service for his, no some unfortunate bastard's, company and she was going to top that off by paying the man directly for sexual services rendered. What in the hell?

He was stumped.

Now that she was out of the booth, he could take in the full beauty of her body. Full figured, with curves so prominent and thick they could make a man's mouth water. Shit, what the hell did he care about any other man? He'd been salivating heavily practically the entire time he sat across from her listening to her run on about her rules. List of don'ts was more like it.

When all he'd wanted to do was pull her over the tabletop and have her straddle him as he acquainted himself with her ample form. He was a Were. His kind came big. He preferred women that could hold up to the fierceness of his love making. A slip of a woman scared him. Sex was a pretty intense affair and he always had to keep his sexual exploits to human women of the thicker variety. A beautiful figure with large breasts, narrow waist and wide, round hips and ample thighs to cradle his hips and take the power of his thrusts. Ebony, in her perfectly tailored green suit, was that kind of woman.

Casually strutting behind her fast, long strides through the lobby, he allowed himself to think on something else—the strength of his desire and attraction for her. He hadn't missed the electric heat that coursed through his arm when he'd laid his hand over hers. It felt as if he'd tried to hold on to a live wire—his blood sizzled. The hot flash of pleasure swirled through his body and landed dead center in his lap. His cock had been rock hard the entire time he sat across from her. Even now, it was semi-erect hidden behind the lower end of his suit jacket.

If the long-lasting erection hadn't been enough of a response to jar him in the gut, the fact that his gums had been itching in four specific places had the hair on his arms raised. He couldn't figure out why he was responding to her in such a way—this strange woman.

As her pace slowed, she drew closer to the elevators, he allowed himself to close the gap some so that he could take in another direct dose of her scent. Cloves and apricot—there was something about it. Something he couldn't put his finger on. Like a vapor, the clarity of who this woman was eluded his grasp.

He intentionally kept his distance from Were-females in his county and found a reason to be far away from town during the First Frost Moon. Finding a life-long mate wasn't on his agenda. There were too many favorite flavors of women in the world he'd yet to taste to find himself in the same bed night after night for the rest of his life. No thank you. Yeah, he felt the pull the week prior like all other men, but he hightailed it quickly beyond Den County's limits. Usually, he locked himself in a hotel room for a few days until the intensity to mate wore off enough that he could trust himself to find a willing human woman and slack his lust.

So, why he was willing to trail behind their aphrodisiac delight and risk the warning connection was beyond him. What he should do was confess the truth and tell her he wasn't the man she'd been waiting for—the one she'd paid to service her.

But his bear growled and urged him forward.

~YH~

When she arrived at the bank of elevators at the back of the lobby, she could feel the heat of his body behind her letting her know he had followed her from the bar. He wasn't close enough that their bodies connected, but it didn't seem to matter. Her breasts felt heavy and the urge to cup them herself assailed her.

Finally, the doors parted and she stepped in and moved as close to the panel as possible.

Her shadow flowed in next.

Cutting her eyes toward him, she was arrested by his direct gaze. He stood against the opposite wall, giving her space. She was grateful for that. However, the way he was looking at her, as if she was his favorite treat that he wanted to consume, made her hands shake.

For a moment she paused with her finger on the button for the floor where her rented suite was located. The protracted stare was doing a number on her. If a man had ever viewed her with such intensity before, she couldn't recall.

Maybe I should just end this. Take the loss of the money I paid and send him away.

The car began to ding, letting her know the doors needed to close and it was awaiting her selection.

Her mind told her having sex with him could be dangerous. Her loins told her it would be worth it. Her heart had yet to voice an opinion other than the firm, steady beat that pulsed through her eardrums.

"I think I've chan—"

"Hold the elevator!" A man came slipping through as the doors started to slide shut. "Phew. Thanks." Out of breath the intoxicated man slumped against the back wall.

"Hey pretty lady." The drunk wobbled closer to her and with a hand stretched toward her. "How about joining me in my room for some holiday che-ee-r?"

A growl pierced the elevator car before the man had

completed his offer.

Ebony and the balding drunk both snapped their heads in the direction of the big, silent man in the corner.

She could have sworn that she felt the steel box shake beneath her feet.

Dainton took one step that brought him to the center of the enclosed space as he focused his gaze on the inebriated man. "Don't touch her."

His voice that was already heavy and rough, in a sexy way, now was menacing and sounded more like two rocks being ground against each other—grating. She also noticed instantly that those intense gorgeous eyes of his that were making her melt across the table now almost seemed reddish in color as they held the intoxicated man pinned to the spot.

Mr. Drunkard, seeing the hard look, swallowed once then twice. He rubbed his hand down the front of his face swiping away the river of sweat that began to pour down from his bare scalp.

The big man that was her date made her a little nervous at the moment, even though his ire was raised by her and he wasn't giving her the cold glare. Would he hurt this man?

She'd never had a man step forward so protective of her before. It had always been something she'd had to do for herself. Unsure of how she felt about her body guard for the night, she surely didn't want him to hurt this man.

"Umm…ugh…haha…umm…" The man shuffled back more.

The beast of a man, her date, took two steps and had the man backed into a far corner away from her. Dainton looked so fierce it almost seemed as if the expanse of his shoulders was swelling bigger.

Impossible.

She knew better than to jump between two grown men that were squaring off, but she had to do something to stop them. "Dainton."

If she hadn't witnessed it with her own eyes, she would not have believed it when she saw his body actually shiver when she called his name.

He turned and fixed his gorgeous eyes onto her. The longer he stared at her the more it appeared the ruby tint faded and those golden flecks began to take over.

She was truly becoming fond of that metallic color.

The elevator dinged announcing its arrival onto a floor; too early to be the one she rented for the night. When the doors were barely open the drunk hustled past Dainton quickly and shot through the slowly widening gap, stammering his apologizes the whole time. Most likely, hoping to stave off any beating that may still be coming his way.

Dainton only shifted so that he was resting his shoulder against the shiny metal side of the elevator, appearing all too cocky.

She folded her arms and pinned him with a look. "I don't care for violence."

"You don't think a man should stand up and protect his woman?"

"I'm not your woman. I don't need a man to go all Neanderthal on my behalf."

A single corner of his mouth curled up. "I think you do."

"And I think you need to step back." Oh, hell what was wrong with her? Why didn't she just tell the man to get off on the next floor and keep away from her? "What are you, some kind of bully?"

"Never to you, love."

Finally, the elevator signaled it had arrived at the twenty-third floor where her suite was located.

"I'm not your love. I'm your client. Since I'm paying a hell of a lot, think of me as your boss." She liked that term. It was something she was familiar with, a way more comfortable for her to deal with such an overpowering man. She'd have him firmly in his place before he slid inside of her.

That thought caused warmth to spread through her thighs and made her clit press into the seat of her panties.

Stepping from the elevator, she led them down the hall. Before her door, she paused with the keycard in hand. For a moment she wondered if she was making the right choice. Not because she'd paid for sex. Hell, she was a modern woman and took control of her own life. More because of this man, a man that seemed so virile, so untamed.

Glancing over her shoulder she looked at him.

"Have you changed your mind?" His question came out in a low timbre and for a moment his gaze became less intense and warmth more than fire filled his eyes.

Was he concerned about my feelings?

She shook that away. This man didn't know her well enough to have such a concern. He was probably more worried about not getting his tip after services rendered.

"No. Of course not. You know the rules…I expect you to stick to them." With that she opened the door and stepped in first.

A soft rumble was the only response she heard.

The suite door closed behind them.

"One thing about rules…I've never been good at

following them."

Before she could respond, he had her pressed to the wall beside the open bathroom door his mouth covering hers. Breaking rule number one, doing what she told him to do and only that. No kissing was the first thing she expressed she didn't want.

Why aren't you pushing him away? Her mind taunted.

However, her body disregarded the question and gave in. She never recalled being kissed so well—it stole her senses.

His lips were firm but gentle. They felt like silk moving over hers. He didn't press his body against her, but kept a small amount of distance so that she barely felt his chest brushing her breasts.

As if reaching for him, her nipples were drawn tight, stretching forward.

The kiss deepened as he slid his tongue into her mouth causing electric currents to shoot into the tips of her breasts and her fingers. She needed to touch more of him. Raising her hands, she placed them on his sides and resisted the urge to pull him closer.

She sighed and yielded to his oral guidance.

He glided his tongue over hers then curled it so that every time he drew it away the tip of it grazed the roof of her mouth. She shivered and moaned in response.

Over and over again he claimed her mouth, turned her core to jelly and made her mind spin. She needed more. More kissing. More of this man.

"Rrrrrrr…"

Did he just growl? Even as the question came into her mind, her body acted on its own to the sound. She arched her back, pressing her breasts to his solid chest. She moved her lips back and whispered, "Touch me. I want to feel your hands on me."

He stared down at her, his eyes were definitely more metallic, the ebony color now flecks in the golden pool, barely noticeable.

If she wasn't half out of her mind with desire she may have stopped them and inquired about the shifting in his gaze she kept seeing. However, with the blood rushing through her veins—hot and fast—she couldn't drag herself to do anything but wait anxiously for his touch.

Smiling, he leaned closer and glided his tongue over her bottom lip as his hands palmed her breasts. Large breasts that most men in the past had struggled with handling. Not Dainton.

He cupped them through her suit jacket as he resumed kissing her.

Her fingers flexed at his waist and felt the hard muscles concealed beneath his clothes. For a moment she felt hesitant about having her body bared before this sculpted man. She was fit. She worked hard daily on the treadmill, but sometimes no matter how hard someone dieted and went to the fitness center they couldn't fight genetics. Her curves were thick and prominent.

In her experience, men liked slimmer woman. They were all over Hollywood and plastered across billboards and the covers of magazines. Even in the corporate field when she first got started she was passed over a few times for lead positions for the thin, athletic type, until she proved time and again how much of a go-getter she was and how well she could produce above expectation results. Then the men in charge couldn't overlook her. Would this man be disappointed in what he saw revealed before him?

She wanted to not care. Wanted to take the haughty road and recall she wasn't paying him for his opinion but his performance.

However, even as a strong, confident and business-minded person in her core, there was still a sliver of the young woman that wanted favorable attention, love, and for someone to see her as beautiful—the things that had been denied to her in her life.

Pulling back, she pressed her hands on his chest, needed a bit of space. Catch her breath. Her head was spinning.

"Ah," she cried out at the sharp sting. She reached up and placed two fingers on her bottom lip.

He set his lips along the shell of her ear. "My apologies. I seemed to have gotten a little carried away." His voice was rough and intoxicating. "Let me take care of that."

His brushed small kisses along her cheek until her arrived at the corner of her mouth. There he licked along her bottom lip and removed the soreness and sting of the scrape. His tongue swiped over it once, twice and returned two more times as if he couldn't get enough of the small taste of her.

She could understand on some level, because those delicate licks were doing something to her. Something she couldn't explain. The single word need seemed to explode in her mind.

This time she initiated the kiss, burying her hands in his hair, she fisted the thick black locks holding him in place as she claimed his mouth.

As strong as he was, she didn't fool herself for a moment in believing that she was overpowering him or making him remain still as she feasted from his mouth. Oh, no.

He was permitting her the lead. He wasn't a bystander by any means. The big man participated but allowed her to control the depth of the kiss.

When she left his lips and dragged her mouth along the column of his throat, she felt the vibrations along her tongue of the rumble that passed through his vocal cords on its way out of his mouth.

His skin had a salty/sweetness to it that she savored. However, it was nothing compared to his scent—a nutty fresh smell that reminded her of enjoying a slice of pecan pie in the park while the leaves were falling. The sensory image didn't make sense since she never allowed herself to consume sweets and she couldn't recall the last time she went to the park to just sit and relax. Usually, the natural scenery was a blur in her periphery as she ran her five miles four times a week.

How could the smell of this man make her long for something she'd never had?

"I'm sorry about your suit."

"What happened to my— Ah!" Shocked at the sight of her jacket, shirt and bra lying in tatters around her feet like confetti, she stared at him.

"I had to see you…touch you and I couldn't wait another minute." There wasn't an ounce of remorse reflected in his gaze.

She told herself to be scared and appalled at his behavior, but she couldn't draw those emotions up. They were overpowered by the urgency within her to feel his hands on her skin.

"Touch me…feel me." Was that a pleading sound in her voice? Who was the woman in this room?

"You're in charge." He winked at her.

She almost giggled at his words. She doubted she

ever had charge of this man. Maybe that was the allure to him. Was she perhaps tired of being able to make men cower in her presence? Jump at a single word from her?

She didn't know and at this moment, she didn't fucking care either, as Dainton's lips were creating a direct path from her collarbone to her breasts. She arched her back and offered herself to him.

He licked between her breasts, designing along her sensitive skin there. Then he moved right and brushed his cheek along the inner slope of one globe.

A sigh slipped from her mouth at his gentle touch.

Her wrapped a single broad arm behind her back and lifted her up from the floor, angling her chest directly before his mouth.

Men didn't lift tall thick women from the floor. However, that was exactly what Dainton had done with ease as if she were no heavier than a feather-as if she weighed nothing at all.

He took the first nipple into his mouth and drew on it hard.

Her palms smacked against the wall behind her, the feeling of sucking and his tongue flicking hot pulses of heat from her nipple to her clit. Her hands on the cool wall aided in her keeping her sanity…some.

When he cupped her free breast with his hand and began to squeeze and pluck the tip, all was lost. She began mumbling his name.

There came a feeling of something piercing and sharp sinking into her. Before she could question him about what he was doing, the world was kicked from under her.

"Oh, Oh…" With her head tossed back, mouth gaped and her pelvis pushed forward grinding against his hard cock, her body exploded. The instant, violent climax caught her unaware. Bucking and screaming in the arms of this big man, her mind turned to mush.

There was a popping sound as he released her nipple from his mouth.

"Fuck! Did you just come?"

She tilted her head forward and stared at him as she gulped in deep breaths of air. She wanted to tell him no. That it was impossible for her to orgasm simply by a man sucking…and biting…on her breast. However, the true answer to his question with the cream now soaked through her panties and the humming throb of her sex was yes.

"I guess so." It wasn't the most intelligent thing to say, but at the moment she didn't have much else.

"I have to taste you." He kissed her as he lowered her feet back to the floor. He stepped back still cupping her hips, his golden gaze holding hers. "Discover more of your musky, intoxicating scent…from the source. I want to feel your pussy on my tongue."

Such words. The wickedness of them shocked her. Men didn't whisper such things to her in the bedroom. Normally, she preferred for them not to speak at all. Just get the job done. However, the same could not be said for how her body quivered at the things he said.

When he was resting on his knees before her, the memory of what he had done to her jacket and top popped into her mind. "Wait, I'll take off my—"

Too late. A loud ripping sound tore through the room as Dainton pulled her pants and underwear in half as if they were paper. Each side sagged down to her ankles.

"Damn that is one pretty, creamy pussy. I need to

taste you," he said, his voice gruff.

When he leaned in, she clutched two handfuls of his hair. "Wait! No more biting."

As she gazed down at the gorgeous man, she could clearly see the teeth marks that decorated the edge of her left areola. It shined from the combination of the small amount of blood and his saliva. Even as she chided him, her breast and body were still throbbing deliciously. But, when this night was over, she didn't want to have bite marks all over her body. Her mind may have been firm on that, but her core seemed to tighten with a sadness she refused to acknowledge.

Reaching up, he circled the tender nipple, his finger stroking the marks he made—taunting her. "Whatever you wish."

Yeah, right. She thought, as a sigh slipped from her mouth at his enticing touch as she bowed her back away from the wall wanting more.

CHAPTER THREE

Staring at the treat before him, Dainton took hold of her thighs and widened her stance. He wanted to see all of Ebony's pretty pussy. He understood that the view would have been better if he had laid her down on the bed and spread her legs wide, however, he didn't have the patience to move them. His bear was clawing at him for a taste of her honey — now.

He'd been with women that came easily before, but none so responsive to him. His gaze, touch, and even his voice. But, Ebony's body was like an instrument that only he knew the cords to or how to play. Why was that?

Even greater question rolling through his mind, 'Why did he bite her?' Not once, but twice. The initial nip of her lip had happened by accident. Or rather he was enjoying kissing her so much that he didn't care that his canines had extended. Besides, he'd never been even close to tempted to bite any of the other women he'd lain with. Why Ebony?

But, once he'd had that small taste of her, her sweet taste had detonated something wild in his body and freed something in his soul. All he wanted to do was sink his teeth into her and claim her. Then the second bite happened and something inside of him shifted. The world he had known folded back and became something different—more vivid and clear it seemed. And that scared the shit out of him.

He knew she had no clue what biting meant to his kind, but he did. The first time had shocked him, the second time had seemed to kick start his heart, something he didn't quite understand. There couldn't and wouldn't be a third bite. He couldn't risk it. That act would mate him until death to Ebony. Something that was not fair to a human female. As well as to a constraining situation he told himself he never wanted. The best thing for him to do would be to just walk away from this woman who seemed to pose a threat to his sanity. However, he knew that if he even tried to walk away from her now, his bear would cause him to shift right in the middle of the hotel, without a care for appearances, just to get back to her. A situation which would probably frighten the hell out of Ebony, seeing a huge bear scratching at her hotel door.

"No more biting." He declared and refocused himself to the task at hand. Bringing the woman more pleasure.

With a single finger he glided it from the opening of her sex through her swollen, glistening lips to just below her clit. He wanted to keep her on edge—panting for him. Pulling his hand away and toward his mouth, he inhaled deeply and took in the heady aroma of her scent. The clove and apricot blend was stronger and more gripping as it pooled around her sex.

Gazing up at her, watching her heavy breathing, he waited until she met his stare before slipping his cream coated finger into his mouth. He groaned at the potent taste of her, making him anxious to dive in for more.

"Hmm, like honey." He wasn't referring to the taste, more of the affect it seed to have on him. Consuming honey for a Were-bear was something they could never live without, now that he had experienced her unique flavor, he would be hard pressed to keep himself from hunting her down frequently just to savor her again...and again.

"I wouldn't know," her words came out breathless.

"How is that possible?"

"I never allow myself to eat sweets of any kind."

He froze for a moment, shocked by what she said. He understood that honey to humans didn't mean what it did to his kind—strength, life, health and sanity—but never to have tried it seemed to be the most preposterous thing.

"We will have to rectify that somehow." He took hold of her hips and slid his hands around to cup her ass and drag her forward. "Enough talking, I'm a hungry bear who's ready to eat."

He didn't hesitate as he pressed his tongue right over her clit, licking and circling the tight bud. She thrust closer to him then shied away a little as he burrowed deeper in her pussy.

However, he wasn't having that. Gripping the plump flesh in his hands, he held her in place. There was no way such a delectable treat was getting away from him. He laved and suckled up and around her labia drawing her supple skin into his mouth, cautiously keeping his teeth away.

The sounds of her moans and whimpers stoked the

embers heating up inside of him, urging him on. Lowering his mouth, he glided along her slit until he could dip his tongue inside her sweet pussy. He pressed deep, teasing her walls and loving the feel of her clenching around him.

He growled, purposely sending the strong vibrations along her sex.

"Dainton..." She parted her thighs wider as she fisted his hair at the crown of his head with one hand, while the nails of her other hand scratched the surface of the wall.

Her cream coated his tongue as he moved in and out capturing every droplet.

That's when it happened. A picture in bold, bright Technicolor unfolded before him. All he could see were images. Odd images that he would never think of. Ebony was lying in a field, the grass brushing and caressing her bare body as he lay between her spread legs pleasuring her. The sun was shining but pecan pies rained down around them igniting and combining the scent of earth and nuts. Her face appeared dark with arousal, but open and at peace as well.

The vision shifted and he saw two animals running through the forest, nipping, playing and tumbling over each other. One, large and dark he easily recognized. However, the other was a mystery to him until it turned and gazed upon him with a white patch of fur in the center of the head. Ebony?

Shaking and quivering, she climaxed showering his tongue with her warm, wet essence.

"Bears? ...bears..." she murmured.

The gasping shocked sound of the woman before him, as well at the illuminating image had him jerking away, ceasing the mental picture. His brow was drawn tight, almost to the point of pain, as he attempted to sort out not only the scene but how Ebony had guessed what he'd imagined.

Mind-link. That one word shot through his mind like a cannon—loud and piercing. It wasn't possible. Ebony was human. Even for those members of his county who had succumbed to their desire for a human and married them, they never had the same deep connection. The couple never mind-linked and the human never gained the ability to shift. The reason it was such a precarious situation and usually strongly advised against.

"What's wrong?" Her light brown eyes searched his face.

The concern in her voice caused his chest to ache. The last thing he wanted to do was worry her. He'd promised her a night of pleasure and he wouldn't renege on his vow just because he wanted to run fast in the opposite direction of whatever the underlining situation was happening between them. There would be plenty of time afterward for him to think about what transpired during his drive back to Den. One thing he was sure about, as soon as the right moment presented itself, he needed to get the hell out of the city and back to familiar territory—literally and emotionally.

"Nothing, sweetheart." He rose, shucking his suit jacket and starting on the buttons of his shirt. "I'm just ready to get you on that bed and bury myself deep inside you."

"Oh."

"Put those soft hands on me and help me out of my clothes so I can fuck you properly." He needed to keep things on a strictly sexual level, the place he was most comfortable — like himself.

She hesitated for a moment as she stepped out of her heels and shoved her torn pants and panties to the floor. He only felt a smidge of sorrow for ruining her suit and hoped since she already had the room booked she also had another set of clothes available.

"I'll replace all that I've destroyed."

Looking up at him, she shook her head. "No need. I'm more than financially able to provide for myself." Taking hold of his belt she worked it loose quickly.

There was a bite to her words, a tone similar to the one she'd used downstairs when she was rattling off her list of instructions.

"And I take care of what's mine."

Her fingers halted in the act of dragging his zipper down, leaving it halfway undone. "But, I'm not—"

He pulled her to him and sealed his mouth on hers. The feelings of possession and aggression had him silencing any disavowing she was prepared to claim.

She grunted and pushed against his chest, struggling against his dominance.

When his tongue brushed the tip of hers as he sank into her mouth, her sounds turned to whimpers and sighs.

A wildness over took them as they began to clutch, stroke each other — both needing and wanting more.

Pulling his mouth away, he said, "I must have you now."

"Yes."

Urgency took hold of him, not willing to wait the steps it would take to get to the bed. He flipped her toward the wall and planted kisses and licks along her spine.

She moaned as she shimmied her hips.

He growled his pleasure at her response as he shoved his pants to his hips then took hold of one of her legs. He pulled it high, opening her for him as she pressed flush to the flat surface before her. She'd need that support. He knew now that he would finally get inside of her, he couldn't even hope to be gentle.

He located her sex and slipped one then two and finally a third finger inside of her, attempting to prepare her for the size of his cock. From years of experience he knew she would adjust to him, but didn't want to cause her anymore discomfort than he had to.

Removing his hand, he pressed the broad head of his cock to her.

"What are you—"

He entered her, guiding himself in slowly.

"Ahh..."

Unsure if the sound was a scream or a sigh, he pulled out and moved in again slower, going deeper. He made sure she felt every inch of his dick as he claimed her.

"Mmm....ahhh... Dainton."

He enjoyed the passionate sound of his name from her mouth.

"I should get a condom."

He parted her legs wider as he positioned the head of his cock at her pussy. "No. I can't carry your diseases."

"What? I don't understand."

He groaned as he stroked along her slit, coating his crown with her cream. "I'll explain later." He was shaking and everything around him was covered in a rich golden haze, unsure how much longer he could keep himself from sinking into her. His body, soul, and beast yearned for a connection with her. An ultimate bonding, something he could not give into. But even with that knowledge, it didn't remove the desire for it.

He pressed forward, feeling her pussy part, opening for him. Pulling out he pushed further along her walls.

"Take all of me, Ebony." In and out he fit his length inside of her. Her pussy was so damn tight and hot along his shaft. He never wanted to be separated from her.

"Ooooo...." She ground her ass against his hips. "But what about—"

Groaning from the sensation, he thrust forward, unsure of what she was going to say. A part of him cared, but the animal part of him was aimed on one thing, mating.

"Ah! Yes..."

"Ebony...so...fucking...perfect..." He moved back, hooked her knee over the bend of his arm and dragged her leg up higher then drove back inside.

For purchase he held her other hip as he took them both to ecstasy. Their rutting was hard and fast, but if his bear couldn't bite her, it still needed to mark her as his.

Leaning his chest away from her back, he palmed her ass. The thick, round, chestnut hued flesh teased him, beckoned him to play. He stroked the crease and followed it to the furrowed opening. He brushed the ultra-sensitive area.

She moaned.

Gliding his cock out, he collected her wetness from his shaft then smoothed the dew over the puckered skin as he thrust inside of her again.

She whimpered and bucked her hips back.

He wondered if Ms. Controlled and Straitlaced had

ever allowed a man to enter there and take her to an untamed climax. He doubted it. And tonight in his anxious state, there would be no time for him to coach her through it. After this, there would be no other chance for them. His chest ached and his bear whined; he ignored both.

"Wait, Dainton." She went still as he slipped the tip of his thumb inside her ass.

Moving his dick out, he leaned toward her and licked the shell of her ear as he guided back into her pussy and pushed his thumb a little more.

Tremors rocked her body and her moan came out in a stutter as if she tried to fight her response to the act. "It's...too wi—"

"Wicked?" He started a rhythm. Thrusting both of his members inside of her openings.

"Yes...Ooo, terribly so."

"Do you want me to stop? Stop the wickedness?" He taunted her with one of her many rules and made her face her own desire.

He worked her body, waiting to see if she would tell him to end the nefarious pleasure.

"Ebony, do you want me to stop fondling you? Stop fucking you?"

She rotated her hips along his shaft and thrust back onto him and took his thumb deeper.

He understood her response. He didn't need her to break her own code verbally. "Take your pleasure, sweetheart."

And pleasing her was his aim. He spread his feet as wide as his slacks would allow and angled his hips for the deepest penetration into her. Their flesh slapped as their bodies pounded against the wall.

A grating sound exploded into the room as her

short, manicured nails clawed and scratched along the antique wall paper.

"I'm-m-m....I'mmmm—" she screamed as her release broke forth.

Her clutching quivering sex pulled his own orgasm from him.

~YH~

Dainton stumbled blindly toward the bed. His vision obscured by the lust haze, hindering him from clearly seeing anything but Ebony. One climax had not been enough. His cock was still hard, his bear still demanding.

When they finally landed on the bed, he turned her to face him. He ground his shaft through her cream and over her hardened clit.

"Don't stop." She gripped his shoulders, embedding her nails in his muscles and pumped her hips.

The sting of pain excited his bear. He growled, "That's it, sweetheart." Leaning down, he laid his chest over hers and kissed her as his hips rocked a hard rhythm greeted by the woman beneath him.

Pulling back he pushed inside of her and was delighted to feel how her pussy welcomed him in again. The folds of her labia surrounded him, holding him like a perfect glove. He never wanted to be separated from her.

When he felt the vibrations around his cock, a signal that Ebony was about to be overtaken by another orgasm he flattened his palms on the headboard, to protect her. Sex wasn't a gentle affair with his kind, and normally he could temper his passion and response to a human woman, but not with Ebony. He was having a hard time keeping his animal side in check.

He set his lips on the shell of her ear and whispered a warning, "Hold on...this ride is about to get real rough."

She looped her hands under his arms and clutched his shoulders from behind. "Give it to me, Dainton...I can take it."

Somewhere inside of him, he detected the truth of her words. With a growl, he buried his face in the curve over her neck and began to pound his cock into her.

True to her statement, Ebony raised her knees and cradled his sides with her supple thighs.

With her acquiesce his bear took over.

~YH~

Dainton's thick, hard shaft slammed into her. It stretched and reshaped her sex for his possession. His loving was fierce and wild and she felt just as untamed and feral. She couldn't keep the images of the two bears out of her mind. Unsure of where the thoughts came from she allowed them to roam free in her head, in some inherent way she sensed there was a connection between the animals and her and Dainton.

She couldn't explain it. She refused to use her energy to decipher it at the moment. No, her whole being and focus belonged to the man taking her to the end of the world with his passion.

As he thrust harder and deeper into her, she arched up to him, rotating her hips and pressing her sex up along his shaft, meeting him. She moaned, having never felt so alive before.

Gazing up at him, he appeared feral—those thick black locks of his were unruly around his head, ravaged by her fingers during the night's events. Dainton. Her mind brought up the image of one of the bears, the larger of the two, held it there like a still frame. As if intuition guided him to gaze down at her, he lowered his head and stared at her with stormy golden eyes — captivating eyes.

"Beautiful." Reaching up, she caressed the skin over one metallic orb and followed an invisible path around it to the lower lid. She couldn't explain her reaction to the odd appearance of his eye. However, seeing them did what it had been doing all night, causing a burning ball of desire to spin down her spine and land in her core — heightening her arousal.

She felt her sex tightening around him as another orgasm started to build and spread from her center out. "Don't stop....please...Dainton." She begged him as if she hadn't had any other climax all night but this one, which was not the case. There had been too many to count.

"Never." Grunting, he leaned down and kissed her. He took possession of her mouth, as his dick claimed her body. After tonight there would never been another man for her, but Dainton. Never be another man she wanted or desired as much as she would this man. And he would be walking out of her life, all too soon.

Over and against her, his body began to shake and his thrusts became erratic — no longer so precise.

As she returned his kiss, she became aware that he must have released the headboard because his hands gripped her ass and held her up away from the bed as he rose to his knees and administered his final forward drive and showered her walls with his heat. His roar of pleasure vibrated along her cheeks and down her throat as if she were the one making the fierce sound.

The intense warmth catapulted her into the heavens

as she screamed her release into the mouth of the man still kissing her.

His movements slowed and his kiss gentled as they settled onto the bed, their breathing rough and fast.

CHAPTER FOUR

When Dainton rolled to the side and attempted to bring her with him to curl up at his side, she wiggled away. After sex cuddling was something that lovers did. They were not lovers. Not in the truest sense of the word.

Ebony dragged her tender body to the side of the bed. She needed to get control of the situation again. Even as aftershocks of pleasure still had her quaking inside, she needed to get herself together. Time to show this man out before she didn't have the strength to send him away.

With a deep breath of fortitude she rose to her feet and moved a little unsteadily to the door. She picked up her purse from the floor where it had fallen when Dainton had pressed her to the wall and kissed her, carrying it to the dresser and reaching inside of it. Her body ached and throbbed all over in a way she'd never experienced with a man before. The kind of soreness she'd heard women whisper about across tables or in fitness center locker rooms. Keeping her back to him she allowed herself a small smile of satisfaction. The man had been more than worth the money she paid for him and had earned one hell of a tip.

Tip the man. Once she pulled out a wad of cash, he would get the hint.

She turned to face him, expecting to find him enjoying an after-sex sleep like most men. Instead he stared at her, allowing his gaze a slow roam over her body.

The impulse to hide herself, shield her curves from his sight assailed her. However, she kept her hands away knowing that he'd already seen all of her through the rambunctious sexual antics.

Thoughts of all they had done made her shiver. She gave herself a moment to admire his large, built form. The man took up over half of the queen-size bed with his shoulder span. His chest was broad and chiseled through his abs. A woman could get lost in all the hills and valleys of his defined muscles. She lowered her gaze to the dark thatch of hair above his reposed shaft as it rested to one side. She noted that the crown of his thick dick reached beyond his hipbone. It amazed her how she'd taken all of that, and more, inside of her…and loved every inch of it.

The urge to lick it from his heavy sack to the tip had her moistening her lips.

His cock twitched and began to raise some. "You know it's a much better view from over here."

Her gaze shot to his face. He had a wide carefree smile stretching his mouth as he lifted a hand and beckoned her to him.

Shaking her head she maintained her distance. The man had to be on something. How in the hell, after all the energy they had exerted over the last few hours, could he even be able to get it up? Even as she asked the mental question about him, her own body shocked her and began to react—the sensitive walls of her sex started to clench and moisten.

With a vengeance, not sure if it was directed at the beguiling man or herself, she snatched a fistful of bills out of her wallet and held them out to him. "This has been great fun, but our night has come to its end."

He scowled and glanced from the money to her face. "What the hell are you doing?" He shoved himself to a seated position.

Why did he look angry and insulted?

"I'm paying you your tip. Do you think it is not enough?" She was fisting over four hundred dollars in her hand. It was twenty percent of what she'd paid Lady Salista. Was the percentage higher than a waitress made at a fine dining restaurant? Ebony had no clue.

"What I know is that you have me confused with someone else!" He stood up, his hands fisted on his hips.

She laughed. Is he trying to fleece me? "Who? A streetwalker. Do they make this high of a tip? Lady Salista really needed to spell that out better in the contract." She waved the money in the air.

He growled. How was it that the man appeared more menacing standing on the other side of the bed nude than when he was clothed downstairs?

Swallowing, she calmed herself. The last thing she needed was to be trapped in the room with a big man. She didn't believe he would hurt her physically. However, what did she really know about him besides how well he could get her off?

"You paid someone to fuck you." He shoved a hand through his hair and gripped the back of his neck.

That sounded like a question instead of the accusation, she was confused. "You are the person I paid...am paying even more to screw me." Had his orgasm scattered his brain?

It would be just her luck that her first escort would be the one that needed around-the-clock meds for some mental condition.

"I don't take money for giving a woman pleasure." It came out low as he spoke through his tight lips.

She tossed the money onto the top of the dresser beside her purse and shoved her wallet back into her name-brand bag. "Fine. If you are too high-stepping to take a tip for services rendered that is all on you. Our night is still done."

"No, it is just beginning."

"Ha!" She pointed a finger at him and squinted, attempting to give him the same piercing stare that had her old staff running from the office to do her bidding. "Just because you want more sex, you think I'm going to submit myself to your lusty demands?"

"Absolutely, because something is going on between us." He took a step toward her.

She stepped back and gripped the dresser behind her. "If you think for one moment that I'm going to lie on that bed and spread my thighs for you again, you must be mad."

"Insane, hot, horny, and confused." He moved around the foot of the bed in two, long strides.

"I'd say you are a little more than confused. I don't do all-nighters with men."

"You don't do a lot of things." He now stood before her, his arms crossed over his chest. "Why were you in the bar earlier this evening?"

"Waiting for you, duh?" Damn he'd reduced her to a short-verbiage teenager.

"Try again. Who specifically were you waiting for?" Those intense eyes of his held hers. They were more blackened now than the gold color they reflected earlier,

Chills began to race up her arms at his question. An uneasy feeling was starting to build in her stomach. She wanted to cross the room and remove her trench coat from the closet and put it on.

"I really don't like to repeat myself—" The ringing of her cell phone cut her off. Turning, she rifled through her purse until she located it at the bottom. Who would be calling her in the middle of the night? The number that came across the screen seemed familiar but she couldn't place it right off hand.

"Hello," she answered.

"Hi, Ms. Scrooge I'm so sorry to call at such a late hour."

Ebony recognized the woman's elegant, velvet voice immediately.

"That's no problem, Lady Salista? Why are you calling?" Ebony eyed the giant still standing too close to her. Maybe his employer wanted to warn her that the man she'd set Ebony up with had just recently been released from the looney bin.

"My apologies for just now calling, but I just found out myself."

"Found out what?" Ebony insisted.

"Marcus, the escort I'd assigned for your evening, had an allergic reaction to something he ate this afternoon and has been hospitalized. I guess his throat was too swollen until an hour ago to even talk. I will fully refund your money or arrange someone else tomorrow night for you."

Ebony's heart plummeted to the bottom of her stomach and her blood turned to ice in her veins. Closing her eyes, she squeezed the phone tightly in her hand, the metal biting into her cold fingers. "So, what you are telling me is that Marcus, who works for you, was unable to show tonight?"

"Co-rrect." Lady Salista spoke slowly as if Ebony lacked intelligence to understand.

However, Ebony was beginning to understand one thing clearly, the man before her was an imposter.

"Is there something wrong?"

"Oh, yes, there is, but I'll take care of it." Ebony hung up the phone, dropping it onto the wooden surface. She needed some space away from the imposing man. Keeping her silence, she moved away from the big man toward the nightstand. Glad he didn't attempt to stop her. "Who the hell are you? You better talk fast before I start screaming or bash your head in with a lamp." She wrapped her hand around the base of the lamp.

"I'm Dainton Armel, I run a business liaison company up North."

A businessman. "What? Are you in town trolling bars to pick up easy women?"

He chuckled. "Nothing about you is easy, Ms. Scrooge. To your question, I'm an unattached male, so if I'm attracted to a woman and she has the same for me, I have no qualms about satisfying us both." He paused and took in her body from head to toe and back up. "Were you not satisfied, sweetheart?"

Her body hummed in response. "That's beside the point." She tightened her grip on the lamp to keep herself focused. "You're an imposter. Why did you pretend to be someone you aren't?"

"That's my question for you." He moved closer to her, but stayed an arm's length away.

She stabbed her thumb into her chest. "I'm not the one pretending. I'm a grown, single woman that hired a service for a few hours of fun. Plain and simple."

"Why?"

Like he was an idiot, she glanced from him to the bed and then back to him. "Ah, sex."

One side of his mouth lifted in a crooked smile. "I know that. But, why would a woman, as pretty, vivacious, sexy and passionate as you feel the need to pay for sex? When you can have any man you wanted with a smile."

Her heart that had sunk into her belly began to lift at his words. No man had ever complimented her in such a way. They called her smart, sharp and a corporate barracuda, but never pretty. "I don't smile much."

"So, I've noticed." He rubbed his chin, the scratching sound of his new stubble echoing around the room. "You're so much more than meets the eye."

"Thanks. I think."

He sat down on the bed and stared down at the rug between his feet for a moment.

She remained where she was, not sure of Dainton's next actions.

"All night something has been bothering me." He linked his hands together between his knees. "After concluding my meeting, I was actually on my way home when I was drawn to the bar."

"By what?" Had he been following one of those giggly women from the company holiday party that was being held in the bar? She wouldn't doubt it. Most of the tiny women were strutting around in small, tight red dresses, looking more than available for any man that asked. "Or who?"

His gaze rose and met hers. "You?"

His declaration struck her like a lightning bolt to the heart. Jumpstarted it and sent warmth racing through her veins.

"What?"

CHAPTER FIVE

Dainton heard her question. Saw the shock illuminating her light brown eyes. The knowledge of what he'd been feeling all night was consuming his mind and as much as he wanted to shove the truth away, he couldn't. What he didn't know was how much to share with the woman before him.

"You didn't even know me. We'd never met before. So, how could I have pulled you into the bar?"

He enjoyed seeing her so passionate. She'd forgotten about her protective grip on the lamp and was waving her arms around her as she stated her case. When he first met her, she'd kept up a controlled façade. He wondered if the people she worked with ever witnessed this side of her.

"That's the part that troubled me. The reason I never stopped you while you explained your mountain of rules to me or dragged me up to your room to have your wicked way with me." He winked at her. Even as he attempted to keep this conversation light, he knew the situation before him was not a joking matter at all.

His life as he had known it was over. Internally, he was struggling to come to grips with that. His bear on the other hand, was pawing with excitement inside of him.

She stared at him through squinted eyes. "Have you taken a look in the mirror big guy? No one is carting you off anywhere if you don't want to go."

"What can I say? The males of my kind grow this way."

"What are you...Native American? White...Samoan?"

"We'll get to that. How about you sit and answer a few questions for me."

Shaking her head, she caused loose and unkempt hair and that captivating gray lock to dance around her shoulders as she said, "I don't want to play twenty questions, I just want you gone."

"Not going to happen anytime soon." He patted the mattress beside him.

She glanced at the spot beside him, but crossed her hands over her chest and remained where she stood. "Not going to happen." She tossed his words back at him.

He chuckled. He always enjoyed women with a little bite to their personality, and Ebony had more than her share.

"Fair enough. Before we talk do you know a woman named Greta?"

Her brows furrowed. "Never heard of her. Who is she, the woman you were looking for?"

"My cousin." He exhaled. It had been a glimmer of hope that possibly Greta had set him up. Sent some Were-female from another county to the hotel where

Greta knew he'd been having his dinner meeting, just to try and catch him out there. His cousin made it a weekly habit to remind him she believed it was time for him to settle down and produce some cubs. If he'd given Ebony a third bite the possibility of her breeding now would almost be fact. Thank the Great Spirit he had restrained his bear.

Dainton's bear scratched at his gut not in agreement of his supplication at all.

"Oh. Well, I don't know her."

"Figured as much." He ran his hand through his hair. "Tell me where you're from Ebony?"

Strutting to the dresser she pulled the drawer open and removed an article of clothing. Once it was on, he practically laughed at the long white conservative gown. The long sleeved item covered Ebony from her throat to her ankles. He bit the inside of his cheek not to laugh. A woman with a body like hers should be adorned in something short, lacy and black to compliment the brown hue of her skin.

"Not that I see it as any of your business, but I'm from...well I was a division president at JP and Rickland Insurance Investments and Consulting. Until I discovered the head of the company was embezzling from our middle-class client. I resigned and threatened to call the FBI if he didn't resign as well and see that all the money was return—"

"I don't give a damn about your business pedigree."

Her mouth dropped open.

"I'm more concerned with who you are...not what you do. Your family. Your kind. Is your sleuth located in the city?"

"What? My kind. I'm an African-American. And the only sleuths I know about are the group of bears at the zoo."

The growl broke from him. He gripped the mattress at his side. None of his kind cared anything for zoos or any other animal exhibits. Even if there weren't other Were's that were being held captive, they were still a type of genetic descendants of them, just as much as humans were.

She held her palms out to him and he noted the fear in her scent.

"I'd never hurt you, Ebony. Never. I'd give my life to protect you."

Dropping her hands loudly against her side, she asked, "Don't you think that is a little extreme for a woman you just met?"

"Doesn't matter. It is the truth of our situation."

"What situation? You're leaving as soon as I can get your large ass out my suite."

"This would all move a lot quicker if you just told me who your family is."

She rubbed her hands over her head. The tight bun she'd been sporting earlier had come completely undone during their lovemaking. The dark brown, ebony locks hung wild and wavy around her shoulders.

Remaining silent, she moved toward the window beside the small kitchenette on the other side of the room. Staring out of it, into the still parking lot, she stood there with her back rod straight and quiet.

For a moment, Dainton thought she wouldn't say anything and that she'd wait until he couldn't take her stoic display any longer and leave. She didn't know Were-males around their mates very well if she thought that.

He rose and crossed the room until he stood behind

her, not touching but close enough that he was sure she could feel his presence. That close, it allowed him to pick up on the tension in her body. If he'd have given her the third bite he would be able to connect with her on a more open mental level and know what she was thinking, feeling.

"Ebony, talk to me. Please."

Still, she was reserved. Finally, she spoke. "I don't know who I am. Or where I come from."

"How is that possible?" Reacting, he reached out and spun her around to face him.

That's when he saw the water glaze over her eyes.

He went to pull her into his arms, but she stepped back.

"Don't." There wasn't even a quiver to her voice.

He could tell she was used to keeping her emotions under a tight leash. "Then explain."

"I'm an orphan. Literally from birth you can say." She moved back toward the other side of the room and collapsed onto the bed as if some weight was pressing down on her.

He picked up a chair from the small table and placed it before her and sat. He yearned to be close to her, but he didn't want to crowd her. The woman before him was struggling with some internal safe where she'd locked up all her pain and it was hurting him to see the anguish on her.

"What happened to your parents?"

She shrugged as she stared down at her hands. "I don't know the story. What was in my file, when I took it from the orphanage director's office, said my parents were shot in the woods outside of Yosemite Park. Some rangers heard the gunfire, a truck was speeding off by the time they arrived to find my father dead from a shot to his head and my mother struggling to stay alive with a bullet in her chest.

"One of the rangers reported the last thing my mother said was baby." Ebony glanced up at him. "You see my mother was pregnant with me. Instead of trying to save my mother and get her to a hospital, they cut me out. My mother died during the process. They took me to the nearest hospital."

"What about the rest of your family? Did they come looking for you?" Dainton could not imagine as close as the people in Den County were that they didn't go on a hunt for whoever had committed such an act. And knowing that the female Were was breeding they would have searched every hospital until they discovered where the child was. It never went well for Were-bears to be raised outside of a sleuth.

"In my records it stated that my parents were naked and without identification or any means of transportation around them. The authorities had no clue where they came from or why they were around the park area. Vagabonds are how they were characterized. Until I was sixteen I was moved from one foster home to another. I had a lot of problems fitting in and was labeled a troubled child. Frequently running away into the woods no matter the distance I had to travel to get there. At thirteen I was placed in an orphanage. It took me three years to get free of that place and this time I went to the city and never looked back. Put myself through school by falsifying my records and changed my name to some 'most likely to succeed' girls name from a yearbook I found left at a fast food restaurant. She must have been really smart because the state school gave me a full scholarship. Once I'd graduated and got my entry-level job at JP, I had my name legally changed and to this day I give an annual scholarship to the college for an at-risk youth. So, have I given you enough of my soul to leave now?"

"What's your real name?" He ignored the sarcasm and recognized it as part of the shield she kept around herself. Taking her hand, he kept his gaze on her face.

She tried to pull it away, but he held firm.

"Rhonda Parks is the name I was given by someone at the hospital. Ebeneza Scrooge was the girl in the yearbook. I preferred Ebony."

"I like Ebony as well." He traced her delicate fingers as he continued to look at her and tried to gather his words.

"There is only one other person in my life who knows the truth about me."

"Thank you for confiding in me." Raising her hand, he kissed the palm. "There's something I need to tell you, but I don't want you to freak out."

"Let's see…I've discovered that I took the wrong man to my bed and had said man pull out all the horrid tales of my life, I'm beyond freaked."

"We need sustenance before we go further." Releasing her hand, he stood and walked to the other side of the bed to the phone resting on the nightstand.

"I don't recall telling you that you could stay." She turned and faced him.

"I don't recall asking." He winked at her.

She rolled her eyes.

When the line was picked up by the room service attendant, he placed his order. "I would like two orders of your honey and walnut encrusted salmon, with a side of asparagus and a whole pecan pie if you have one."

"Hey, I don't eat sweets and I always eat poultry

over seafood."

He thanked the man on the line and hung up. "Not eating salmon is a crime in my county and why don't you eat sweets, especially honey?"

"When you're a foster child or in an orphanage, there aren't a lot of sweets that get handed to you. When there was time for it, it was never worth defending myself against the bullies that wanted to punch you for it. So, I just learned to skip it altogether. With my curves it didn't seem to make a difference."

"I love your curves, first of all." He reclaimed his seat as he stared at her body. When he met her gaze again, he allowed her to see the hunger there.

Ebony placed a hand on her stomach and caused the gown to press tight against her breasts. He could see the points and shadows of those blackberry-colored nipples through the material. She was just as turned on as he was.

"Second, I think you will have a different outlook on sweets when you get a taste of honey. Now, tell me you don't want a slice of pecan pie."

Her eyes lit up, he knew he had her there. He'd seen the vision in her head when his tongue was buried inside of her.

She licked her lips. "I've never had it before. I don't even know if I'd like it."

It saddened him to hear how underprivileged she had been in her youth and how deprived she'd kept herself in her adulthood. He figured it had more to do with her fear of needing anything or anyone too much.

"Well, it is one of my favorites. My grandmother makes me two every year for my birthday."

"Two of them?"

"Hey, if you haven't noticed, I'm a big guy."

The chestnut color of her cheeks darkened to show off a cherry undertone. Oh, yes, he was sure she had noticed quite a bit about him.

A knock came to the door and he rose.

"Um, Dainton, you planning to put on some pants or shock the hotel staff?"

He glanced down. Were's weren't modest at all and he was so comfortable being in the buff when he wasn't in his bear form he hadn't even noticed he wasn't wearing clothes. He smiled. "For your modesty, I'll put something on."

She shook her head, but he did see the corner of her mouth twitch.

Swiping his pants from the end of the bed, he stepped into them and had them zipped part way before he opened the door.

"Room serv—"

The woman on the other side of the door holding the tray gaped at him. First she looked up to his face then down to ogle his chest.

Flipping her blond hair over her shoulder she gave him a sultry look. "You ordered service?"

Before he could respond the door was ripped wide and Ebony was standing between him and the flirty server. Her hands were balled into fists as she gave the woman a hard stare. "Yes we ordered food not floozy. Which did you come to deliver?"

The woman shuffled back twice. "Umm. Y-y-your food." She stretched her arms as far as they would go and held the tray toward Ebony."

Swallowing down his chuckle, Dainton wrapped one arm around Ebony's waist and lifted her as he grabbed the tray with his other hand. "Thanks," he told the scared woman as he kicked the door closed behind him and ushered the fierce she-bear back into the room.

"The nerve of her. I have a mind to find her and give her a dressing down that I'm sure her boss should have given her a long time ago." Ebony was fuming and pacing as she waved her hands wildly around her body.

He wasn't put off by Ebony's aggressive action to the server, he understood it for what it was…a mate challenging someone she assumed was encroaching on what was there's. Ebony's bear, no matter how suppressed it had been in the past, was starting to change her.

Dainton didn't know the full process or how long it would take for Ebony's bear to show herself, but he knew time was of the essence, especially once he began providing her body with the nutrients it had lacked. Honey and salmon, the two most important factors of a Were-bear's diet. Berries and nuts also provided additional vitamins they needed.

"Sit. Eat." He pointed to the small table. Grabbing the chair from the bed on his way to carry the tray to the kitchenette area.

Still upset, she plopped down in the seat at the table.

Getting everything set up, he picked up a fork and broke off a piece of the salmon special and held it before her mouth.

She twisted and scrunched her face, a recalcitrant child. However, as he began to wave the bite beneath her nose her face relaxed some and she leaned in to smell it again.

"Just one taste." He knew the bear buried extremely deep inside of her picked up on the syrupy delight and detected the honey notes. He waited and remembered what Cord, Den County's new Mayor, had gone through with his mate Rena. Rena's bear had been suppressed as well. Dainton only hoped he would be as successful as Cord in coaching her through the coming days and weeks.

"Fine." Parting her lips, Ebony took the forkful into her mouth and closed her lips around it.

Gently sliding the utensil out, he watched her take in her first taste of honey.

She moaned, closed her eyes and stopped chewing for a moment and just allowed the food to rest in her mouth. Groaning, she consumed the food in her mouth fast then snatched the fork form him and began feeding herself. Bite after bite, she ate and moaned. Ebony let go of all etiquette and decorum.

Her face remained less than two inches from her plate as she demolished everything there.

Chuckling he started on his food. His laughter ceased when she snatched his plate and finished off what he had left.

"Hey!" he growled.

A look of shock crossed her features as she seemed to come to her human senses and stared, appalled at the two empty plates on her side of the table.

"Oh, my gracious. I'm-m-...why...." She gazed up at him. "I'm not sure what came over me."

He relaxed his features and smiled. "No worries, sweetheart, I can order more." He handed her a cloth napkin.

Wiping her mouth, she murmured shyly, "That is so good."

"So you like it do you?"

She lowered her head then met his eyes again. This

time she was smiling. "It was good, especially the stickiness of the honey."

The sight halted the beating of his heart and restarted it again. The stretch of her thick, full mouth made his core tighten. "Oh, shit...just beautiful."

Her face darkened, but the grin held. "Thank you."

He moved their plates to the side and picked up the pie and set it between them. Handing her back the fork, he took her hand in his and held it to keep her restrained for a minute. He'd been a witness to what she had done to the food with a taste and now that her bear was unleashed and hungry he had to be cautious when he set something before her.

"Before we both take care of this pie, do you know why I ordered it?"

"Because it's your favorite, right?"

"Yes and no."

A single eyebrow quirked up at his response as she stared at him.

He took a deep breath as he stroked the back of her hand. It was time to start them down a road they needed to travel. "I saw your vision."

Now she was frowning, but he could feel the slight quiver in her hand. "What vision?"

"The one you had while I had you against the wall and my tongue inside of you. We were making love in a field and there were pies floating down from the sky around us."

She snatched her hand away, her fork clattered onto the table. "You're crazy." She rose to her feet.

He stood.

"Ebony...sweetheart, listen to me."

"What are you some David Angel character or something."

It didn't matter to him that she mixed up the names of two different illusionists, what he cared about was getting her to remain calm, things never went well when an untrained Were's emotions were high.

"Please sit, and allow me to explain."

She folded her arms over her breasts. "I have a better idea. How about you leave and we forget we ever met?"

"No!" he roared, louder than he intended, but his bear was fretful inside of him. The beast didn't want to lose its mate when he'd finally found her.

Startled she jumped back.

He took a deep breath. "Sorry. Remember you never have to fear me."

"I don't even know you."

"A part of you does." He sighed and sat. He was fucking this up royally. When he got home he was planning to put in a petition with his Mayor to create some kind of manual...guide or course on how to handle situations like this.

"That is not possible, for me to know you but not know you."

"I'm going to tell you something that is going to be hard for you to believe and understand." He gestured toward her vacant seat. "It would be best for you to hear it sitting down."

Ebony didn't seem like one of those females that passed out at the sound of shocking news, but he wasn't taking any chances in her hurting herself.

She hesitated for a moment, but finally took the seat across from him.

"The second vision was mine. I know you saw it. The two bears playing in that field. They were us."

She shook her head. "Do I look like a bear to you?"

She questioned, holding her arms out wide.

"Yes." He didn't even hesitate. "I see you as the beautiful woman that you are before me, but when I look at you, I also see your secondary form. Some of our kind says it is our true form."

Nodding, she said, "I was right, you are a loon." Tossing her head back, a cackling laugh exploded from her.

"I could prove it to you."

She went silent and pinned him with a suspicious, squinted stare. "How?"

"Before I do, I want you to understand something. You're not the only person who has had their whole life and self-awareness flipped upside down."

"Are you going to try and convince me that something like this happened to you?"

"No, I'm not. I was fortunate enough to be raised in a sleuth that is located in a place called Den County. We've been there for many, many years. We are very private and keep to ourselves for the most part. Both to enjoy our way of life fully and for security and safety of everyone."

"Understandable if what you say is true." Her voice was still filled with disbelief.

"It is," he declared. "There is a woman in our county. The Mayor's wife, our new First Lady of Den. Rena was raised away from the county and made to suppress her bear-side even though she didn't even realize she was doing it. She was both shocked and horrified to determine who she truly was. But, she came to embrace being a Were-bear. I want you to come home with me for Christmas and stay through the New Year. Take the days to meet my family, talk to Rena." He hoped she would decide to stay a lot longer.

Permanently.

"I don't thin—"

"Don't think, Ebony." He slid out of his seat and kneeled before her, his great height still placed him on eye-level with her. "Being a Were isn't a thought, it's instinct. Whether you accept what you are or not, sooner rather than later your bear will come forth. I'd hate for that to happen in a mall, or at your next job...anywhere that something could happened to you."

Taking her hand, he pressed it to his heart. "You feel this?" He remained still so she could feel his heartbeat. "It would stop if anything happened to you. When a Were loses its mate, it can tear them apart, cause them to go mad and even kill them." Raising her hand, he placed it on the side of his face absorbing her warmth. "Honestly, I never wanted this, sweetheart. I thought I was happy living as an unattached male. But now that my bear has found you and I've had you in my life...don't make me be without you."

"I'm not sure what to say...or even how to feel about all this, Dainton." She brushed her thumb over his mouth. "This seems like an odd dream that I'm going to wake up from at any moment. Truthfully, a big part of me is hoping it is a dream and I'm screaming at myself in my head to wake up."

He could hear the trembling in her voice, fear and apprehension present.

"Is there another voice? One that may be softer, one located in your belly somewhere?"

Her light brown eyes darkened and her brows creased with perplexity.

Placing a hand on her stomach, he rubbed it slowly. "What is the voice saying, sweetheart? That tiny roar is the one I want you to listen to."

"I don't know…"

"Fair enough." He couldn't push her. Moving away, he stood. "Will you at least give me a moment, trust me, and promise not to yell or run from the room?"

She licked her lips and fingered the gray lock of hair behind her ear. "I'll try."

He gave her a small smile. That was all he could hope for right now. Removing his pants, he tossed them toward the bed then stood before her nude of body and bared soul.

Holding her gaze, he inhaled deeply, once…twice…three times then shifted. His legs shortened, dropping him to all fours as the trunk of his body expanded. His skin tingled as every hair of his body grew longer, covering him. The change wasn't painful, but dizzying as his internal temperature increased and the strength of his senses sharpened. He could see the tiny spider crawling in the corner by the door. He could hear the laughter and discussion of a group of people in the other suite—writers and readers discussing books. His nose even detected the stench of oil and the musk of the elevator mechanic who was walking passed their suite door.

All of those things his bear turned off and tuned out until he only saw, smelled and heard the woman before him—his mate. The intoxicating, rich smell of her apricot and clove scented musk made his core hum and his soul fill with peace. She was his life. It didn't matter that he'd just met her last night, or that she hadn't even performed one single shift, her bear was his bear.

Resting on his hunches before her, seeing her light brown gaze take in all of him, he waited. A half whine/half roar croak from his throat. He wanted and needed her acceptance. Ebony didn't know it, but she held the power to destroy him emotionally; cause him a grief he could never recover from—the rejection of a mate.

She moved on trembling legs, extending a hand toward his bear. Her breathing was coming out rushed as she placed hesitant fingers on the top of his head, far away from his mouth.

He licked her arm.

Squealing, she pulled her hand back and stared at him.

He whined and leaned his head against her stomach, trying to show her that he meant her no harm.

Her body was quaking, but this time she gingerly touched him with both her hands. She slid her fingers from his crown around the back of his ears, in a way most people pet their dogs. It had the same effect on bears, his skin tingled and he pushed his bulk closer to her and whimpered for more.

"Whoa, big fella."

The quivering of her laughter started in her belly before it ever came out of her mouth. She scratched him on the back of his neck between his shoulder blades…the sweet spot that all bears searched out trees to reach. His bear became putty in her hands at the moment. It took all of his strength not to drop, like a big lump at her feet.

Kneeling before him, she gazed into his eyes as if searching for the man inside.

From within his bear, he could see the tears streaming down her cheeks. He could sense how mystified and confused she was.

"Dainton...Can you hear me?" Concern shadowed her features.

Closing his eyes, he inhaled deep and shifted back to human form on the exhale.

She gasped when he was kneeling before her in an instant.

Cupping her face, he whispered, "I'm here, my Ebony-girl."

Her body shook and a loud cry came from her as more tears poured from her liquid brown eyes.

He pulled her to him, burying her face against his neck as he held her tight. As she cried, he continued to stroke her back and murmur words he hoped were reassuring. He wasn't sure how he'd react if the situation was reversed. His heart beat with hope that she wouldn't allow her fear to cause her to run from her true self.

"I don't know who I am. I feel like my whole existence has been a lie."

Leaning back, he looked into her face. "No. It was unfortunate and you got sidetracked a little from your expected path, but all that led you to me." He placed a light kiss on her mouth before continuing. "I think that your parents were in those woods on a run. Maybe their first run of the spring before you were going to be born."

"Why did someone have to kill them?"

"That, we may never know. People harm animals a lot of time out of fear." Brushing the tears away with his thumbs he went on to say, "I'm just sorry it had to happen to your mother and father."

Sinking her teeth into her lower lip, she nodded. Perhaps she was thanking him for his words or just trying to make a little sense out of something that was senseless.

"I'll do it?"

"Do what?" He didn't want to make any assumptions where Ebony was concerned.

Resting a hand over his heart, she said, "Go with you to Den County, meet this Rena bear person."

"Are you sure this is what you want?"

Lifting a hand, she grazed a finger along the stubble on his chin. "I'm not sure of anything right now...but the fact that I want to trust you. I'm going to trust you. I want to know who I am, not what some file down at the county says about me. But the real me. Will you teach me, Dainton?"

Rising, he scooped her up in his arms. "I will teach you everything you want to know and help you discover the wonders of each item on your 'I don't' list." He winked at her as he sat down in the chair at the table with her in his lap.

Wrapping her arms around his neck she giggled.

A sound that he was sure the old Ebony Scrooge had never made before.

"You have changed me this Christmas, Were-bear." Pressing her breasts against his chest, she asked, "So, where do we start?"

"With your first taste of pecan pie." He leaned in and laid his lips along her ear. "Then I'm going to spend the rest of the morning buried deep inside of you and showing you our bears at play again."

"I do so like the way your mind works, Dainton Armel."

Dainton gazed at the woman in his arms. Now different than the one he'd met downstairs, the one with no reason to smile. Now there was life reflecting in her eyes. There was so much for her to learn and he looked forward to showing and teaching her all the wonders of their kind. He and his bear were aligned, understanding that one day the time would come for the final bond, the third bite. Until then his bear was at peace that she had accepted him. Dainton couldn't ask for anything more.

ABOUT THE AUTHOR

A *USA Today* Bestselling Author, I've been penning erotic tales since 2006, on the hedonistic side of the romance genre. However, I've been writing romance under a different pen for a while. I'm eclectic by nature. My stories range from paranormal, contemporary, BDSM, sci-fi and historical. Mostly short stories, but occasional full-length novels.

If you'd like to find out more about my books, visit my website. http://yvettehines.com

Made in the USA
Columbia, SC
03 July 2022